# Home

# Blues

## Archie Thorn

First published in Scotland in 2021, by Pelters Press

Copyright Archie Thorn 2021

ISBN: 9798472521963

The moral right of Archie Thorn to be identified as
the author of this work has been asserted in
accordance with the Copyright, Designs and Patents
Act of 1988.

Pelters Press
email: pelterspress91@gmail.com

# Tuesday, 0608

Thorn's morning began, as it often did, with stirrings of discomfort in his groin. He never knew which came first – the anxiety that it was morning and the need to pee, or the anxiety that he needed to pee and that it was morning. He hoped it was the former.

This early wakefulness was very much a term-time phenomenon – and a weekday one at that. On a Saturday, the alarmed early rising of the five-day week echoed into the weekend and led him to stir, grumble and roll over. Sunday was often the only morning of real rest.

But today was Tuesday and it was eight minutes past six.

She, Polly, was taking the car. If it was warm enough to bike – this cold, dark February morning – he would bike. Too cold and he would take the service bus.

Less than five degrees centigrade and he did not risk the cycle path. Past experience and severe bruising of elbows and shoulders told him that hitting a patch of ice in near darkness was something best avoided.

He reached from beneath the covers and felt the chill of the room. Moving his hand to the pile of discarded books on the floor, he found the phone. With sleep clouded, failing eyes, he peered at the awakening device.

The weather app told him six degrees. At 7am there was a sixty-five per cent chance of rain. During his homeward ride, this evening, he would ride into a headwind gusting to thirty-five miles per hour.

So, bike it was. It was warm enough to cycle, but cold and wet enough to curse every second of the forty-two minute journey to work and to swear every pedal push of the forty-seven minute drag home.

*Fuck.* If he was going to cycle, he had to hit the floor.

1

*Fuck.* Bed – warm, snug, enveloping bed – could not detain him.

It was his sworn duty and obligation to go to his bloody work. "Wage slave", a colleague called him a dozen years ago. A wage slave he was still. *Fuck.*

The alarm clock beeped. He silenced it with a deft flick. She stirred. 'It's not time to get up is it?' she breathed warmly, heaving the covers and turning her back on him.

He leaned towards the alarm and set it again. She was in bed for another forty minutes. *Lucky fucking...*

With no natural light, he used his other senses to shuffle from his side of the bed to the shower room.

After clicking the light on and pulling the door to, he leaned his forehead against the slope of the ceiling, opened his plaid pyjama pants and let the darkly yellow liquid splatter into the white pan.

As he emptied, he looked up through the angled skylight and saw plastered leaves, a darkened sky and heard a rattle of slates, as another blast from the south-west shuddered across the nail-sick roof.

He didn't flush. No point in wakening her.

The glare of the recessed downlight was unflattering and unkind at this time in the morning. Creeping the surface of the planet for more than fifty years had taken its toll – he reflected daily, as he looked on the mottled, sleep-creased face in the toothpaste-flecked mirror.

He gave his uneven rugby features a sluice with the warming water and, with still wet hands, rubbed at the bristly bedhead, until the greyed hair lay more or less flush against the bony dome of his skull.

With the Gillette Mach 3, he made quick strokes, avoiding cuts under his ear, where the skin was soft.

Grooming complete, the razor – tapped to discharge hair and dead skin – was returned to the shelf for use next day – and the next.

Dropping pyjama trousers to the floor and kicking them to the bedside, he dressed, using as few movements as possible.

Leggings, padded shorts, base layer, threadbare fleece. A few moments and it was all in place – tight in places, saggy in others.

2

He never dreamed that it would come to this – a middle-aged man clad in Lycra… *Fuck.*

Picking up his shirt, pants, socks and phone, he creaked downstairs to the kitchen to flick the switch on the kettle.

*Fuck.* He was going to see that class of S4 bastards today. Why the hell was he going in? What the hell was the matter with him?

The last thing he wanted to do was to stand again, in the same dismal space, before the same mirthless children, meaninglessly extemporising about whatever futile task they had to complete.

And wholesome fucking muesli again. Hellishly hard on crumbling teeth.

Munching grains, he scanned his news app. An article justifying extrajudicial drone execution made him spit. Even the liberal elements of the press were a bunch of conning bastards.

Bag packed, there was nothing left to do but seal the joints in his clothing and venture forth into whatever weather February could offer.

Each time he stepped onto his street of bleak, brick-built repurposed MOD semis he blasphemed.

From the concrete front step, the cycle track was only a few hundred metres through the houses and a short rumble along the ruts of the main road. The real struggle, on dank mornings, was to push his stinging nose and cheeks through the wall of clinging, frigid damp and to fill his chest with those first gulps of icy air.

At this time of year, there was little to enjoy about cycling. Nothing to relish. Not like a planned dip in a cold sea or a snort of air as you stepped onto a glacier. Nothing like that. Just a dismal ache in his joints and the dread, not just of pricks of rain, but of the day ahead – the grim tedium of wasted opportunity, for which he was paid – yet another thankless shift.

Deprived of daylight, he suspected his spirits dulled further. The poverty of natural rays – on his bike, in his teaching space, at home, day after day – made him want to creep into a warm, dark place and hibernate till spring.

Today, however, there was no option but to go on.

So, at just past seven, he threw his leg over the bike, pushed off and bumped down the slabbed path into the stark sodium glare of the street.

3

# Wednesday, 0750

Thorn opens the door and something immediately catches his throat. It is an awful faecal smell.

The room sometimes smells bad, but it never stank like this. What the hell has happened here?

It is really terrible. He chocks the door open, with the wedge of wood and veers towards the windows, opening them from the back to the front of the room. As he does so, he scans to see if he can locate the source of the stink. It is still powerful, even as the cool breeze blows through the tilted panes.

It must be a stink bomb or something, but he cannot see any broken glass vial – a tell-tale sign.

'Fucking hell,' he mutters and moves towards the filing cabinet, where he has some air freshener. Maybe the draft and the chemicals will take the stench away before the bell rings and the kids come in.

Sometimes, after lunch, the kids complain about the smell of his food as they come into the room – especially when he has broccoli cheese. They complain when they come in after a malodorous class has left – which is perfectly understandable. But he doesn't want to be held responsible for this thick and noxious smell, because, as sure as hell, it does not belong to him.

He reaches his desk and leans towards the drawer to pull out the tall pink aerosol can of air freshener. He hates the chemical smell of it too. It is called something like, oh yes, he reads, *'Zen Blossom'*. *Aye, right.*

But, *jeez*, the smell is even worse here. *What the hell?* he thinks. It is pretty much unbearable. He puts out a hand and spins his revolving chair to sit down.

As he does so, something catches his eye on the seat. Just before he drops his behind onto the chair with a thump, as he often does, he recoils, bashing his knee on the desk.

'What the fuck?' he says. Repelled, he leans on the desk and gags involuntarily.

He is mightily thankful that he took evasive action. His reflexes kicked in. Reactions like a cat, almost. Most importantly, he avoided sitting on the big turd that is sitting perkily on the cheap grey polyester fabric of his chair.

Yes, where he usually sits there is a great gleaming shite.

It is enormous.

It is a brown colour, in variegated chocolate tones. He covers his mouth with his hand, then with the sleeve of his jumper, which he pulls down over his hand, so that he can better cover his mouth and nose. There is no way he wants to suck any of these savage smell molecules up his tubes to be ingested into his system.

It is not completely fresh – as in, just laid. Thorn can see that. It is shiny, but it is not steaming. If it was steaming, the smell would be intolerable.

It is definitely human, he knows that. It is not dog shit scooped up off the street. Dog shit smells different from this.

No, what is obvious, from the way it is perfectly piled, is that someone has hovered over the chair, pants round their knees, arse out and dropped this mound of excrement as a perfect monument. The tapered end, where it snapped off, is still visible. As an example of what it is, it is flawlessly formed. It could even be a colossal model for that cheery little shit emoji on the mobile phone.

But it is first thing on a Wednesday morning. Who the fuck has left this big bit of shite on his seat?

Thorn takes a step back. This is fucking it. This is the bloody morning to end all mornings.

This is his workspace, his dominion. Now, there is a monster jobby staring at him from his own bloody throne.

He leans against the desk again to look at it. He rubs at his knee – the one he battered off the desk.

Then he thinks, *What the fuck?* and takes a step away from it. He leans against one of the kid's desks and studies it more – from afar.

'You dirty fucking bastard,' he says, shaking his head. 'You dirty fucking bastard!' He does not know who he is talking to, but he sure as hell means it.

He realises that his heart is thumping. No wonder. His insides are going like the clappers. Stepping back, he can see that this is one of those purely school-type situations. It couldn't feasibly happen anywhere else. This kind of thing doesn't happen in *'real life'* – only in the rarefied atmosphere of a secondary school. Only here.

It is fucking manky. He is taking this personally. Every day of his working life he rests his own arse on this cheap chair. Every day he lolls and leans and farts and eats biscuits – and now some irreverent wanker has abused the resting place of his sacred ring. They have desecrated it.

*This*, he thinks, *this is something else.*

He can barely believe it. Surely no wee bastard pupil is dirty enough, no wee tosser is clatty enough to do this to him, because he is taking it as flat-out, one hundred per cent personal.

He rubs his eyes. Maybe, he thinks, maybe he is dreaming. Maybe he will wake up in his bed beside Polly and realise it was all a daft nightmare…

He opens his eyes and refocuses. It is still where he found it – a near perfect and bloody ginormous expression of the movement of the human bowel.

It is a masterpiece of balance, curvature and coiling. The perpetrator might have practised to produce something like this. If an artist sculpted a pretend poo from chocolate truffle, they could not have done a better jobby. Describing an almost perfect circle at the bottom, then spiralling gradually to a peak, it is almost as tall as it is wide.

But what the hell is he going to do about it? There is no way that he is going to be using that seat again. They can fuck off.

But where will he get a new one? This one he stole from the theatre, when it was used as a prop in a drama production. There is no saying that he will be able to get another half-decent chair. And there is no way he is not going to replace it. Not after some eejit has soiled it like this.

And the chair is set quite high. It must have been one hell of a tall person who placed it – or a contortionist. There is no way a normal person could stand on the seat and drop a perfect mound like that. It would have been all over their feet. If anything, the chair has been let down, then raised again. That is the only way that someone – other than a masterful giant – could have rendered it. Unless it was performed somewhere else and then transferred to the chair. But surely not. It appears to be well stuck. It has been dropped from an arse, surely – not done in a box. No, surely not. It is far too gooey. It is easy to see that its moisture has soaked into the fabric of the chair. There is no way it could have been pushed off the edge of a box or a plate or a newspaper. It would never have been so perfectly composed. No, it has been expelled with skill from a carefully co-ordinated orifice – with laser-guided precision and panache. The shitter ought to be complimented.

# Tuesday, 0658

At the entrance to the cycle track – the old station – he chicaned the railing and his light flashed across the graffiti on the tiled tunnel walls. Standing on the pedals, yawing from side to side, he lifted his weight upwards through the gloom.

Turning at the top, he looked both ways and eased onto the cycleway.

'Well, good morning,' he muttered – to himself.

Same bloody track – the bends and gradients. Same bloody journey.

He dropped a gear and lifted his cadence. Heading for work now, there was no turning back.

The gentle drop away from the houses, hardly noticeable on foot, allowed him to find rhythm, pick up some speed. He rolled unhindered.

His hands and the front of his body were already cold from cutting through the freezing droplets hanging in the air.

Upright in the clips, he crossed the gentle arc of footbridge – over the arterial route from the coast. Yellow cones of light punctuated the grey at regular intervals. Headlit forms came and went.

Thorn felt brief pity for the poor bastards in the lanes below, stuck in their crash-tested steel. Lemmings hurtling.

He was relieved not to be amongst them. Astride his rusty steed, he had at least a fleeting sensation of nature. For a moment, he was pleased to forgo the steamy windscreens, commercial radio and inevitable nose-to-tail traffic.

Seconds later, he cycled down the ramp and halted at the superstore lights. There was once a mill there – a pocket of industry, sending products across the planet. Now there was no room for manufacture – just the empty thrill of shopping.

Breathing heavily, he did not miss the rain.

He rumbled across the river on the old railway bridge and ran atop the embankment near the haulage yard. A brightly lit container lorry thundered abreast of him on the access road. The cold had sapped his bedtime warmth completely. His resistance was ebbing. His face was glacial below his glasses and his nose was oozing. He spat as the snot dripped to his mouth.

'Yawp!' he growled, 'Fucking yawp!'

This was the unbearable bit – the next kilometre or so. After that, if the drenching rain did not fall, he would gradually heat up and his burning breakfast would repel enough discomfort for the rest of the ride.

He shimmied onto the main road and merged with the traffic. Often it ran too close. On a grim, grey morning, the commuters were unforgiving. He could reach out and grab them. Bus drivers mostly knew what to do. Cars had a bit of conscience – they didn't want scratched paintwork. Vans were the worst – swerving out, then, half past and unsighted, swerving back in. They cut it too fine.

Back on track, swooping down an incline amongst disheveled birch trees, he passed a worker – short, in heavy boots. Shuffling along, huddled in fluorescent orange, he oozed vape smoke – the sweet smell of summer berries.

An S-bend on the track bed took him over the main road, where a clear run and good visibility made it easier to see the strewn litter.

Next, a run of brick-and-tile cul-de-sacs – stamp-sized front lawns, a car or two on monoblock and backyards of whirligigs, faded plastic furniture and rusted bicycles.

He swore. Imaginations stunted by advertising and algorithms, people behaved like rats in ruts, gorging on inadequate housing, gaudy shopping malls, vapid working lives and gruesome package holidays.

He pinged the bike bell.

A dog walker did not respond and made him slow. No logic to these people. Thorn was cautious about them. There was no saying when a dug would dart. He would break its back – or it would break his.

Social media claimed that bikers rolled too fast, scared dogs and alarmed pedestrians. Maybe some cyclists were rude, but

9

doggie folk were cracky – with their retractable leads, doggie treats, frantic shouting and shit-picking. Completely nuts.

# Wednesday, 0755

Thorn hears footsteps in the corridor. He thinks they belong to the probationer, who is about twenty-five and very wet behind the ears. She is usually in early.

Something disgusting like this he almost wants to hide from her. But why should she be sheltered from this fact of life? She'll hear about it anyway. What the hell.

She is slowing at his door.

'Agnes!' he calls, just as she appears.

'Yeuch!' she says, wrinkling her nose, 'what is that smell?'

'Eh, I think this might be the source of the problem,' replies Thorn, pointing her in the direction of the chair.

She approaches warily. No wonder. He looks at her moving – all small, clean, naïve and innocent. He looks back at the chair. The dirty big turd is still there. It is not a dream. He did not just imagine it. He looks back at Agnes.

'Oh, Jesus!' she says, uncharacteristically. 'Who did that?'

Thorn narrows his eyes a bit as he watches her watching the jobby. He can't imagine that she did it. She is too young and probably too short, even with the seat at its lowest setting. Her reaction rings true.

'I have no idea,' says Thorn, 'but it is definitely not the sort of thing that I want to be faced with first thing in the morning when I come to my work. But some dirty bastard did it and I bet they won't be tidying it up.'

Agnes looks pale. She is a lovely girl from a small town in Cumbria. Thorn expects that she has never encountered this sort of situation before.

To be honest, though, neither has he.

Now she is paler. Thorn isn't absolutely sure that this is because of the shit, or because she heard him using a swear word. It could be either – or both.

'What are you going to do about it?' she says. 'Do you want me to get the janitor?'

Thorn is quite taken aback by this, but he plays it down. 'No, no, I don't think we need a janitor yet. There are a few people who will need to see this before the janitor deals with it.'

'Like, well... who do you mean?' asks Agnes curiously. 'I mean, surely you want rid of it.'

'Well, the boss has to see it, at least,' replies Thorn. She has to see it, Thorn thinks – if she is prepared to deal with the likes of him, that is. Although, it might be the sort of thing she passes on to one of her minions. But he is not having that. No way. This is her school. This is going all the way to the top.

Agnes steps back. It is not her situation to deal with and she is not sure how to react.

It probably does feel strange for her, he realises – standing there while he leans on the edge of a desk, gawping at this masterpiece of anal sculpture.

So, he moves himself towards the door. He has to break an awkward silence. They don't know each other very well.

'I cannot believe this,' he says. 'I just came in to get an early start and now I have to deal with this. It's given me a bit of a shock. I don't know who's responsible, but it's a dirty trick...'

They both move into the corridor. 'You go and get on,' he tells her. 'Don't worry about me. I'm going to phone downstairs to get some help. It needs some sort of investigation. It's absolutely disgusting. It's already spoiled my day.

'They better not try to sweep this under the carpet,' he continues. 'Somebody will need to get to the bottom of it, for sure.'

Obviously unsettled, Agnes leaves him at the door and walks off smartly towards her own room. He sees her wriggle her shoulders as she retreats.

He is not sure which way to turn. He could phone downstairs, but he doesn't want anyone else walking in on this and getting a shock. It could have given Agnes the fright of her life, if it had happened in her room. It would have been enough to give the old science technician, Mrs Hertelmann, a stroke.

# Tuesday, 0733

The catchment area of the school was typical of many urban areas of Central Scotland. Unfortunately. A once prosperous town on the outskirts of the city, it grew significantly during the industrial revolution. For past generations, it was a colourful, vigorous burgh, with a multiplicity of mills, a bustling high street and a vivid sense of place.

Now, the high street, which Thorn remembered from his youth as a busy thoroughfare, was bleak, pedestrianised and bereft of shops – never mind shoppers. The bigger stores had left the town centre for the out-of-town development, set in acres of car parks.

The big department store died too. Derelict for a decade, the facade was scaffolded. Most was to be knocked down for flats. Elsewhere, factories were demolished and low-cost housing erected. Industry had disappeared.

There was nothing desperately wrong with the vicinity of the school, but nothing to recommend it either. It was just grey-rendered urban sprawl – adequate dormitory accommodation for the city.

Thorn's workplace was in the miserabilist architectural style of the 1970s. Two linked, flat-roofed boxes of grey brick and cracked roughcast were bookended by a tatty assortment of annexes. That the replacement double-glazed windows were a whimsical yellow did nothing to divert attention from the otherwise cheerless appearance.

In front was a large space, barren of everything except pitted tarmac and a few rarely used concrete litter bins. This was the 'playground'. On the other side, adjacent to the main entrance, was another weedy patch of bitumen, edged by crumbling kerbstones and a rusting steel fence. This was the 'car park'.

The school was a leftover. Many other buildings in the authority – brutal 70s blocks, with cell windows – had been demolished and replaced. Thorn had visited these gleaming palaces of education, on the edge of green woods – adjacent to acres of artificial sportsgrounds – shiny new structures, with modern teaching spaces and airy, plant-filled atriums. On the contrary, Thorn's workplace represented the nadir in institutional design. It signified an absence of imagination and flair and, possibly, a complete disregard for the role of education in the community. Cleverly contrived to contain the minimum amount of space legally necessary and to be completed in the cheapest and most basic of materials, nobody with one tiny speck of creativity appeared to have contributed one pencil stroke to its planning.

Every time the building came into view – five mornings a week, as he strode in the front gate from the bus stop, or rumbled on two wheels through the back gate, past the rubbish skip – Thorn's heart plummeted.

He glimpsed the place sometimes, across rooftops, when driving the motorway to Glasgow. But, most of the time, when he wasn't there, he preferred to pretend that it did not exist.

Its routines wearied him and made him ashamed of who he was and thoughts of it sullied the life he led outside of work.

In the recent winter holidays, when lying snow brightened the day, they went for a walk. From a high point in the countryside, behind their house, they looked across the valley in the midday light. Even at that distance, the edges of the dismal grey boxes became visible to him. He turned away immediately – any benefit from the crisp walk dispersed.

Polly asked him afterwards why he was tetchy.

'I'm not tetchy,' he snapped.

'Because I just saw the workplace that demoralises and debilitates me completely,' he said to himself.

And within was worse than without. The bottom corridor accommodated a shadowy and ill-conceived social area, crammed with benches, racks and lockers. There, especially on one of the many wet days, crowding bodies and the stench of damp coats and squalid boys' toilets was enough to unsettle any sensitive stomach.

Above, was a series of corridors, each one too narrow and dark to safely accommodate the traffic that filled it every fifty minutes. Thorn was more used to it now, but, when he first arrived, one dim December, to be in one of the stairwells at change of period was to be caught up in a swirling mass of Breughel's humanity – seething, noisy, many-shaped and drab.

Despite the legend inscribed on the dented sign at the front gate – *'Welcome to Hopeton High School'* – the fact remained that, if there was a more oppressive and less welcoming-looking educational establishment built in Europe at the rear end of the twentieth century, it was not built on this side of the Iron Curtain.

15

# Wednesday, 0757

He needs something to warn passers-by. He wants to guard against anyone else coming in and getting the shits when they see this sizeable jobby. It would be awful if it gave someone a bad turn. What he needs is something like that blue-and-white police tape – something to show that the room is off limits, until the crime scene has been investigated.

What he will do is phone the business support manager. She must know. If there is to be an inquiry, there will need to be alternative provision made for his class.

Fleetingly, he acknowledges that the kids might not even bother. They would see a big shite sitting in front of the class and think it as good as many a teacher. Indeed, given his own experience here, there have been times when he felt that he had as much cultural and social significance as a big shite.

He goes to his bag. He left it on the table as he stepped away from the crime scene. He takes the key fob and locks the door behind him. If nothing else, he can contain the smell.

He readjusts. *Hang on*, he thinks. He unlocks the door again.

Going back into the room, he pulls his phone from his trouser pocket. He selects the camera and directs the lens towards the chair, capturing the scene, with context.

He moves to another angle, looking towards the table. If he squats and tilts the camera, he can just catch the filth in one corner and the wall clock in the other. Thus, he records the time and crime for posterity.

Next, a close-up shot. He has become accustomed to the aroma by now, but it is still mightily unpleasant in close proximity. He wants an image of the pile and the glisten of it while still relatively fresh. With every minute it will shrink in size, especially with the warmth belting out from the radiator panels now that the day has nearly begun.

He locks the door again and makes off for the English base. He finds the number on a sheet of paper on the wall, lifts the receiver and calls downstairs.

'Hello, Lorna speaking,' Lorna says brightly.

'Hi, Lorna, it's Archie here, in English,' Thorn says, in a rather world-weary way. 'I have a bit of a problem.'

At this minute, Lorna is thinking – illness, heating, water leak, furniture, computing – any one of the multitude of mundane issues faced by the population of the school and relayed to the business support manager – all part of her daily grind.

Thorn guesses this issue may throw her.

'I wonder if you could come up for a look,' Thorn suggests. 'It's not the sort of thing I want to discuss over the phone.'

'I'm sorry, Archie, I've got the class cover to do. It will have to wait,' she says, without the faintest awareness or understanding.

'Well, I need help up here,' replies Thorn, unsurprised. 'Is the boss in yet?'

'I don't know,' Lorna says. 'Her number is 145. You would be best to try her yourself.'

'Thanks for your help,' says Thorn, curtly. He has never spoken curtly to anyone in the management corridor before. Plenty of times he has felt like it. Many times he has bitten his tongue, but not today and not this time.

Already he is turning it over in his head. He rang downstairs. He said he had a problem. He was denied help. He is not going to phone the janitor. This is not a janitorial problem. He is going to phone the office of the head teacher.

He sits down on a chair in the English base. It is similar to the chair he uses in his room, but it has a lower back. His hand automatically goes down so that he can adjust the seat height. He lifts himself five centimetres before dialling the heidie's number.

It rings out. Sometimes she is in at the crack of dawn, sometimes her silver BMW Coupé rolls in about half eight. He looks at his watch. It is about three minutes past eight now.

There is no answer from her office.

He calls the school office on 100 and it rings out there as well. By the book, they only have to start answering at eight thirty.

17

He is sick of it already. He felt sick when he went into the room, sick when he left it and, with the prospect of teaching in there in fifty minutes, he now feels pretty nauseous. He phones Lorna again. She must have known that he was unhappy. He is never rude and always professional. On the other hand, she has a knack for being abrupt with people and rubbing them up the wrong way. But surely she is sensitive enough to realise that she pissed him off.

'Hi, Lorna,' he says. 'Sorry, it's me again. Sorry, but I have an issue in my room. Please make sure that you send the boss up when she comes in. It is something significant. Also, could you make arrangements, please, because I won't be teaching period one, at least, and I won't be teaching in Room 117 again, until the issue has been properly dealt with. Okay? Thanks.'

'But I can't...' says Lorna.

'I am sorry, Lorna, I understand it's not your fault, but I will be in the English corridor until the boss comes up. I hope that's clear. Goodbye.' He places the receiver down. In fact, he slams it a bit, then he has to resettle it.

He is feeling quite determined now. This revolting excrescence is a bullying issue or personal abuse. For that reason, he is not doing a thing until the matter has been dealt with and dealt with properly.

# Tuesday, 0757

After changing, he sat down at the computer. For more than ten years, he had inhabited the same space during his working day. When he first arrived at the school, he was rather rootless. He moved from class to class – a symptom of being the last teacher to join the staff. He was at the mercy of the timetable and, with a succession of troublesome classes in a ridiculous number of far-flung rooms, he spent most of his time in largely futile attempts to prevent all-engulfing chaos breaking out.

The pupils had little awareness of this – he affected to have a calm demeanour – but inside he was screaming hysterically and imagining heedlessly throwing his weight around in an unprofessional and very threatening way.

When a colleague left, taking early retirement – an opportunity few were willing to refuse – Thorn gathered the courage to ask the principal teacher to adjust the timetable, which would allow him to occupy the vacant room and create a space of his own.

The then principal teacher, a strange, puckish, twinkly-eyed little man, looked at him as if he was a genius. 'Of course, that would make perfect sense. Why didn't I think of that?' he said, smiling broadly.

*Why? Because you are a twinkly-eyed halfwit, a completely ineffective leader and utterly remiss in your duty to your junior members of staff,* Thorn said into himself, whilst returning the principal teacher's broad smile.

Pleased as he was to get the room, it didn't take long to see that its previous occupant had been a clatty, messy midden. He had joined the school not long after it opened and was on the staff for thirty years. And, during all of those decades, he had thrown nothing out.

19

Apart from the cupboards and drawers being full to spewing point with past papers, prelims, publications, portfolios and other printed material, the whole place had the smell of somebody else's dead skin. There was also a suggestion, a little soupçon here and there, of stale, pissy pants.

Whilst the average teacher does not care that their room smells of their own dead skin or farts, Thorn had no wish to inhale the DNA of the previous occupant.

He bought electric air fresheners for the sockets and atomiser air fresheners for the high ledges. He tried every available fragrance – lilac, lavender, rose, mountain pine, peppermint, lotus flower, cool lemon. He scattered perfumed powder over the carpet ... repeatedly. He even borrowed the cleaner's Henry Hoover. But to no avail. The fake chemical pong would ebb away and the foul tang of retiree would roll back in, undeterred.

When he was not at war with classes, seventy-three per cent of whom were treating him with complete contempt (and the other twenty-seven per cent as if he was not there) he would fill the green wheelie bin with two-kilo lumps of solid paper, as he emptied cupboards and drawers and cleared surfaces and floors.

None of the piles of documentation had any relevance for Thorn. Names, initiatives, planning sheets and official documents were from times long gone. Whether they were five months or twenty-five years old, he cleared them out with uncharacteristic and ruthless efficiency. *Roll on the paperless school,* Thorn thought, as he tidied. There was no point in keeping any of it – he would soon enough accumulate his own heaps of soon-to-be-forgotten curricular materials and pupil files – for future recycling.

In those days, when Thorn first entered that room, he cleared up, put up posters, stamped his identity on the space and prepared for a better future.

Now, he reckoned, already ten years into that future, after the termination of his own career, yet another member of staff would experience the same revulsion, dispensing with his drifts of paper and erasing his biological legacy.

* * *

At the threshold of that room, every morning, Thorn believed he left his self-respect.

Everything that he held to be meaningful – values, theories, social obligations – none of it had any integrity there. It was a world of perpetual and disabling flux.

All he enjoyed of it was a view to the outside – across the sloping membrane roof – with leaves and rubbish clotting the distant drain grids. In this panorama, through trees to the rooftops of nearby houses, he imagined a world where real life continued, untroubled by the anti-intellectual vortex that he experienced within the confines of the classroom.

For months on end he sat virtually unnoticed in that benighted place, with almost no contact with the world of the adult mind.

He had imagined success once – in education, politics, society, in the world. But he had fallen some way short of his own expectation. Now, his daily darg – the unending cycle of 'teaching' and 'assessment', in an endlessly hostile environment – meant that the last remnants of energy and hope were squeezed from him, like the last bit of dry toothpaste from the tube.

Desk-bound and futureless, captive to mortgage and standing order, Thorn's dreams no longer featured a bright horizon or even better money. All that he could foresee was an inauspicious end in this graveyard of ambition.

21

# Wednesday, 0808

If nothing else, it is a slight on him. His personal space – or the area where he spends his working hours – has been broken into and defiled.

He remembers now how furious he was when he was out of class and an obnoxious little shit called Dunbar – one of the irrepressible little bastards who absorb sugary, caffeinated drinks by the litre at lunchtime – doused his chair with water when he was out of the room – that same chair. At least that was what Thorn assumed had happened when he sat down. Dunbar cackled, the class sniggered and Thorn felt liquid soaking through his trousers and underpants. However, he affected not to notice and pretended to remain comfortably seated for the remainder of the period. He did not want to give the little shit any morsel of success – or a glimpse of his sodden behind.

Here, today, however, the situation is much worse than that, much more grave. This attack is not just personal, it is gross and disgusting. It is almost a desecration.

He believes that old-time burglars relieved stress by shitting inside houses. Obviously, there is nothing in this room to steal, so this is malicious. It is vandalism, nothing more.

He wonders if the boss will call the police. The way he feels, it would be appropriate. As well as being vandalism, it's an issue of health and safety, a public nuisance, a breach of the peace, a breach of something. And it's abusive. Without some sort of action, there might be a succession of these incidents. There might be a domino effect and a serial defecator at large – or defecators. For all Thorn knows, there could have been other incidents like this. Maybe other cases have been hushed up. Maybe he is not the first victim.

He spins round on the chair as the principal teacher, Judith, comes into the base.

'Archie,' she says, 'are you okay? You look as if you've seen a ghost. Is there anything I can do?'

'No.' Thorn half turns to the phone again and pointlessly waves his arm at it. 'I was just on the phone to the boss. I'm wanting a bit of help. I've a bit of an issue in my room. I just wanted to get it sorted out.'

'What sort of issue, Archie, can I help?'

'No,' answers Thorn, 'I don't think there is much you can do – unless you have a face mask and a shovel.' He stands up. 'Come and I'll show you.'

The PT looks anxious, but she shrugs out of her wool-mix coat and leaves her imitation Mulberry handbag down. She kicks it under the table with her Hobbs-shod foot and quickly follows him along the corridor.

A few short steps and he is at the door again. He feels the irritation rising, even before he unlocks it. In fact, he does not want to go in. He swings the door open and points the way through. 'On you go,' he says. 'Look, but don't touch.'

'Eurgh!' she says, 'what is that smell? That is vile. What on earth…?'

'On you go,' he says, pointing her in again. 'Look over there at the desk. See if you can guess where the smell is coming from.'

She advances slowly towards the source of the problem. She couldn't be more cautious. The stink is warning enough. She looks as if she is approaching an unexploded bomb.

Unfortunately, the device has already gone off.

'Oh, my god!' Judith turns to him, a look of abject horror on her face. 'Who on earth would think to do that? That is disgusting! We'll need to get that cleared up before the class comes in.'

She walks back towards him. 'Have you phoned the janitor?'

'Hang on a minute,' Thorn says, lifting his hand and shaking his head. 'No, no! Nobody is clearing this up.'

She looks at him, aghast. 'You mean you want to keep it?' she asks. He always knew she thought he was some kind of weirdo. 'You can't teach in here, Archie, not with that thing lying there.'

'It's okay,' he replies, 'I told Lorna I'm not teaching. And I'm not – not till I get some satisfaction over this.'

'What?' She is exasperated. She doesn't know what he is talking about. She sees a shit on a chair, not her own, and all she can think about is the operation of her bloody department. Nothing else.

Not one thought does she give to the teacher whose day has been ruined by the appearance of this grotesque specimen. All Judith's little principal teacher brain is thinking about is how to get her job done. She does not understand that Thorn feels like he has been shat on himself.

However, he does not care in the slightest that she is going to be inconvenienced by him withdrawing his labour. He is going to stand firm on this issue.

'No, Archie, listen to me. This is no use.' She looks more swivel-eyed now. 'I can't have a classroom out of use. We have five third-year classes coming first thing this morning. We need all the rooms.'

'No,' says Thorn, 'you listen to me – for a change,' he adds rather maliciously. 'I am not going to teach in this school and I am not going to let anyone tidy up in here until this incident has been properly recorded, investigated and reported. As far as I am concerned, I will be phoning my union for advice and you will just need to make other arrangements for the third year class. I am not moving from here until I have seen the head teacher, until she has had a good gander at that jobby and until it's clear that she is going to do everything within her power to ensure that the perpetrator is caught and brought to justice.'

By now, the principal teacher must realise that he is serious. She may not think he has a valid point, but she must know that this sort of behaviour, from him, is not something she has experienced before. Surely, he thinks, she will recognise that he has drawn a line which will not cross. Surely.

But no, she has another go at it and he can't quite believe it. 'Come on, Archie,' she says, in a faux calm manner, 'just come along to the base. I can make you a cup of tea. We can have a word about this in a while. I can phone the janitor.'

She doesn't get it. *Idiot*, is all Thorn can think. She can see the shit. It is huge. It is a very real, extremely tangible blot on his teaching day – or his teaching year – or his teaching career. It is

24

a blot on his upholstery and a mark against him. It is a dirty great jobby-stained assault on his character.

'Naw!' he says, with gritted teeth. 'You're not going to soft-soap me. We're not going to pretend that this didn't happen. Don't get it into your head that I am the one at fault here. I'm not accepting that idea, so that you can get cleared up and pretend that this was some kind of mirage. This is meant to be an inclusive school. We stand four square against sexism. We don't put up with racism. We're working hard to eradicate homophobia. Are you telling me that you are just going to ignore the fact that someone came in here and deposited a great big angry shite on the seat I sit on every day of my working life? My rights have been infringed here.' He shakes his head slowly and emphatically. 'You have got to be bloody joking. I will wait outside this door,' he tells her. He is teetering on the verge of angry now. 'I will wait until the head teacher comes up the stairs to witness this abomination and I will not, I repeat not, move from the door, neither to allow a janitor in to clean up, nor to allow a school pupil to see what sort of behaviour I have been subjected to.

'So, I suggest that you go downstairs and you speak to the business support manager, so that she can organise cover for my classes. Then we will wait until the head teacher crosses the threshold, because she has to see this. She can't be protected from this. You might as well accept that I'm going to make a big stink about this and I am not going to shift one inch until the right people are contacted and the issue is resolved to my satisfaction.'

The principal teacher is flushed now. Her neck is blotchy. She does not know what to say. She has never seen Thorn like this before, because Thorn has never been like this before. However, she must realise that she can't convince him of her argument. The penny is dropping that she will need to concede at the moment. She cannot do anything else.

Agitated, Judith steps away, back to the base, to the telephone and her silly, phoney handbag. One of her heels has lost its rubber tip.

# Tuesday, 0834

Ten minutes before the bell, Sandra Cameron appeared at the door. Her recent lengthy absences have given the department a headache, because her colleagues have had to cover her classes. Thorn did not know why she was absent and he didn't want to indulge her by discussing her issues. She should have taken the chance to retire several years ago.

And he had a class coming shortly.

She was nearly ten years older than him, but, because they were amongst the oldest in the school, she thought they fell into the same age bracket. This was simply not true. Thorn had no interest in Fleetwood Mac and could guarantee that he would never listen to Led Zeppelin. Ever.

Also, while Thorn was in a fairly stable relationship, Sandra had enjoyed an interminable series of marital glitches with her husband, so they had recently separated. That was the big reason why she was still working.

*Shit!* he thought when he heard her voice.

She was usually wise enough to know that folk were tired of her and took her with a pinch of salt, including Thorn, but today she looked as if she had forgotten that detail. She came in and quickly sat on the front desk. She was clearly desperate to confide in someone, to turn back the clock, to pretend it was just like old times.

'You remember I told you the last time I went to the lawyer?' she said, without a hullo. 'I went because of my new flat. You remember, don't you?'

Thorn was preparing for classes. He didn't have patience at this time in the day. 'I think you did say,' he agreed. 'The lawyer in town, aye?'

'Yeah, the one I've seen for ever. Remember I said I thought he was getting fresh when he said he always enjoyed seeing me in his office.'

26

'The lawyer said that?' replied Thorn, thinking when he heard this that Sandra was going to tell him she went to the police. 'That's not very professional, is it?'

'Och, I've known him for ages. He lives near where I stayed when I was married. His wife is an ugly old bitch. She wears a twinset and pearls and drives a blue Ford Kuga.'

'Tory, then, is she?'

'Aye, he's an old Tory wanker too. He's been my lawyer for years, since before the girls were born. He's more like a good friend than a lawyer.'

'Right,' said Thorn distractedly, 'what are you going to tell me?'

'Well, I was just going to say, he has been perfectly professional for about thirty years now – always friendly, always nice manners.' She had a big, broad smile. She could hardly contain herself. 'And he has been keeping in touch with me every so often for a decade now, just to make sure I am okay, about Leslie and that, you know.'

'What, to give you legal advice?' Thorn said.

Nothing would surprise him about Sandra. She lived in a parallel dimension, where normal scruples had little value. He used to see her in the staff kitchen, necking handfuls of multicoloured tablets and washing them down with San Pellegrino. She said it was all she ever drank – when she was working.

She lifted a coy shoulder to her chin now in some kind of black-and-white movie pose.

'It's not a problem,' she said, 'he's done it for a while now. He's going to retire soon anyway. But that's not what I wanted to tell you about. I've got a wee secret. I can't let the girls find out, or Leslie. It's between you and me.'

Thorn had met Leslie, Sandra's estranged husband, a couple of times, poor sod. He lectured at the further education college. He had also met both of Sandra's daughters – by chance, in Glasgow, with their mum – surprisingly nice girls. They lived with their dad now.

Thorn did not have time to listen, but morbid curiosity compelled him to find out what kind of trouble this bit of walking insanity had attracted.

27

'Who would I tell?' he said. 'It's not as if I see Leslie and I won't see the girls, unless I bump into them.'

'Well, it's just that you can't tell. It's a secret.'

*Jesus*, he thought. She was a fucking teenager. She was regressing.

'What's the secret? Has he been giving you something else as well as advice?'

The thought made him feel bilious, but he had struck her happy nerve now. Her lived-in face lit up.

'I went in to see him a fortnight ago. That's when it started. I was sitting on the couch in his office. And he said that same thing – about enjoying having me in the office. Then he actually touched me.'

'What the hell did you do,' asked Thorn, 'scream the place down?'

'It wasn't like that. I had a skirt on. He just put his hand up my skirt. And I said he shouldn't do that. I said someone might come in and he said that no one would.'

'How did he know that?' said Thorn, exasperated. 'Is it something he does a lot?'

'No, no, he said it was just me. He said he had admired me for a long time and always thought that we would be good together.'

'Yeah, but, because you are a mature woman, you pushed him away and said you were flattered, but that you had to go.'

'Not really.' She gave him direct eye contact and a huge smug grin. 'We did it in the office.'

'Did what? Had sex? In the lawyer's office?'

'Yep, and on the desk, on all of his legal papers and contracts. It was so good.'

Thorn really did not know what to say. How could he? Here was a completely mental woman, telling him she had been shagged in a wooden-panelled lawyer's office, by an old Tory pillar of the community. He hoped he was blushing.

'But it gets better,' she said. 'He came round to my flat last night.'

The woman was virtually flying now. What the hell was she on today?

'He was in my bedroom with me and we were nearly naked when Leslie came to the door.'

*What the hell!* thought Thorn. Poor bloody Leslie. The silly, psychologically abused old bastard would have been absolutely mortified to find his estranged wife in the arms of her lover.

Thorn was speechless. Leslie was a daft old duffer, who looked like he had to be persuaded to drop his pants to conceive his own kids. He certainly didn't look like he had an insatiable sexual appetite. So, if he visited Sandra the previous night, it would be for old times' sake, because he wanted to keep in touch with the mother of his children.

Sandra was snorting with wild laughter. 'I'd forgotten he was coming to plunge the U-bend in my kitchen sink. It wasn't draining properly. He said he would come round and give me a hand, because he doesn't stay far away. Haha! You should have seen Alec's face when the doorbell rang.'

This was Carry-On style bedroom farce, Thorn thought. He couldn't bear to think of the poor guy, standing there, plunger in hand, ringing the doorbell, while his erstwhile partner was having it off with, of all things, a true-blue Tory, several metres away in the bedroom.

'What did you do?' Thorn asked, trying not to visualise the sagging flaps of leathery skin and brittle bone being disentangled before Sandra grabbed her gown and rushed to the door – leaving the lecherous lawyer panting on the pillow.

'Och, it was fine,' she said, with a lopsided smile.

'What was fine about it?' Thorn was horrified. 'What did Leslie say?'

'Och, I just said I had forgotten he was coming and I was just about to go for my bath.'

'And he believed you?' Thorn was incredulous.

'Of course he did. He gave me a peck on the cheek and tried to hug me, but I didn't let him. I said that if he wanted to get on with fixing the sink, I would go and have my bath and we could have a cup of tea and a biscuit when he was finished.'

'For god's sake, Sandra, I hope you weren't messing Leslie about. He's a harmless guy. He doesn't need you shitting on him from a height. You've already kicked him out of your life.'

'No, it was fine. It was no problem. He cleaned out the sink trap and I came back through after a quick bath and made him Earl Grey and gave him a caramel wafer. He thought it was just like old times.'

'Oh, that's okay then. What the hell did your lawyer say to that?'

'Haha! It was hilarious. When I went back into the room and closed the door,' she was sniggering again, 'Alec was on his tiptoes, trying to get dressed. He was still full of Viagra. He could hardly get his trousers on. You should have seen him. Then he started looking for his sock under the bed. He was frantic.'

'I'm not bloody surprised. Did he climb out of the window?'

'Naw, he couldn't.' She was really enjoying it. It was ghastly to witness. 'My flat's on the second floor. I gave him a big hug to settle him down. I think he thought I was wanting to have it off again.'

Thorn's stomach took a lurch.

'Then he whispered in my ear about wanting to escape somehow. I thought he was about to have a heart attack. I just about pished myself.'

Thorn thought that this situation could never have played itself out in real life unless Sandra was doped up – on something strong. More fool the lawyer, though, for pursuing her. She was completely irresponsible and amoral – and he had a law firm, a wife and a reputation. If he had jumped from the window, he would have been front-page news. Stupid bastard.

'So did you pish yourself?' Thorn asked. He had stuff to do. This charade was tiring him out. It was car crash social life and he had no wish to rubberneck. He didn't want to hear about the squalid little pantomime. He just wanted to clear his head of the sordid affair and prepare for his next class.

'I took him into the bathroom and put the taps on. I said he could lock himself in there if he was worried. Then I splashed some water about and pretended to have a bath. Alec was terrified. He locked the door and sat on the toilet. I was just laughing at him the whole time. It was his own bloody fault.

'About five minutes later, Leslie was at my bedroom door asking if I had a plastic basin for under my sink. I just shouted back to him to take a bucket from the cupboard in the hall. Even hearing Leslie's voice gave old Alec palpitations. Haha! He was brave enough when we were at it in his office, but he came over all grey and scared-looking when he was caught – the dirty auld bastard. It was hysterical.'

Thorn just wanted to hurry Sandra out of his door. 'How did you get rid of him then?'

'How did I get rid of who, Alec or Leslie?' She sniggered psychotically. 'I didn't get rid of either of them. It was a scream. After a minute or two, I went through in my bathrobe and put the kettle on. I made a couple of cups of tea, then said to Leslie I was going to get dressed.

'I took my cup of tea with me and gave it to Alec. He was livid. Then I put on my baggy sweatshirt and went back through to the kitchen. I think Leslie thought his day was made when I went back with my legs out, but we just sat down for a bit and chatted about the kids.

'And he made a good job of the sink. He was always handy to have around for that sort of thing. I told him I missed having him around, for practical reasons. I said maybe he should come down sometime and have his dinner or we could watch a movie. His big brown eyes lit up when I said that. I think he's lonely up in that big flat, when the girls are out, rather than sitting with me in the evening. I don't know...'

Thorn could not bloody believe it. This conniving woman had outdone herself. She didn't realise that all she was doing was convincing him how much of an utter nutcase she was.

Did she think he was going to be impressed by her complete mastery of the two feeble-minded old men?

He would not endorse this. He could not. It was implausibly true, but it was also truly awful.

'Then I told him I had a bit of work to do, which was a lie, and I gave him some milk to take home for his cereal in the morning, because he said he had run out. I even gave him a wee peck on the cheek when he left. That brought a wee tear to his eye.

'Then I went into the bathroom again and the other one was sitting on the edge of the bath like a wee boy who was in trouble.

'When I told him Leslie was gone, he started rushing around and getting his clothes together. Then he sat on the edge of the bed to put his shoes on and I went over to him and put my hand on his shoulder and, it must have been his pent-up energy, but he...'

'It's okay,' said Thorn, 'you don't need to go into the gory details. I think I can imagine...'

'Oh, can you?' she said, smiling coyly at him.

Then, fortunately, the first bell rang and Thorn was saved from his thoughts by the sounds of the hallway door battering open and eager learners climbing the stairs and clattering down the corridor to the department and his classroom.

# Wednesday, 0820

Thorn steps out of the room and locks the door again. Outside, the smell is not so penetrating, but it lingers.

He recognises how bizarre his situation is. Here he is, standing in the corridor, outside his room, guarding a pile of faeces against any interference. He reflects a minute.

What else could he do?

He could clean it up. He could ask the jannie to clean it up. He could pretend that it didn't happen and then continue with his day. Yeah, he could do that. But surely he has gone too far already.

Should he make a fuss about it or should he just go and apologise to the principal teacher and go along with her plan – to erase all trace and ignore the fact that it ever happened?

But that would not be right. It might be satisfactory in some ways – if he could just pretend it did not occur, stifle his revulsion and sense of injustice – and just suck it up...

But he realises that this is exactly why he took a photo of the crime scene. It is proof that it definitely happened – so that it can't just be brushed up and hushed up.

He could, he thinks, cement it as reality – or an imitation of a reality – by publishing the photo online. That's what the kids do. Maybe that would give him some sort of audience. At the moment, all that exists is a big jobby and the only person that it has any meaning for is him. Maybe social media is the right sort of forum for this kind of behaviour.

But would Facebook post it? They don't do breastfeeding, so perhaps they wouldn't do shit either. They might remove it.

On the other hand, it might provoke a response or some sympathy or something, because, Christ sake, it's surely some kind of harassment. No one should expect to work in an environment where this sort of thing happens. As a paid-up member of the union, there must be some recourse in this

33

situation. It might not be detailed in the policies and procedures, but he can't be expected just to ignore this incident and return to the chalkface without some recognition of his plight – some consolation or compensation.

Agnes passes again, as he is leaning against the wall. She smiles awkwardly, but doesn't say anything. She understands that there is an issue, but perhaps the principal teacher has spoken to her already and coloured her opinion about him – about his professionalism, about his overreaction.

But no one can tell Thorn, or Agnes, for that matter, that this is an everyday event or something that he should take in his stride. Surely any common-thinking citizen would accept that this is an unwelcome infringement.

Nonetheless, the situation is crazy loco. What the hell is he doing? He is trained to deal with unruly teenagers. He has years of experience of breaking up fights and making diplomatic interventions in disputes between colleagues, but, realistically, how many people in the school know how to deal with this sort of episode?

Unbelievable.

Agnes walks into her own room and, at the same time as she closes her door, he turns to see the double doors at the top of the stairs being pushed open. The principal teacher appears, a little ahead of the head teacher.

# Tuesday, 0850

His S3 class was almost bearable and it was a bonus. Despite the received wisdom that most kids in the first three years were bored shitless and struggled to engage, he actually had a modicum of educational rapport with these kids.

It didn't happen often – only once or twice in a decade. But here, by chance, through some mistake in the timetable or quirk of fate, was a bunch of hormone-riddled teenies thrown together to produce a class with a measure of natural intelligence, charity and good humour – rather than the customary blend of stupidity, meanness and ill-temper.

Usually, by the time Thorn saw kids in third year, they were badly jaundiced by the whole school experience. They bounced up from primary school, jam-packed full of optimism. Then, after being held captive for a thirty-three period week, forty weeks a year, in the perpetual fog of curricular misdirection, they were disenchanted, frustrated and hard to manage.

With this bunch, however, with this bunch, Thorn felt – what? – almost encouraged…

It took time to get used to them, because, with typical S3 classes, he was always on the defensive. He always knew everything would end with a bang soon enough, when some error – his own or a kid's – poisoned the atmosphere.

But, so far, and improbably, with this class the honeymoon period seemed to run and run.

Thus, for some bizarre, almost blessed reason, the class was now a group that he felt almost a 'kinship' with. He even speculated – and he didn't think this frivolously – that they were a class of 'motivated learners'.

They were so overwhelmingly amenable to what he said, that sometimes he imagined a complex set-up. Was he being lulled into a false sense of security by kids complicit in some wicked jape? Were they preparing some complicated joke at his

35

expense? Was he going to be trapped in some horrendous gag and then exposed to ridicule, *Candid Camera* style?

To date, nothing like that had happened, so, in the meantime, he forced himself to try to relax and enjoy it – the bizarre sense of control he felt in the room and the ambience of calm and civility. It was such an alien experience that it might even sell someone on a career in teaching – as a profoundly worthwhile and life-enhancing endeavour. It was quite remarkable, but quite bewildering. For every fifty minutes he spent with them, he was transported into the realms of the almost bearable.

Another thing that made this particular period bearable was a film study – the thing most kids liked best. It was spoiled by an essay later, but, watching the film, the kids did enjoy.

He had dumped *K-PAX* – an old favourite from his movie archive. Unpleasant revelations in the press and Kevin Spacey's spectacular fall from grace guaranteed that, as a naïve extra-terrestrial, he was no longer convincing. And, whilst the class might be oblivious, Thorn could no longer endorse it.

He opted to show them *The Truman Show* – a sufficiently complex film, with a rather irritating star, but at least one who had not been implicated in sexual impropriety with minors – to date.

# Wednesday, 0823

The head teacher strides out down the corridor towards him. She bristles. She is not doing a good impression of someone who has much empathy. To be realistic, she has never shown an iota of interest in the fact of his existence before, so there is little chance that she has brought her warm, caring aspect with her today.

'Morning, Mr Thorn,' she says icily, looking straight through him. Eye contact is a meaningless detail to someone with her power and status. Never does she make it. Also, it would mean looking upwards at a thirty-degree angle – even at this distance.

*My goodness, she is a pocket battleship*, thinks Thorn. *Or is it battleshit, in this case?*

'I wonder if you can help out here, Mrs Butcher?' he says pleasantly, turning from her and beginning to unlock the door.

'I think that what we have to do is make sure that you have somewhere to teach your displaced class,' she replies. 'We don't want your pupils to miss any teaching time.'

*For fuck sake*, Thorn pronounces, to himself. *Here we fucking go.*

He hesitates. He doesn't want to scream like fuckitty, fuck, fuck in her face – not just yet.

'Maybe you can have a look at the problem first, before we discuss it,' says Thorn. 'I think that before you advise me of what to do, you should be in possession of the facts,' he hesitates, 'Mrs Butcher.'

He goes to enter the room. The stench has accumulated in his absence and he turns and sees Butcher's face clench as it wafts into her.

'If you would like to follow me, I'll explain the problem to you.'

'I think I get the idea, Mr Thorn. It's my opinion that we should ask the janitor to deal with this. We'll replace your seat and, when the room has had a chance to air for a couple of hours, it will be useable in the afternoon. Your principal teacher has already identified a room for you to use this period. We will make sure we get something organised for the rest of the morning too.'

She is standing in the doorway. Although Thorn is halfway across the floor, she has done nothing to follow him. In fact, she moves to turn back into the corridor.

Thorn is astonished. 'Mrs Butcher!' he says, without raising his voice much, but with sufficient force to make sure that he has her attention.

'I am going to speak to the janitor,' she tells him. 'I think you should make ready for the rest of the morning. I can assure you that this will be dealt with in an appropriate way.' And this time she actually does move into the corridor.

'Hey, Mrs Butcher, a minute of your time here, please!' shouts Thorn, with what he imagines might be considered due authority in a situation like this.

He strides across the carpet towards her, in what she might think is a potentially confrontational way. She is right. Thorn is again on the verge of angry. In fact, he is thinking about stepping onto the brink of furious.

But she is now a few metres off in the corridor. She looks up at him, briefly.

'I think you should come and have a look at what I have on my chair here, Mrs Butcher. It's only fair. I think if you'd gone into your office this morning and something like this was staring you in the face, you might have felt a bit disenchanted – a bit like I feel now. You would want some justice.'

'I have things to do now, Mr Thorn,' she insists. 'Make preparations for the day and I will do likewise. There is nothing for either of us to do in this room just now. We both have duties. I'll ask the janitor to let you know personally when the room is ready to use again. We'll make sure that you have a suitable chair.'

'No, hang on a minute, Mrs Butcher. I don't think you understand.'

'No, Mr Thorn, I do understand and I think you need to understand that you have a job do I, so I suggest you get on with it.'

Thorn looks from the head teacher to the principal teacher, who looks away from him, and back to the head teacher, who, this time, is steadily meeting his gaze. She has a beady, watery little eye and there is grit and determination in it. Then she peers down at her diamanté watch.

'If you will excuse me, Mr Thorn, I think we both have things to attend to.' With that, she turns and walks away.

Only now does the principal teacher look at Thorn to see what will happen next.

He shouts, 'Listen! You have not heard the last of this, head teacher, I mean, Mrs Butcher. This is going further. This is a ridiculous situation and you are making it much worse by walking away just now. I am going to take this further!'

But now he is speaking to her back as she strides down the corridor. Her shoes are far too high. She is giving her hips and her feet a pounding. It can't possibly be comfortable.

Thorn can feel the blood bumping in his chest. He is exasperated. He has been defied and he is infuriated. The leader of the establishment did not even pay him the courtesy of looking at the big shit on his chair. It was beneath her to even look at it. Either that or she did not have the stomach for it. Whatever the case, it was a complete abdication of responsibility. So what if it is a sordid little event in the course of her professional life! So what if it is a squalid little stain on the passage of her week!

Thorn knows that it is a silly and trivial crime, but it's growing out of proportion.

In essence, his territory has been invaded, his personal space despoiled and his managers are, so far, washing their hands of the issue. It is preposterous that they cannot at least acknowledge the gravity of the situation and the hideous effect that it is having on the beginning of his day.

He wants to take the item and place it on one of their seats or smear a little excrement around their rooms and see how much they like it. If they suspected him, there would be no suggestion of ignoring the action. Therefore, for them to turn up their noses at his request for an urgent investigation – so that the perpetrator can be caught and chastised – demonstrates that they have a complete lack of respect and an absence of understanding about his rights or any sort of natural law.

He has growing desperation to see justice done.

# Tuesday, 0950

With the bell and the departure of the little S3 blighters, Thorn would have liked to kick back and relax. He had a preparation period. In other departments they could do just that. But he had work to do.

This February morning was getting close to folio time in the English department. Thorn didn't know if there could be more than one nadir in a year, because there were several low points, but folio time was a real trough in the calendar – a time when everyone was one step closer than normal to the psychological abyss.

A minority of kids took due care with the work they were going to send to the exam board and were responsive and punctual. They tried to produce something of which they could be proud. Their teacher breathed a sigh of relief, because, by some miracle of motivation, they gave a bit of a shit about what the teachers, their parents or the exam board thought of them.

These kids were not the best company or the paragons of virtue or the geniuses, they were just the kids who, at the appropriate time, when duty called, took some of the burden on themselves.

Unfortunately, from Thorn's point of view, most older classes were made up of kids who were so chronically unmotivated that the teacher had to drag every misspelled word and underdeveloped sentence out of them.

It wasn't fair. Teachers laboured to produce plans, scaffolding and exemplars. They offered pupils the support they needed to generate good work, as evidence of their ability. They set deadline after deadline.

But pupils, being pupils, did not bother that their work avoidance and poor effort reflected badly on them. In fact, many could not have cared less.

It was an ongoing mystery to Thorn why churning out a couple of mediocre essays was such a monumental task for so many of the dingbats. But, sweet mother, waiting for a redrafted essay from one of these kids was like bending behind a cockapoo in a rainstorm, poo bag in hand, waiting for the damned dog to shit gold.

And anything that they wrote made it look like they had never expressed anything in written form before – despite having been more than ten years in the system. It was as if their creative powers and their vocabulary had peaked in primary five. So little experience did they have of reading and so little understanding of extended writing, that it often felt that the march of civilisation had stalled and that education was going into reverse gear.

Therefore, for the 'teaching professional', in the English department, it was an exacting time. For someone like Thorn – who did not identify as a 'teacher', in the traditional sense, and who felt professionally challenged at every juncture – it had the potential to feel like full-scale psycho-torture.

Added to this, was the undoubted fact that management held individual teachers responsible for poor pupil performance.

For this reason, some of his peers bowed to temptation, played the system and gave levels of support completely contrary to exam rules.

One colleague, desperate to secure a promoted post, provided pupils with copious amounts of alternative phrasing for inclusion in their final work.

Another 'team-mate', someone with an exemplary record, took a memory stick home for two sick days every year. There, every folio essay was doctored, to ensure that each pupil achieved the excellent grades that teacher had predicted.

Therefore, in February and March, as the deadline approached, Thorn, unwilling to stoop to any chicanery, felt nearly overwhelmed. In fact, through many nights, he was besieged, in half-sleep, by dark visions of scrawled handwriting, printers spewing blank pages and clocks ticking. An uninterrupted night's rest was hard to come by.

# Wednesday, 0826

'You have to take your class up to Mrs McCready's history room,' says the principal teacher flatly. Standing about three metres from him, reluctant to come any closer, she makes brief eye contact. She is standing at a defensive angle to Thorn. He knows she is speaking more in hope than anything else.

'I am sorry,' returns Thorn, 'but I won't be taking the class today and I won't be taking another class until I have spoken to the union rep.'

Thankfully, Thorn is in a union. He has never had any cause to speak to a representative before, or any desire, but he thinks that this is one of those instances, which no one could have foreseen, when a union rep or, potentially, legal representation might be necessary.

'I am not sure that's the best thing, Archie. You are just going to make things difficult for yourself,' she says.

'Wait a minute,' Thorn returns. 'I am not doing anything other than demanding that this situation be taken seriously. I am not going to come into school, find this mess in my classroom and pretend that nothing has happened. You have got to be joking.'

'Come on, Archie,' she says, trying to pacify him, 'it was just on a school chair and we can easily throw the chair out and get you a new one.'

Her comment does nothing to relieve the pressure. He is bullish. 'For your information, a shit in my room is a shit in my room and no one is going to diminish the importance of that. If someone had broken into your house and shat on your sofa, I don't think you would be best pleased. Can you not see that? In fact, you might even have called the police.'

'Come on, Archie, the bell is going to go soon. You have a class. You should really teach them. You have responsibility for their learning...'

'Aye,' he says, 'maybe in normal circumstances that's true, but what about your responsibility for me and the heidie's responsibility for me? Are you just going to ignore that, just because this big bit of shit is something neither of you is prepared to deal with – or even look at, in the head teacher's case?'

'Right, Archie, I think you've said enough. Mrs Butcher and I agree on what you should do. If you are not prepared to follow instructions, then perhaps you should go and sign yourself out, so that we can get things organised for someone who is prepared to teach a class.'

'You are completely out of order saying that to me,' insists Thorn. It is all he can do to stop from spitting it at her. 'I suggest you go and get the class and the work organised. They are your responsibility now. I am going to get some help from the union rep.'

'I am not sure that Mrs Capaldi will be interested in your story either, Archie, but go and see her if you want. Just make sure that you leave that door open, so that the janitor can get in to clean up.'

Thorn bristles again. 'You have got to be joking,' he says. 'There is no way the janitor is coming in here to clean up – not yet. I'm not satisfied that anyone has even acknowledged that there's a problem here, far less that they've recorded the incident. It's so typical of the management in this school. If a situation arises and they feel they might get their hands dirty, they're reluctant to do anything. They're quite happy to ignore the issue and hope that it will either just die a death or disappear into the past.

'This issue is not, repeat not, going away. You can plot with the head teacher as much as you like. You can try to strong-arm me into teaching, but I am not going to do it. Just get someone else to take the class. I am staying here.'

At this she wrinkles up her face. She has never really had much interest in him. He's been a number in her inherited department – someone she would not have appointed herself. He's someone else's legacy to her – hired by someone she did not know and someone she cares nothing for. He's older than her and, in some respects, she knows, more personable than her. For her, in the longer term, it would be a relief to get rid of him. So, deep down, beyond the more immediate problem of covering his class and finding work for it, she would love to be shot of him, to replace him with a younger model – a person with their whole professional life in front of them – someone interested in what they are doing, but, more importantly, someone more biddable and pliable.

'You'll need to make your own decisions, Archie, but you know there'll be consequences if you decide not to teach your class.'

'My mind's made up. I thought that was clear. I'll stay here until I've decided what to do. If you tell me where you want the class sent, I'll redirect them. But there's an issue here and I'm not prepared to be walked over. Sorry.'

Taking that as his last word, the principal teacher turns and strides away, trying to look purposeful and authoritative, but, in reality, just looking as if she has been drinking too much red wine and eating too much chocolate over the past couple of years, as means of coping with the stresses and strains of a job which she often thinks she does not want.

To an extent, Thorn is sincere in his apology. He doesn't want to make work for anyone. He does not want to piss off his immediate boss, the principal teacher, or to leave the kids at a disadvantage. But he is not moving or letting anyone into his room who is not treating this complaint seriously. He has a genuine gripe, so he is not going to let anyone clean the mess, because then the evidence will be gone and all of his fuss will appear to have been about nothing.

He locks the door and stands, leaning against the corridor wall – like he is waiting for a bus.

# Tuesday, 1015

Thorn sat quietly in his room, trying to concentrate and focus on shoddy essays. The agony of reading the miserable offerings killed him inside. There was so little time left to read so much of the spectacular literature that remained unread on the surface of the planet. And there he was, condemned by contract to reading the half-baked, ill-considered output of a bunch of disinterested juveniles.

Then he heard a rising, screaming voice from across the corridor. It was the penetrating sound of a teacher, Chambers, imparting some of his strident words of belittlement.

Although not physically imposing, the teacher responsible for the manic screaming made even Thorne uneasy. He was the possessor of a bizarre and mesmerising malevolence.

As he strode the corridor with heavy and deliberate steps, his shiny brown brogues thumped, pupils went quiet and a bow wave of ill-nature moved ahead of him. He occasionally gave a cursory glance of acknowledgement to a colleague, but he was selective. Anyone who had ever said a wrong word to him or disputed his authority in all matters teaching felt his withering disapproval.

His cantankerous personality poisoned the place. He was the one irredeemably rotten egg which made the atmosphere of the department close to unbearable and one more reason why Thorn spent as little time in the establishment as he was contractually obliged to do.

Thorn did not completely understand the dynamics of his classroom. Very seldom was there a raised voice. Very rarely was a class member disciplined or removed. But, if he was honest, Thorn sometimes felt the same mortal fear that the kids must feel when they were in this man's presence. It was intangible, but it was as if there was some barely concealed fury and searing contempt always breaking, just below the façade – a sort of bubbling, putrid rage – ready to spew forth as soon as the opportunity arose.

Only once every second month or so did that happen. At those times, Thorn heard that unearthly scream.

Then, the whole corridor fell silent. In every room, pupils sat rapt and staff stood appalled.

Shocked by the violence in his voice, Thorn – even with solid concrete walls and stout doors between him and its source – felt the scalding shame of the pupil.

Not in the furthest bounds of his imagination could Thorn identify with this caricature of a teacher. He only recognised the wilting of the kids.

When Chambers ramped up his ferocious invective, time stood still. It was verbal assault no longer legal, never mind fashionable – like something from a Dickensian nightmare – from a time of grave inequality and vicious punishment. In Thorn's mind, the rows he meted out to miscreants in his room probably bore much similarity to the chilling confrontations which the perpetrator had experienced from his own father.

'How dare you?' he would shriek, seeming to waver on the very threshold of insanity, 'How dare you?... Do you think I come into my workplace to suffer this sort of behaviour?... And you have the gall to interrupt my lesson... You... you should be ashamed of yourself, spoiling the lesson for the people who are prepared to listen.

'How dare you?... Now, I don't know how you have been brought up...'

The pauses were shocking, but, whenever Thorn heard this sort of phrase, he was doubly aghast.

In reality, Chambers did not have the faintest inkling of how any child he screamed at had been brought up. And everybody knew that an accredited professional should not be making that sort of proclamation in state school.

Then he would say, 'but I am sure your parents would be appalled to think of you behaving in school in this manner...'

Again, he had not one idea whether the child had one or two parents, lived with a granny, a foster carer or even if the carer cared – even in a modest manner – about their child's behaviour in the secondary classroom.

46

But, this guy's myopic focus meant that, if there was a child in his class who stepped over the border – between his middle-class Victorian ideal of what a child's behaviour should be and the way the rest of the world actually behaved – they would be verbally flayed until left in no doubt as to what his voluble view of the situation was.

His behaviour betrayed an innate and repellent conservatism – a continuing belief in a mythical and better past, where children learned in an atmosphere of fear, bordering on terror – a world in which they were seen and not heard.

A succession of senior colleagues left him undealt with for years. They had no notion to take him on, such was the unpleasant dynamism of his character. They muttered about it from time to time and made eyes about it. Then, when they heard him scream again, they danced from foot to foot and listened guardedly, since they were the person identified as responsible and senior and professional.

But they were loath to act. That Chambers treated people like he was living in the 1850s reminded all of his alleged superiors of their personal dread of inflexible, old-time authority. It made them shy away from the nose-to-nose confrontation, which was their undoubted duty.

He should have been button-holed, reprimanded and re-educated or fired.

Had a member of management spoken to a member of staff like that, within the earshot of colleagues or pupils, they would have been out of the door like a shot.

But, possibly by intention, Chambers screamed often enough for everyone to be aware of his capacity, but seldom enough so that there were many quiet periods, when confronting him dropped from the top of anyone's to-do list.

Thorn imagined, sometimes, that a video posted on social media of one of these theatrical tirades would ensure that the issue was soon addressed. But, so far, that had not come to pass. He also suspected that any mobile phone, misused in class, should it ever be detected, would probably melt in the heat of this teacher's wrath.

# Wednesday, 0835

There are ten minutes left before the first bell. The principal teacher has beetled away and is in the base on the phone – no doubt speaking to the business manager and the head teacher. She brown-noses all the way. There is not a smidgeon of a chance that she will stand by Thorn. Not one scintilla of an iota of a possibility. She is a company body and she is promoted one stage above her ability level – at least.

*What to do now?* Thorn is thinking. He is not the only one with a key for this room.

It is as if he is guarding the crown jewels.

Surely there is something wrong here. This is just not right. His seat has been shat on, by god knows what little bastard – assuming it's a little bastard – a little bastard no longer bunged up with one hell of a big shite – and not one person is acknowledging it or doing the first thing to investigate it.

It is almost as if he is being set up.

He cannot leave, or someone will tidy up and things will carry on as normal. He cannot stand here indefinitely, or he will be removed from the building. He feels outgunned.

In a few minutes the pupils will fill the corridor. The bell will ring and they will steer themselves to their classrooms.

His own class will be mystified. They won't understand what is going on, unless someone has an idea of who is responsible for the deposit. With that in mind, Thorn decides he will watch them like a hawk when they approach, for signs that they know what he has discovered.

Any shifty-looking individual should raise his suspicions – any little blighter with an awkward grin or one talking too intently to a friend in order to deflect attention.

He must stay at this post meantime. He cannot afford for the evidence to disappear. But he needs to contact the union rep.

Maybe he can ask a kid to get her. Maybe she will pass this way. Her classroom is further along on this floor.

Just as he thinks of the union rep, he strikes lucky. Her neighbour, another science teacher, approaches in the corridor. He doesn't usually talk to her. She is a bit odd and not used to normal human interaction.

'Hi, Helen,' he says, jauntily, 'how are you doing?' It is his usual sort of greeting, but Helen doesn't know this, because he doesn't often meet her in the corridor and she does not expect people to make eye contact when speaking.

'Have you seen Jen this morning, I wonder? I have a union matter to discuss with her, eh, urgently.'

'Oh, I think she'll be in her room just now. She usually comes in early. She goes up the end stairs. I would try there, if I were you.'

'Okay, Helen, that's great, but I wonder if you could run a message for me, please? I can't really move from here. I have a class coming.'

'Yes, of course, that's fine. I'm just going along there myself.'

'Yeah, I thought you might be,' says Thorn. Then he reminds her, 'Could you tell her I need a word with her as soon as possible, please, Helen? Yeah? That would be great.'

Helen is not quite clear what happens now. She is unaccustomed to being engaged in any communication outwith the science and technologies faculty. It is throwing her somewhat. She hesitates.

'So, if you could just say I want a word with her, that would be great,' says Thorn, just to prompt her. 'And it's urgent, so, really, the sooner the better, thanks,' he says, urging her onwards.

Helen might want the conversation to continue. She has likely not spoken to anyone since she issued homework to her S5 class at three-thirty yesterday, but Thorn needs her to get her arse in gear. He doesn't know how much time he has before someone insists on him moving, or him going home, or before someone tries to get into the room to clean it up.

So he gives Helen a broad smile.

She flinches. She is surprised when anyone gives her what appears to her to be a genuine smile. It makes her start and turn away, which gives her legs the cue to carry her down the corridor. 'Thanks,' calls Thorn. 'If she could come along now, it would be even better.'

As he is watching Helen's retreating back, with its awkward bottle-green coat, black polyester school trousers and comfortable pumps, he muses on the nature of teaching and its tendency to include in its fellowship a more than representative sample of social misfits and the conversationally inept.

# Tuesday, 1030

Thorn climbed the stairs two at a time, just after the interval bell at 10.30. He was in a rush to reach the staffroom.

He didn't normally have the notion to go, but today was different.

Today, there were cakes in the staffroom – a significant enticement – and bought at someone else's expense.

He hoped to get there in time for a pineapple cake, bought in from the local bakery.

It would be the sensual highlight of this working week.

Yes, highlight. In the midst of the grey slurry of the teaching regime and the drab sludge of curriculum, that one pineapple cake – a sweet little jewel of thick pastry, sticky pineapple jam, sugary fondant cream and vivid yellow icing – could outshine any other pleasure – social, intellectual or culinary – in his grim, timetable-bound existence.

It was a sense explosion of colour, texture and taste – an almost miraculous confection – an unambiguous contrast to the cheerless passage of his salaried hours.

But then he was delayed on the stairs. A fifth-year child asked about her essay – asked if he had marked it yet.

She claimed to have handed it in.

Thorn was sure that she did not.

She said that she left it on his desk at the end of a period. This in itself suggested that she was duplicitous, because she knew that Thorn's desk, untidy at best, was a talking point.

If he was honest, in the fug of his memory of all things scholastic, she might be right.

But, regardless of the facts, her hope was that Thorn would admit fault, which would be the sign of weakness she needed to declare victory.

But Thorn could spot a liar. He knew that, if this particular girl was not a liar, she would not be wasting her interval time in this exchange on the stairs. He had seen this strategy used before. He could not let it triumph.

He said to her that these things happened. He asked if the essay was word-processed. He always recommended that. If so, she could print it out again… however, if not…

These comments pushed her onto the back foot.

He could barely be civil to her. She was taking possession of his free time. He was not being paid for supervision. His only focus – the one that kept popping in and out of his mind as he spoke to her – was the ever-dwindling chance of staking a claim to a pineapple cake.

He left her on the stairs, dodged a scattering of crisps, a spilt can of Irn Bru – a pupil breakfast – and breenged through the double doors onto the second-floor corridor.

As soon as he entered the staffroom, he clocked one of the probationer teachers making off with one of the near-fluorescent, lemon-coloured beauties in a paper towel.

A glance at the dark-blue bread trays on the counter told him that the probationer had taken the last one. All he could see were yum-yums, cream cookies, carrot cakes, doughnuts, French fancies, toffee cakes, fly cemetery, vanilla slices, two Chelsea buns, millionaire's shortbread and, still within his field of vision, that damned probationer with the last delicious pineapple cake.

He was thwarted.

His instinct was to jump at the probationer and demand his bloody cake back.

It nearly stopped him in his tracks. He had no wish to go on. Even those trivial hopes were dashed. The pitiable balloon of his only optimism collapsed.

Only the coincidence of his life and Jim Malone's retirement conspired to bring him into close proximity with a pineapple cake, but now, in his interior monologue, or dialogue, there was a tiny voice crying out, because the fulfilment of a cherished dream had been torn from him.

Just beyond the endless drizzly drivel of his working day, a little yellow light of hope had been shining. Now that light was extinguished.

The ruthless power of chance deigned to leave him bereft of any pleasure and he began to feel more feeble, more deprived and more isolated than usual.

However, rather than dropping where he stood – which would have been his preferred option – and rather than scream out, or retreat into catatonia – he trudged up to the remaining cakes, levered up a deep slab of toffee sponge and made a beeline for a space on the stained, brown corduroy banquette in the distant corner.

Once perched there, he took a big gobful of the sticky cake and waited for the compensatory sugar hit.

A few folk still milled around the coffee bar. The school intended the staffroom to support collegiality and to foster fellow feeling amongst professionals, but it did not even have enough chairs for everyone to sit down together.

It was a long room, the size of three classrooms. Situated on an upper floor, it looked out over urban sprawl to the wind-turbined horizon. Mostly empty and usually cold, it was an odd place for anyone to relax.

A clique of people used the place at intervals and lunchtimes, so it was used for one hour and five minutes a day. Even then, only a small portion of space round the coffee bar was used – where there was an urn, a microwave, a sink and an empty paper-towel dispenser.

Decorated with pink-and-grey embossed wallpaper, it was adorned with a few framed and fading works of art, created by fourteen-year-old pupils fifteen years ago.

There were some dog-eared union posters, pinned at various angles and one of those dartboards with imitation veneer doors. The recently discarded Christmas tree was stuck out of the way in a corner – still fully decorated.

A large patch of rusty-looking spillage stain on the grubby pink carpet – about the size of a full-size snooker table – was evidence of a leak in the roof, in the storms three years ago.

Furnishing was minimal – just an assortment of pieces, garnered over decades, from hallways, offices and cupboards. When chairs outlived the purpose for which they were purchased, they found their way there. It was the waiting room for chairs before they went into the skip. 'Faded, blemished and nearly broken' was the design concept for furniture in the staffroom.

Enticed by a very superficial level of empathy for Jim Malone, a retiring colleague, but mostly by the prospect of free cake, the attendance was exceptionally good.

There was the usual assortment of people, with no apparent order to their distribution, but Thorn identified that they were gathered in vaguely departmental groups, with a few cross-curricular allegiances.

Compact and once muscular, Jim Malone was sitting and smiling in a prominent position near the coffee bar. He was unusually well dressed. His pale-grey shirt looked ironed and he was wearing a self-coloured purple tie – without soup stains or loose threads. And, whilst he wore the same typical teacher trousers as usual, his abraded, steel-toed work shoes had been swapped for a pair of shiny, tan loafers – which wore all the hallmarks of being one of his wife's Spanish holiday purchases.

Malone believed that he was an 'institution' in the school, because he had worked there since he was a young man and the building was new.

The reality was that Malone had worked in the school since the building was new and he was a young man. Other than that, all that actually happened was that both he and the building had grown older, tattier and more frayed round the edges.

He was never an 'institution' – not in the school, not in the department and not even in his own classroom.

This was just the day when the education system spat Jim out. His best years were drained out of him – by the steady torrent of terms, timetables, calendar entries and other pointless shit. And now he was an ageing man, with a few years left – if he was lucky.

*But why so smug?* Thorn thought. As the oldest guy there, on the surface of it, he didn't have much going for him. Also, on the inside, if you sawed right through, all anyone would find would be 'science and technologies teacher' gunge. There might be plenty of understanding of rudimentary chemistry and physics – how to light a Bunsen burner, oxidise iron filings and fire light through a glass prism – but there would surely be little else.

Thorn knew that he was a pleasant and well-intentioned enough guy. He had done the porridge. For all of his working life he had scuttled through the shadowy corridors of the science and technologies faculty and, now, he was emerging, joyously, into the heart-stopping oblivion of retirement.

*But why so little self-awareness?* Thorn thought. Everyone was only there to scoff cakes, not to listen to any of his clumsy jokes and historical anecdotes about people who no longer worked there.

However, before Malone had the chance to speak, there was the issue of the head teacher, Mrs Lucille Butcher – Butcher by name, slitter of throats by nature.

Thorn had heard it said that she sought out a man with a suitably scary surname, married him, adopted the name, then sliced him, diced him and devoured him.

She was no longer a lover of men... or women, for that matter. Five foot two, in her not inconsiderable heels, she power-dressed in a manner which no one else dared. Her frame – four foot eleven by two foot three of ample flesh – was corralled and constrained by plush upholstery fabric and durable double stitching.

It was unclear why she was ever appointed. Personable, she was not. Caring, she was not. Human, barely. Thorn suspected that, in the days when female applicants were less common in secondary head teaching, she was the gesture. Either that or she was a fully paid-up member of the previous party in power.

He did not like to think of her climbing the greasy pole of promotion – his imagination shied away from challenges like that – but the truth was that she simply could not have done it on her own – and certainly not in that close-fitting suit.

Butcher often passed him in the corridor, which was two point seven metres wide, without setting her wicked little eyes on him – passing him, in fact, as if he was not there.

Whatever the reasons for this behaviour, Thorn sometimes mused that she had the appearance and the social aptitude of an overstuffed armchair.

Her efforts at public speaking, at events like this, were stilted and insincere. Some people laughed – in an involuntary, forced sort of way. The majority did not want to appear rude and were inclined to be sycophantic. But there was nothing to laugh at. Far from being genuine, the tone of the address was painfully artificial.

Perish the thought, mused Thorn, that she would be in post to oversee his departure. He might not be able to contain his feelings.

Now, she was standing to make her speech. She knew that people were looking her up and down, which did not take long. They looked at the cut of her dress, her expensive, asymmetrical haircut – with highlights. And it was clear that she had her nails done. For this occasion? Surely not!

Then, when she spoke, she used appropriated language – because she was unaccustomed to any positive statement of approval. Malone was 'well-respected, organised, someone who was happy to express an opinion at a meeting'. It was all written down. She was capable of no spontaneity – nor wit, nor compassion, nor humanity.

Thorn guessed she had a folder on her USB stick labelled 'Generic Retirement Speeches'. She changed the name on the template and inserted one or two new phrases from a word bank – in order to maintain her integrity.

If anything, he detected some resentment in her manner – probably because Jim Malone was retiring and she could not yet leave. Perhaps she resented that he was centre of attention. Perhaps she resented that people were eating free cakes.

Listening to the sound of her voice took Thorn back to the first day after the summer holidays, six months ago, when Butcher addressed the staff.

He remembered it well, because returning to school after a long summer was never easy and the previous summer saw him in his most positive frame of mind yet.

In late June, the tent and books were packed and off they went to France. Then, when they got back, Polly was cool and he settled into painting bits of the house, without grumbling too much. A few outings on his bike kept the black dog at bay and he enjoyed the tail end of the holiday. Visiting school – something he had never done before – he reacquainted himself with the workplace. He felt a new resolve that there would be none of the previous histrionics – just because he was going back after a long break.

On the first day back, he dropped his bag in his room and went off to the staff assembly.

On a bright, late-summer morning, when everyone was bright-eyed and willing, bloody Butcher spoke from notes from nine o'clock till ten-twenty.

She gave the slightest of nods to their good work, but used the majority of the time to browbeat them and incite fear and alarm. That an inspection was due, everyone knew. That it was a chance for the reputations of the staff to get a real duffing up, no one had thought about until Butcher used it as a threat.

Thorn's main objection was merely the implied menace in everything that she said. No one was buoyed up with any encouragement, only threatened with failure.

He could not believe it. He wondered in what hell such a zealot had been fashioned. He could not understand how she could dredge up such bile.

He had not forgiven her for that morning. He knew that positive sentiment was not her thing. Her thing was criticism and spiteful negativity. Her thing was not to lift people up, but to smack them down.

Then the bell rang. It always did. There was never an extended interval. Butcher resented the staff having an extra five minutes. Teaching time was her thing. It was sacrosanct in the establishment – for some bizarre reason. She thought that the kids' results were reliant on it. And, to her, the results were all that mattered – certainly more than any sense of well-being amongst staff.

She wrapped up her trite commentary. Perfect for her – the timing of the bell – because most staff needed to rush from the room, which meant no time for Jim Malone's comments.

Thorn was caught between a rock and a hard place. There was no reason in the world why he wanted to sit and listen to Jim Malone, but, equally, there was no way that he wanted to present himself before the class in his room.

He muttered and left.

57

The only motive he had for going up was for a bloody pineapple cake. A bloody pineapple cake he did not get. It was just another one of his life's wasted opportunities.

# Wednesday, 0847

Then the bell rings. It is on the wall nearby and too close to his head for comfort. It is the three-minute bell, which rings early to alert those pupils in school that they must make their way to classes. It also rings loudly enough to remind those within two hundred metres of the building that, if they hurry, they will manage to get in before the doors close. Those slightly further away know that there is no point in hurrying. They will be late, will receive a slip at the front door and will need to attend interval detention for ten minutes at 10.30.

For Thorn, the three-minute bell is a reminder that he normally visits the toilet. If he leaves his room on or just after the bell, he has time to pee, wash his hands and return to class before the majority of the pupils have arrived.

As a teacher, Thorn's bladder responds to bells – conditioned like Pavlov's dogs. His wife cannot understand it. She has a bladder which Thorn imagines to be the size of a spacehopper. Not him. When he needs to pee, he must pee and, usually, it is at times dictated by the school bell. Before 8.50. At 10.30. At 12.25. At all of these times, if he is within range of a toilet, he will use it. If he is out of range of a toilet, he will pee against a tree or a wall. For Thorn and his ageing bladder, an urgent need to pee sometimes means using an empty plastic bottle. He prefers the wide-mouthed bottles, which contained Lucozade or Oasis. Not because he has an enormous need to pee, but because it makes hitting the target much easier.

Today, however, is an exception. Today, it is 8.47 and, although he would like to pee, he has even more pressing needs. His S3 class is on its way up the stairs and he has to repel them and redirect them somewhere else.

He hears a clack, clack, looks round and sees the principal teacher approaching down the corridor. She looks more haggard

59

than usual, he thinks. Then he realises that he is probably the reason for that.

'Archie!' she calls. She doesn't come any closer than necessary.

He notices a smudge in the mascara on her left eye. *Has she been crying?* he wonders.

'Can you tell your class to go up to History One, please? I don't know who is going to cover them. If you are sure you are going to keep this going, I will send some work up.'

'I'm sorry,' says Thorn. 'This isn't personal, but I am not willing to take my classes until this is dealt with.'

'Whatever you say, Mr Thorn,' she says, with a fully-grown tone of irritation. She is clearly imagining her workload piling up today as she compensates for Thorn's negligence. 'Just make sure you redirect the class to History One.'

'Are we not going into the class, Mr T?' Angie Thripple asks, as soon as she walks up. She is followed by Charlotte Dowd and Fraser McNab.

'No, not today,' says Thorn. 'There is a bit of an issue. If you go on up to History One, there is someone coming to look after you.'

'What's the issue, Mr Thorn?' says McNab. He is a cheeky wee freckle-faced boy. He has earned the nickname of 'McNob' from his peers. Thorn has heard this name used in class and has officially criticised it. Privately, he fully understands the reason for it.

'If you get up the stairs just now, Fraser, I'll tell you about it another time.'

McNob wants to pester him, but Thorn raises his hand and shoos the kids round in the other direction.

'If we go that way, Mr Caithness will give us a row, sir,' says McNob.

'Och, just go, will you?' says Thorn, with teacherly tetchiness. 'And if you see anyone else, take them along with you.'

He realises that he has left his bag and jacket in the room, but he can't go in for them just now, because he sees the union rep striding towards him down the corridor in a rather uncoordinated manner. He lifts his hand in recognition, because she seems to be marching towards him, however, just as he does so, she comes abreast of the door onto the stairs and the young male depute head appears. If Thorn was a suspicious type, he would think he was standing there to ambush her – to speak to her before she reaches Thorn.

Thorn witnesses an urgent conversation between the depute head and the union rep. Then the union rep shrugs her shoulders and follows the depute head through the door and, presumably, downstairs to the management corridor.

Thorn is just about to run after her, but he realises that he cannot leave his post. Now, with the classes settling in around the school and the corridor clearing – as pupils siphon noisily into the other English rooms – he recognises that he is shortly going to be left in the corridor alone again, as guardian of the pyramid of poo.

He nips into the room to collect his stuff. He doesn't want to lose his things if the room is suddenly declared off limits.

# Tuesday, 1050

One pupil was already in class. A nice one. One of the quiet, unassuming girls who sat and tried to do what was asked of her. She had her folder out and was sitting with a pencil in her hand.

'Hi, Laura,' Thorn said, 'how are you today? I didn't see your name on the parents' night list. Can they not come?'

'No,' the mousy girl replied. 'My mum's out.'

'Oh, well,' said Thorn, 'maybe next time.' He smiled at her.

'My mum's out' could mean so many things – out, working in a respectable job – out, working for less than minimum wage – out, unconscious from drink or drugs – or it could just be a coverall excuse, because her mum did not care to come, or her mum was too intimidated by the institution of school to be comfortable attending the parents' evening.

It was another moment before the rest of the class attended, coming in the usual dribs and drabs. They came a measured time after the bell. Today, they were even later than usual – almost provocatively so. Thorn ignored this and greeted them by name as they came through the door. He sensed a bit of bravado about them, a bit of attitude which he did not like. But he ignored it. He could do nothing else. There were a few knowing glances and snickers between some of them.

He quickly ran through the register. 'Is Lindsay not here today?' he said.

'She went to see her pupil support teacher,' one of her minor allies told him.

'Okay, thanks.' Thorn did not like this either. He suspected that Harper was complaining.

There were some knowing glances.

'Well, it will be nice to meet so many of your parents and carers tonight,' he continued. 'It always surprises me how pleasant your parents are compared to you.' It was an old joke he always made. He didn't know why he should change his methods. There were a few of the obligatory sneers.

'One of the main things your parents will be asking about will be close reading, so we are going to continue with some work on that today. I have a passage here, taken from a newspaper, *The Guardian*, I think. We're going to read over the article and then you are going to pick out some of the literary techniques.'

There was a collective groan. That was what it was like. The kids hated close reading because they thought they were bad at it, so he chose accessible articles to give them practice and to help expand their vocabulary and grasp of linguistic technique. But many of them just blanked out.

Thorn distributed the photocopied passage to the pupils closest, asking that they be passed back to the other members of the class.

As always, even though he counted out the exact number, there was a little shit who mucked it up by holding two or not passing them back quickly enough – wasting another minute of the precious teaching time.

Then, because they would never deign to read something aloud in class, he read to them – like teacher did when they were in primary school. Worryingly, some couldn't even follow the text with their eyes. Many declared ambitions to pass the course and go on to tertiary education or responsible jobs, yet they could barely concentrate for the length of a paragraph – never mind focus for long enough to read a whole passage.

It tired him out. It really did. Many arrived in secondary school thinking that they already knew how to read and write – because they learned in the first seven years of schooling. Thereafter, many did no reading at all – other than the instructions for video games or misspelled texts and social media posts. They were not stupid, but their capacity for processing black font on white paper was mostly piss poor.

It was a passage about travelling beyond the Arctic Circle. He often chose travel writing in an attempt to engage the kids – to make them realise that there was a world beyond their own digital, self-encapsulating reality.

When he read a piece like this, he imagined one of them, in the future, instilled with a spirit of adventure and living somewhere else other than the immediate environment – maybe teaching in Japan or working in Europe.

He started reading, but had to stop almost immediately. One of the boys near the window was sniggering with the girl behind. 'Do you want to read this, Chris?' Thorn said, going through his usual rigmarole. 'If you could do that, then I could sit down here and snigger. Then we would see how you like it...'

Chris, a blond footballer, sniggered to the girl behind again, then slowly turned around.

*Fuck it!* thought Thorn, *they are a bit feisty today. Pain in the bloody arse!*

He started reading again.

As he read the first paragraph, he could see at least two kids with their phones under the desk. Another was picking her nose while looking out of the window. Another let fly with a fart.

There were sniggers.

*Boring*, Thorn thought, and, without interrupting his reading, he switched on the fan behind his desk, which returned any flatulence released in his vicinity. In this manner, he dealt with the revolting behaviour with deadpan panache and complete impunity.

Just as he switched the fan on, bloody Lindsay Harper breezed in.

He stopped reading this time. He had not even finished the first paragraph. 'Hi, Lindsay,' he said breezily, as if to demonstrate that nothing was amiss.

'I was down speaking to Mrs…' Lindsay said, fully expecting to see his face fall.

'Yeah, I heard, thanks,' Thorn said, nonchalantly. 'What do you say when you are late to class?'

This was what he said to all of the latecomers who came in once he'd started.

'I'm not late,' she said smugly. 'I told you, I was speaking to the pupil support teacher.'

*Smug rat*, thought Thorn. Why the hell did he have to put up with this shite? She thought she was getting one over on him.

'Okay, you weren't late, but you did interrupt the class.'

This was her grandstanding. She was looking for a reaction from him. She was wanting him to snap or to give her reason to complain again. She was wanting to showboat in front of her peers. She thought she was gaining kudos – but Thorn knew that she didn't have much of a following.

'Maybe you could just apologise for coming in after the start of the lesson. It's what I would do.'

She was in stand-off mode.

In the scheme of things, he didn't give a shit if she apologised.

'Forget it, Lindsay,' he muttered. 'Let's not waste any more time. Sit down now, please.'

That didn't help her. She couldn't stand there if he wasn't going to say any more and she didn't want to be told to sit down. He had won a minor point. She looked stupid for not doing what everyone else was asked to do. Now, she had to sit down, as she was told, because she was, in fact, wasting everybody's time.

He handed her a copy of the article as she flounced past.

Thorn might have been a minor nuisance to his own teachers at secondary school, but he was never like this Lindsay bloody Harper.

Although not particularly popular, she was a poisonous little catalyst. What with her laziness and tardiness and deflection of his criticism, he hoped she wasn't the type of egocentric little dissembler who would turn her grumbles into some kind of a Salem-style witch hunt – with him as its quarry.

It had often happened before with teachers.

On one occasion, he was hauled up by the depute after a kid started telling tales at home.

Some parents had gone over his head to complain about his professionalism. The mistake he made was to play music in class when the kids were working. For fuck sake – playing music!

Any classroom behaviour which challenged parental expectations – extended group work, a new seating layout, an informal test, using coloured pens, an innovative text, an unconventional media study – could come back and bite a teacher on the bum. It was such bollocks.

Tedious was his life and that period played out in a classically leaden way. He worked hard to draw out any interest from the kids – although he believed that he could have worked twice as hard, without any discernible effect. It was closer to the truth to say that he worked hard to keep them awake.

Barely one of them ever allowed a glimmer of even the faintest interest – not today or any other day – parents' evening or not.

If anything, in advance of the event, they were more distracted from their work, more restive – because they were wary of what he could report to any parent who cared to show up and listen to the teacher's advice.

Early on in the term, during the honeymoon period, he felt some sort of affinity for this lot. Now, as they sensed the pressure of looming assessment, he felt the distance between them yawning.

Nevertheless, he tried to keep up his end of the bargain. He plied his trade – word after word, sentence after sentence, paragraph after paragraph. And, as he read, he explained technique and nuance, until he had broken through to the end of the passage.

It was like a conjuring trick. A witty and engaging article was made sterile, by the act of being read to a stolid and indifferent audience.

And then he persisted. He posed questions – often on points he had already mentioned. Doggedly, he persevered, asking each and every one of them about some aspect of the text. Unsurprised, he found that virtually none of them could answer rudimentary questions – unless they were led to the answers with blatantly obvious clues and reminders.

The endless bloody period, which only lasted fifty minutes, felt as if it lasted all morning.

All he did was fill the tedium with the sound of his own voice. Apart from anything else, in this battle of wills, he wanted the kids to remember that he, at least, had been working hard on the day of the parents' night – even if they had not fired a single neuron.

# Wednesday, 0850

The place smells really foul now – like some rotten mixture of rancid and degrading cheap meat – which is at its most horrible when it is stuck to your shoe and following you everywhere you walk. He suspects an omnivore.

Thorn pushes all of the windows, so that they are fully open. He might as well. There is no point in letting the pernicious molecules alight on the carpet, seats and tables, if they can be swept away with a blast of air. He doesn't yet know if he will be back in the room or if other people will be in it. He sees no reason why anyone but the shitter should be made to suffer.

He does not want to look at it, but he does. It is still there, still massive, but less big than it had grown in his imagination. So strange to see the perfectly formed, yet repulsive memorial, which, without him doing much other than object to its presence, is fast becoming a source of peculiarly purposeful direction in his life – an unexpected trajectory in his career path.

He cannot, for the life of him, imagine who might have squeezed this one out. It is a minor masterpiece – quite something. With the size of it, he should have taken a picture of it next to a Coke can. That's what folk do when they send photos of potholes to the council. That would give an idea of scale. But he doesn't have a Coke can and he doesn't want to put his hand anywhere near it, so he just leaves it as it is, sitting there – sitting where he would normally be sitting at this time on any other Wednesday morning – in front of his lethargic period-one class.

He checks his drawers to see if there is anything he might want. He takes his steel coffee pot and stuffs it in his bag. His mug, orange and white and in the style of an old Penguin classic, he leaves behind. He has never felt the same about *The Great Gatsby* since he attempted to teach it to an allegedly able S5 class. He told them it was a monument of American literature – which, through previous study, reading and careful consideration, he knew it to be. They were unconvinced – regardless of his commentary, reference to authoritative sources and the notes he produced. It was an insufferable experience – a battle of wills, which Thorn struggled to win. Eventually, he just had to accept it and move on. The class knew better. The book was complete shit. This is why the Gatsby mug is overlooked and he slams the drawer shut.

What does it say, he thinks, as he leaves his room – the room in which he spends the bulk of his working week – that he has no interest in anything else there? A passer-by would have assumed some measure of affinity between a teacher and room, given that it is the pedagogue's natural environment – their workshop, their stage. But Thorn learned early on, through the days of probationary and supply teaching, that he was far from being a fixture in any classroom. Other teachers might be teachers of vocation or teachers of a different calibre to him, but he and many others are merely part of the daily and monthly reckoning – the internal economy of the school. On any given day, there is a finite number of pupil bums on seats and, in a purely administrative sense, there has to be someone to stand in front of those bums. That someone is often a person like Thorn.

Thorn knows, from his dealings with temporary members of staff and probationers and with full-time teachers, that there are some fantastic people involved in the profession – people that the kids would follow to the end of the period. There are some like that, but there are also some who are the polar opposite – to whom the kids do not listen from the moment they enter the room until the instant they leave it. Indeed, there are some 'trained' teachers, who could stand in front of a class from the very dawn of time until the furthest limit of the expansion of the universe, to whom the kids will never give the slightest bit of attention – not now or ever.

And, whilst Thorn is far from being the very worst kind of teacher, he would never be considered amongst the best. To him, his classroom is a place of penance. It is not his zone – neither a comfort zone nor a war zone – and it is certainly not where he imagines himself strutting his stuff, captivating young minds and moulding their personalities.

No, in fact, what he really does in this room is pass time – often thinking about little more than the fact of it passing. He laments its passing and rues it – and yearns desperately for the end of the period, the day, the week and the term. He is unvarying in that. He has no wish to be in that room, ever, for any longer than is necessary.

He feels nostalgia for the streets in which he played as a boy and sentiment for each one of his family homes. He knows something about how to relate to places, people and time. But, suffice to say, when it comes to the room in which he spends his working day, he never feels anything but a yearning to be out of it – and to never go back.

And, considering this, as he stands in front of the pile of excrement on his chair, he allows himself to imagine that this time might be the last time he stands here.

Therefore, without regret, he prepares to depart. He lifts his stuff, casts a single, rearward glance at the intrusive jobby, swings his bag and jacket over his shoulder and leaves the room.

He locks the door again from the outside and stands a moment in the corridor. Then he places his bag on the floor and thinks – thinks hard.

# Tuesday, 1131

Lindsay first came to Thorn's attention because of her blue hair. He mused that she probably had her heart set on a career as a music blogger or a graphic artist, because the hair hinted at an affinity with alternative music or a mania for Manga.

The hair was probably an attempt to distract onlookers from the fact of her girth – as were her trendily-cut cardigan, black ra-ra skirt and stripy Pippi Longstocking tights.

She was ungainly from too many biscuits and too much Netflix lying in a heap on her bed. And the poor kid was going knock-kneed from carrying the extra weight. It happened to some – those who forsook exercise for comfort eating. It was a symptom of the times.

She affected to have a cheerful demeanour, but often sat apart, as if she was staking a claim to being her own person – or pretending to be. Her real friends were not numerous.

She was in sixth year, which meant that, in the arc of her school career, this was her last chance at Higher English.

Whatever her ambition, the girl thought that turning up late to Thorn's class four days out of five – or, at best, three days out of five – gave her entitlement to progress to whatever stratospheric heights her self-importance would allow.

The honest truth was that the class had a smattering of kids with the ability and temperament to do well. The rest were disinterested or lazy or not very literate – or all three.

Lindsay definitely fell into the latter category.

Unhelpfully, for someone wanting to progress in English, she did not have any interest in reading or literature. When pressed, Lindsay would say that her favourite writer was JK Rowling. This meant that she knew JK Rowling was a writer, that she had seen all of the Harry Potter movies and she had the related books in her possession – bought for her by relatives at birthdays and Christmas. Lindsay likely started to read the first book four years ago, but lost the will to continue, after mouthing her way through just ninety-five pages in six weeks.

She also misspelled the word 'philosopher'.

Pupils like this were many. They had talent enough to flatter and deceive – but often mostly deceived themselves. They were just a subset of the many, disengaged by the system, floating through, ambivalent to the fact that their lives were devoid of much meaning and, as yet, too young and insensitive to be aware of it.

However, as exams and certification approached, they perceived that a reckoning was coming – something over which they had very little control.

Then paranoia set in. Realisation dawned – even in people like the vague and unresponsive Lindsay Harper – that things were getting serious. Then, feedback on their puny, half-effort practice papers and essays made them realise that failure beckoned.

They had swanned along, not giving a shit, year in, year out, then, suddenly, the pressure shot up. They were under official scrutiny. And that was exactly when they needed a convenient scapegoat.

With Lindsay it kicked off when Thorn was going over a close reading paper in class. The kids had spent two periods completing it – a past paper.

He should have known that going over the paper, in some detail, so that they could compare their answers with the exam board marking scheme and ask him questions, would be far too useful to them. It was simply the best thing to do and much better than just giving them a mark. He only wanted to demonstrate that it was something they should attempt themselves – so that they were better prepared, better informed.

That day he started the lesson as planned.

Then, Lindsay arrived eleven minutes late and wanted him to stop the lesson and place her measly close reading effort centre stage in his life. She said that she had not finished the paper.

He told her, perhaps bluntly, because she missed the previous period and was often absent that, nonetheless, reading through the paper and understanding the answers with the rest of the class would be beneficial for her.

However, she argued that the rest of the class should wait until she had finished the paper, so that it could be marked by him – which was his job.

She dug in her heels. The injustice. In an embarrassing display of juvenile self-righteousness, she blazed a trail through almost five minutes of the period. No one else made a fuss. Those who had two legitimate periods to complete the exercise just wanted to get on with it. They knew that there was little value in her show of conceit and that she was frequently absent and prone to blowing hot air.

Maybe she had been unwell. Maybe she did feel some injustice. But it did not matter. The work of the entire class could not be dictated by the absence of one individual – especially an individual with poor attendance, who was shy in applying herself to any task.

Thorn felt some mild sympathy, but he would not relent. She was not the first to feel frustration, as she trundled through the infinitely complex and baffling maze of learning experiences which was the senior school curriculum.

So far, so bad, but perhaps the more glaring mistake Thorn made was to send Lindsay's parents a 'homework warning' letter, shortly after that. He was not a fan of homework. He made no assumption that a bit of irrelevant scribbling would somehow lift the skill level of disinterested and demotivated pupils, but, when it came to the time of year when work for the exam board was due, there was no option but to insist that work arrived in school and on time.

Lindsay had not met her obligations. She provided a first draft of a personal essay – a page and a half of quite neat scribbles about a day which changed her life – but the work was incomplete. That was all. The work was not finished and the deadline for exam board submissions was fast approaching.

The letter must have been a blow to Lindsay. All the trust and understanding between her and her parents, carefully nurtured at home, was shattered with the flick of a teacher's pen and the arrival of a photocopied letter addressed to her mum.

That was when Lindsay's instinct for self-preservation kicked in. This was when her problem with Thorn became less of a personality clash and more of a co-ordinated witch-hunt.

Thorn didn't set out to be disliked. He didn't set out to be a wise-ass or obnoxious, but his status as teacher often meant – particularly because of the ridiculously long holidays – that there was a world of people out there who were keen to hold him to account.

And Lindsay came down hard on this letter of complaint. At her instigation, her mother phoned the guidance teacher. The guidance teacher made it her business to draw Thorn to the attention of his senior member of staff and to respond to the concerns of the mother – little suspecting that the fault could lie with the pupil.

Both were spun a line by Lindsay – the usual one about the teacher – inadequate support, poor teaching, etc – whilst, in the meantime, Thorn's contention – that he had a lazy, underachieving pupil, which was already documented – was completely ignored.

The principal teacher took to the warpath. The depute head was involved. With no remorse about tampering with the narrative – to satisfy her own ends – Lindsay's version of the story gathered momentum.

# Wednesday, 0858

At this moment, he has no allies. He is standing outside his own room and someone, somewhere, is doing his work – because he refuses to. The union rep has been waylaid by the management team and, as far as he knows, only the probationer, his principal teacher, the janitor and the head teacher have any inkling of what has befallen him.

Where are his supporters? He cannot make a case. He cannot hold anyone to account. No one knows. Polly doesn't even know, for god sake. How can he make people aware?

A janitor's head appears at the door to the stairwell – at the other end of the corridor from where the union rep disappeared. The janitor spies Thorn and withdraws her head. She is presumably going to report to the head teacher that Thorn is still there.

Thorn thinks again. He needs to let Polly know. He needs a confederate. She might listen to him. She might know what to do.

Then he realises. He has a picture. He has a phone. He has an internet connection and he has a Facebook account. This really is the perfect medium for getting the message out. Why did he not think of it before? He will use the World Wide Web. He always advocates the use of internet technology in school. At last, he has found a situation worth reporting on social media!

At last!

At least one person follows him in school and several old colleagues. The old colleagues will help. They will know what to do.

He pulls his phone out and retrieves the turgid turd pic. Immediately he crops it. He foregrounds the jobby, making sure there is evidence in the background that the photo is from his room. He includes a bit of computer and some paperwork. The class planner with his name on it is sitting on top of the pile of papers.

Perfect.

His account does not have his full name on it, but it does have his initials. He has to get the word out.

He uploads the edited shot.

He slows a bit as he decides what to write. He has to make maximum impact. He starts to draft.

'*GIANT-SIZED JOBBY*', his headline shouts. That's good, he thinks. It gets some alliteration in.

'*I am an English teacher in Hopeton High School. This morning, I arrived in my classroom to find this item on my chair. As you can see, it was not left there by accident.*

*As the victim, I am interested to know what you think. What should I do?*

*I have informed my principal teacher. She looked at it and suggested it be tidied up.*

*I insisted that my head teacher attend the scene to witness this nasty business. She was not prepared even to look at it and instructed me that it would be cleaned up by a janitor. Then she told me to get on with my work.*

*I am not satisfied with this response. I am a victim. My workplace has been vandalised – in an obscene dirty protest. Surely the fact that a shameless someone shat on my seat should be investigated. I would not expect to dump in the head teacher's office and get away with it.*

*I do not believe that this incident can be ignored.*

*Please 'like' this post and help me in my campaign for justice.*'

Thorn reads over the post and reads it again. He would like to spend more time on it, but he senses that his time in the building may be running out.

He is just about to click when he sees the double doors swing open loudly. The depute head teacher comes sweeping along the corridor. He is the big man on the staff. For some reason, the head teacher has chosen to send her enforcer. He is accompanied by the janitor. She is big herself, in a wide kind of way and has a determined shuffle. It was her head Thorn saw appearing through the door a few moments ago.

She enjoys having the ear of the management team. She will never be Thorn's ally, no matter how pleasant he is to her in the morning. To her he means nothing. He is not her boss. But Thorn will not be intimidated. He is a big enough man himself. He is not afraid of the scary depute, who worries the kids, but, in reality, appears to be quite a genial young man. He might have a bit of youth and flexibility on his side, but, with his residual fitness, Thorn will not go down without a noisy struggle. Surely somebody would get that scrap on camera…

He realises he still has his phone in his hand. He takes one quick look down and, before he confronts the depute, he presses 'POST'.

# Tuesday, 1137

He re-entered the classroom at the same time as many of the class members. Having visited the same unpleasant lavatory for the fourth time that day, he was ready – as much as he ever would be – to teach the S4 class about persuasive writing.

Not that the class wanted to know anything about persuasive writing. And who could blame them?

At once, it was an effort to make them sit down, an effort to have them take their jackets off, an effort to get them to be quiet and an effort to make them listen.

Three kids gave him difficulty about the jacket thing. Sophie Tucker, a wee fat lassie, was reluctant. She was probably embarrassed. She wore her hoody zipped up to cover her grubby collar and tie, but also to cover the food stains on the front of her shirt from last week. Thorn didn't know her story, didn't know where she came from – much less where she was going – but he had sent a guidance alert about the poor child and her personal hygiene – several times.

The second kid he leant on to take his jacket off was Scott Hunter. He was a difficult wee bastard, but mostly elsewhere. Thorn had a run-in with him eighteen months ago – a real forehead to forehead dispute – about a slammed door, but since then he had seldom raised his head. He didn't take much persuading.

That just left Grant McFudden – the most challenged and challenging lad in the class, if not the year. He had a spacer – a shiny silver cylinder with a scorpion shape in it – which was inserted into an enlarged hole in his right ear lobe. His bleached hair appeared to be randomly teased out and fell to one side of his head. This was a pupil who, in the weeks since start of term, had only written his name twice and a garbled answer to a close reading question once. It was now February. He was a kid who clearly didn't give a fuck.

He appeared to be about as dense as they came, but Thorn guessed it was learned behavior. McFudden lived with his ageing mother and Thorn suspected that the angry, spoilt-brat man-child could not be made to lift a finger at home, because he was too busy messaging on his mobile, playing the Xbox or rolling a joint.

It was always a shit start to the period when Thorn saw this class – and he saw them four days a week.

The kids didn't care.

He wasn't able to get their attention.

They did nothing.

There was no tangible evidence to show for his time with them.

It was like spending time in some hellish limbo.

Day after day, hour after hour, time was pissed away, with nothing to show for it. Teaching English in the early twenty-first century classroom could be a thankless task.

Then the class was nearly quiet – not because they had responded, but because there was a temporary lull in their conversation.

Declan Meikle was tapping his pencil on the desk, but Thorn ignored it.

If there was anyone in the class he actually despised for their behaviour, it was Meikle. If there was one child he was likely to explode at, in a fit of frustrated rage, it was Meikle.

Thorn still ignored the pencil tapping. At this stage there was no point in mentioning it. Falling out with Meikle so early in the period would lead to an unpleasant fight. Meikle would draw the laughter and support of the other pupils in the class. They would side with him. Yes, speaking to Meikle about his pencil tapping would be a mistake.

'Okay, does everyone have a jotter and something to write with?' he said.

Shortly, there was an unruly queue of five at his desk, all wanting a sheet of paper or a pencil – from fast-diminishing stock.

Moments later, another boy was at the desk. 'Do you have a sharpener?' he said.

'So, if you have a look at the board here,' said Thorn, as he pointed the boy towards the sharpener on the table at the bin and moved across towards the screen.

The talking had started again. He barely heard himself speak.

'So, if you could have a look at the board here,' he said more loudly, rapping the panel with his knuckles. 'Excuse me, can I have some attention, please?'

Most kids were still distracted by the noise round about them. But a tiny number, the really nice kids, were listening. These were the kids who tried a bit – the kids with a ghost of a chance.

The kids who couldn't care were still talking – about what it did not matter.

'Can ah huv a pencil, sir?' Scott Thomson called out.

'I gave out pencils three minutes ago, Scott,' Thorn said.

There were sniggers.

Scott Thomson was a kid Thorn always wanted to see marked ABS when he looked at the daily attendance sheet. He was another noxious presence in class. In full flight, he had the manner of a Premier League footballer taking issue with a referee. If Thorn did not deal with him warily, he was likely to erupt into obscene language and elaborate gesticulation.

Many kids were scared of Thomson's temper. He travelled to away matches with a team of football casuals and, in a recent essay, confessed to enjoying gang violence. Thorn much preferred him when he came to class with dilated pupils. Smoking weed at interval took the edge off his temper and made him more amenable.

Not today.

'Take a pencil from the top drawer,' Thorn said, 'and quickly.'

From his seat in the middle of the room, Thomson walked to the back of the class and down the next aisle towards the teacher's desk. He opened the drawer and started taking things out of it – a rubber, a board marker, a ruler, a stapler and a hole punch. He placed each item on the desk and then took a pencil out. He checked the point with his finger and waited for chuckles before walking slowly back to his seat. During another extended walk, in the other direction, he jabbed one of his peers in the arm with the pencil.

'Sit down with your pencil, Scott, now!' Thorn called, with volume, but no hostility.

'Ah wis just checkin it was sharp enough,' Thomson joked. He was such an entertainer.

*You are a fucking prick, son! A complete fucking prick!* Thorn said, inside his head.

'Would you stop tapping your pencil, please, Declan,' he said out loud.

'Ah wisnae tappin ma pencil,' said Declan.

'I think you were,' said Thorn. 'If it wasn't you, maybe the person who was tapping their pencil sitting near Declan could stop it, please. Thank you.'

He turned to the board again.

The tapping continued. He knew it was Declan Meikle, but he did not have the energy to confront him. He ignored it.

Someone else started tapping. There were sniggers.

Thorn looked at the clock. Nine minutes down. Only forty-one to go, he thought.

He heard a coughed 'Fuck' from the middle of the class.

*Fuck!* he thought. *Fuck, fuck, fuck!*

'You know I don't want to hear that sort of language, thanks, Scott,' said Thorn.

'It wisnae me, sir,' Thomson scoffed.

Thomson had the attention of most of the class now. They were so gullible, so easily distracted. Thorn knew, with great clarity, that they had scant interest in what he had to say, but they could easily be captivated by an unpleasant teenager, who had a few disruptive ideas and a little imagination.

It made him feel sick, from his gullet to his gut. Again.

If any one of them had a modicum of humour about them, it would be different, but all they wanted to do was bait him and frustrate him, push him and pull him, grind him down.

If any of the little shits had any hope in their sad little lives, it was that he would teeter and fall screaming into the big chasm of their chaos.

There was only so much a body could stand. Some people were chided and teased until they lost it. No longer did they interact with humour or empathy, like humans. That capacity had been gnawed away at until there was nothing left but the hardened husk of the previous person.

One of the languages teachers down the corridor was like that. He had been at the chalk face for so long – the best part of thirty-five years in the glare of the classroom tubes – that his hide was now a leathery shell. He looked human, but the soft, sensate, responsive organism inside had all but wasted away.

'I had to speak to you about it before, Scott. You know that. You know it's inappropriate language for school. If I hear it again, I'll refer you. You know I've got to do that.'

'It wisnae me, sir,' Thomson repeated.

More sniggers.

'Whatever,' Thorn said. 'Now, let's get on. You know we have two pieces of writing to complete for our folios in the next week or two and if that is not done, we won't be making any progress to the exams.'

*So tedious,* Thorn thought, as the seconds of the period ticked sluggishly by and the precious moments of his life slipped pointlessly through his hands. *Tedious for me, tedious for you, tedious for every-fucking-one.*

# Wednesday 0904

There is no suggestion that there will be any rough-housing.

'Mr Thorn,' the young depute, Honnigan, says as he approaches, 'the head teacher asked me to come up and ask what your intentions are. She said she spoke to you earlier, but she is concerned you are going to prolong the situation. I said I would come up and see. I think she was happy for me to come up, because she didn't want to have another confrontation in the corridor.'

'Where did she want to have the confrontation?' asks Thorn. 'I suppose she usually has them in her office, doesn't she?'

'Listen, Archie,' Honnigan says, with what he thinks is his amiable smile, 'please don't shoot the messenger. I'm not here to fight her battles. I just want to know what's happening.'

'I know, I know,' Thorn replies. 'I don't want a fight either, for god's sake. I just want some help here. I don't want it to look as if I am making all this up. I asked the boss to come up and see what the problem was and she couldn't even take a look at the thing. How can she possibly understand that I have an issue, if she is not prepared to look it in the eye?'

The depute is looking through the window in the door now, but he can't see anything, because the small computer table is in the way. 'Can I have a look?' he says.

Thankful that someone has finally shown some interest, Thorn says, 'Of course.' He moves his bag and jacket and opens the door.

The depute steps in. The janitor waits outside.

'Sheesh!' he whistles. 'That is rank.' He takes a well-used handkerchief from his pocket and holds it over his mouth.

Thorn thinks this is a bit melodramatic. Honnigan has clearly seen the discovery of too many decomposing bodies on cop shows. He lets him approach the desk area on his own.

*Yeah, police tape needed*, thinks Thorn again, *for the scene of the crime.* Maybe, given the smell of the bastard, they need some sort of Geiger counter or stench monitor from the Environmental Health Department. It is still absolutely stinking.

'What the hell…?' says the depute. 'That's a bloody work of art! Look at the size of that!' He stands agog. Thorn can see he is astonished. And, he's quite right. It is something else. 'Who on earth was in here early enough to do that, for Christ sake? It wasn't you, Janny, was it?' he shouts to the janitor who, at this moment, is hesitating at the door and howking up the sides of her trousers.

'No, it wasn't me.' She laughs. She comes through the door and catches sight of the pile of human waste. 'Jesus Christ!' she swears through her teeth. 'That's disgusting. I'll need a shovel for that and a big bucket. Christ, was there an elephant in here or something?'

Just then, the depute's radio beeps. It beeps several times before a nasal-sounding female voice is heard. 'Mr Honnigan, Mr Honnigan, please return to the office urgently, thank you.'

Thorn guesses it is a lady from the office. He does not know which one. He does not know any of them by name. They are all very nice, but they are transferred and replaced with greater frequency than the teaching staff.

'I'll need to go, Archie. I am being called. Let me know what your plans are, will you? I'll be down in the management corridor for the next while, by the sounds of it. You can get me there. I think the boss wants to know. Okay?'

Then he turns to the janitor, as he moves towards the door. 'Can you get shot of this, please, Netta. I think Mr Thorn will want his room clear as soon as possible. Maybe you could find an air freshener as well, to get rid of the smell. Thanks.'

'No,' interrupts Thorn, 'that won't be necessary. Someone has to do something about it first. Investigate it or something.'

'I'm not sure what you expect, Archie, but just let me know what's next, okay?' replies the depute, shaking his head. 'We need the classroom and we need a teacher. Be better if that was you – obviously. Anyway, I need to go. Let me know, okay?' he says, more pointedly.

'Yeah, sure,' Thorn says, without much conviction.

The depute strides off quickly down the corridor, jacket too short in the arms and metal-tipped heels clicking like he's important.

Hearing him definitely go, Thorn is concerned that the janitor is going to pull a fast one and wheech the keech away. He turns to her. 'It's all right, Netta, I can sort this out. You must have loads to do.'

'Naw, naw, it's my job,' replies the janitor, unconvincingly.

Then her radio buzzes and rattles too. 'Netta, Netta, please come to the office. Please come to the office.'

'I'll get it when I come back up, Archie. I'll bring some rubber gloves,' she says, retreating. 'I might bring a mask and safety glasses as well and I think I've got a white paper suit. Just make sure you lock the door. That could give a kid an awful fright.'

'Yeah, yeah,' Thorn agrees. 'I'll be here anyway. Thanks. See you.'

He is surprised that the depute shot off so quickly. He was obviously sent up to soft-soap and do some schmoozing. He has the skill set for it. But the unexpected whistle from downstairs sent him bounding off quickly. He's well trained.

# Tuesday, 1225

The bell rang and the fourth-year class scrambled towards the door. If Thorn did not actually stand between them and the freedom of the corridor, he believed they would probably crush each other to death. God only knew how many would be ground underfoot in an actual emergency.

It was as much as he could do not to loathe the wee bastards. And it took a lot out of him. They left him so down and depleted, even though his compassionate inner self often told him that it wasn't their fault that they were insufferable little shits.

They couldn't help it, he knew. With a bit of luck, as time went on, they would understand that he was only a functionary and as irrelevant in the oppressive system as they were.

Looking back into the room, he realised its mess. There were two upturned chairs, tables were in disarray, pencil shavings lay under a desk and, in one of the aisles, someone had popped a tube of barbecue Pringles and ground them into the carpet with their heels.

He could do nothing about the Pringles, but he turned the chairs over and straightened the desks. As he was doing this, his first-year class started to trickle in.

At this time in the week, they came up in ones and twos from physical education. Most were red and sweaty and still in the process of getting dressed.

They struggled with ties. Thorn suspected that most of them left their ties looped on a chair overnight, to save dealing with the complexity of creating anything as sophisticated as a knot first thing in the morning.

It was mostly boys who struggled with getting dressed. They came in with collars up, loose laces, shirt tails hanging out, the lot.

This was a rowdy crowd of first years. Thorn wasn't sure, because he didn't care to recall classes from one year to the next

– they all melded into a grey mass of memory – but he thought this was the worst S1 class ever. Well, not so much the worst, because there were nice kids in it and they didn't mean any harm, but they were definitely noisier than any S1 class he had ever met.

He wasn't shouty by nature, but there were times in the year when he had raised his voice with the wee blighters.

One of the girls in the second row told him that, for a hobby, she did 'sassy' dancing. He thought that summed the class up pretty well. They had very limited skill with reading, writing, talking and, particularly, listening, but they had plenty of 'sass' – plenty of brassy, groundless self-confidence.

And the fact that there was an often-unsupervised kid with several syndromes didn't help create an aura of calm either. This was never to diminish the contribution that someone on a spectrum could make to society, in due course, but this boy loved to play the complete clown. In a room full of pupils who were happy to be endlessly entertained, this led to boundless amusement.

Thorn wholeheartedly believed in inclusion. It was best for everyone that the range of humanity was, as much as humanly feasible, present in the school community, but, if all that happened was that the number of special schools was reduced and most kids were sent to mainstream schools, well, obviously, that wasn't going to work. And it didn't matter how positive the parents, pupils and staff were about the principle.

Thorn liked the kid in this class who struggled with his behaviour. He was a bit better in the mornings, when he had taken his medication, but, jeez, in the afternoons he was bouncing.

If the nice lady classroom assistant wasn't there, he could be ranging around the room and it would take Thorn one hundred and ten per cent of his time to deal with him.

And that, in a nutshell, was it. If the kids couldn't keep themselves in a bit of order, a teacher was completely shafted.

# Wednesday, 0910

Locking the door, Thorn places the key in his pocket and, with the other hand, pulls his phone out. He places his thumb on the screen and the background photo and app icons appear.

He scans quickly. The Facebook icon has a red dot in the corner, with a small number 3 in it. He clicks the app. Just then a message appears across the top of the screen. It is from Polly.

*Call me when you can. P xx*, it says.

He will do that in a minute. He has to check Facebook now. As he returns to the app, another message jumps to the top of the screen.

It says, *I got your number from a friend. Please return call ASAP. Much appreciated.* He will do that in a minute too. He must…

*What the hell is going on in that place?* – another message, this time from a retired colleague.

He checks Facebook. The three notifications have become sixteen. He clicks on. There are eleven likes and five comments. One of the comments is the same as the text message he just received, but from someone else, a probationer teacher from last year, Alan – *What the hell is going on in that place?*

The other messages are:

*That is disgusting. I hope you have some wet wipes.*

*Wheel it down to your boss and ask her what she wants you to do with it.*

*Oh, shit! What did you do?*

*Call the police and say you have evidence of a crime.*

So, a few ideas, but nothing much to go on. He decides to phone Polly, who should be able to take his call.

She picks up first time, which is unusual. 'What on earth happened?' she says seriously. She sounds concerned. The fact is that he hates his job and, every time something vaguely stressful befalls him, she thinks it may be the final straw and he might walk out for good.

'Did you see the picture?' Thorn says. 'That is my chair and somebody has crapped all over it.'

'Who do you think it was?' Polly says, straight to the point. No fucking about with her. She knows the questions to ask and she ain't no head teacher.

'I have no idea,' replies Thorn. 'I don't know if it's a grudge or a wind-up. I was having a chat with some kids the other day and they asked me why I never get annoyed. They were asking what sort of thing would irritate me. I told them I didn't know. I wonder if one of them might be on the wind-up – to see if I cracked up when I saw a massive crap in my room.'

'But have you cracked up?' she says, this time not sounding so sage. This time sounding as if she is levelling criticism at him.

He takes a deep breath. It is a technique he has tried to perfect – something to avoid some of the complex confrontations they endured in the early days of their being together – back in the days when living together with anyone, even someone for whom you felt a great deal of attraction, was a challenge – especially with that excess of youthful energy.

'No,' he says, 'but thanks for considering my feelings anyway.'

She will know by this response that he is jittery. She must know, for god sake, that a great big jobby is not going to kick-start anyone's day in the appropriate manner – unless it is their own jobby and they have dumped it, of their own volition, in the comfort of their own toilet.

'I didn't mean that you have cracked up. I just mean, well, have you shouted at anyone or lost your temper?'

'No, I have not. I said that already. What I want is a wee bit of help here. I'm on a really sticky wicket with this one. I said to the boss I wasn't going to do anything until she helped me to clear it up.'

'You can't expect the boss to clear it…'

'I didn't mean clean it up, I mean find out who did it, because, really, I'm not here just to have my stuff crapped on. It's bad enough being walked over every day by the kids – and the bloody management, for that matter – but, if I don't make a stand, then the same thing will happen again or it will happen to somebody else.'

'But do you think it was wise to post it on Facebook?'

'Listen, I've done it. I had to do something. At the moment I'm standing in the corridor outside my locked classroom door and there's very little else I can do. Facebook was all I could think of.'

'Maybe you should phone the union,' says Polly. 'Maybe they can intervene or mediate or something. You can't just stand there all day.'

'I know, I'm going to do that right now. I'll let you know what's happening, but, the way I feel just now, I think they may ask me to leave, because I have refused to do my job. I don't know if that'll be a disciplinary offence or not. If Butcher has anything to do with it, it wouldn't surprise me. It wouldn't be the first time she threw the book at someone for disagreeing with her.'

'Maybe you should go and have a word with her. We've still got a mortgage to pay.'

'I know we have a mortgage to bloody pay. You know that's the only reason I come to this shithole every day. It's not because I bloody enjoy it. And I've certainly stopped enjoying it since someone shat on my bloody chair!'

'All right, all right, don't lose the rag. I just don't want you to damage your career, you know that.'

'I know, I know,' says Thorn tersely. 'Anyway, I'll have to go. I'll let you know if there's any crisis, but don't worry about me. I've got myself out of worse situations than this.'

'Just don't do anything daft,' says Polly feelingly. 'I was a bit worried when you put it on the web.'

'I didn't know what else to do, Poll. I'll see you later. Bye.'

He looks down at his phone and ends the call. He can't spend the morning on the phone to his wife, much as he might prefer it.

As soon as he ends the call, his phone begins to vibrate. He looks down again. It is a number he does not recognise. As usual, he rejects it.

He goes back to the app. Facebook has another few hits. Then the phone starts buzzing again. He sees that his former colleague is phoning. He cannot answer him just now. He will need to phone Edinburgh and speak to someone who is qualified to deal with situations like this – someone from the teachers' union.

# Tuesday, 1237

*War of the Worlds* went down well with the first-year kids. Even someone with numbers of educational needs could watch most of a movie without blighting the experience for the rest of them. Thorn had no love for whacko Tom Cruise, since he starred in that nauseating Yank crap – *Top Gun*.

He had also aged a hell of a lot better than Thorn, with his bloody gym guns and abs. Only overtime with a personal trainer and guzzling protein shakes and god knows what else kept him in that sort of shape. In an otherwise gripping Spielberg blockbuster, the artistic low point was when Thomas Cruise stripped off his T-shirt and crashed out on the bed for a topless kip. Prick.

And he was a Hollywood Scientology type. So, more than just being a wealthy tosspot, he was a weirdo spiritual tosspot too – which was a hell of a lot worse.

But that the first-year kids did not know. They just sat and watched the movie and willingly suspended their disbelief.

Then one kid asked if the alien invasion in the movie was for real.

*Jeezo!* Thorn thought. But then, with the number of video-game consoles out there, perhaps the line between observable fact and fiction was blurring. Was the kids' world view becoming so distorted that their sense of reality was slipping and being replaced by some surreal and crazy dreamscape? Who knew?

He knew there were kids, mostly boys, who spent their waking lives online. In the worst cases, they barely came out of their rooms – other than to eat and shit – and barely slept.

Some were already growing into computer-generated Jabba the Hutt-like masses of wobbling flesh.

In a class, it was usually quite clear whose social development was taking place online. There was no evidence of eye contact or physical interaction. Their communication was practised through their fingertips, rather than their faces.

He didn't have the faintest idea what would happen to these kids.

Several bedroom-dwellers from his own childhood still walked the streets of town. He saw them sometimes, but wanted to avert his eyes from these boys who never grew up – orphaned, middle-aged children who lived alone in the homes of their dead parents.

Thorn had always struggled to unglue his own kids from their screens. But he always insisted. They could not sit there all day. He would force them out for a walk – or Polly would. He would take them to a club – or Polly would. But they could not sit for days during weekends and holidays, growing marshmallow guts. Something – socialising or exercise – had to punctuate their screen time. He was no paragon, but they would not squander all of their hours transfixed by the retarding rays of television or the stupefaction of social media or video games.

# Wednesday, 0916

As he fumbles in his bag for his wallet, he realises that, rather than using the dog-eared card for the union, which he has kept for years for a situation like this, he can search for the number online.

Within seconds, the relevant number, underlined in blue, is on his screen and he touches it to make the call.

It is a few seconds before the phone starts to ring, another minute before it's answered. Someone with an east-coast accent asks him what they can do to help.

'I need some advice urgently,' Thorn tells him. 'I have refused to teach my classes today because there has been an incident, but I am still in the school. I want to talk to somebody now, please.'

'Can you give me your name, please, sir, and your membership number or date of birth?'

'Archie Thorn, twenty, nine, sixty-six,' he says, sounding as desperate as he can.

'Okay, sir, if you just hold the line for a moment, I will pass you through to the other office. I think there is someone there who can help you.'

Again, he has to wait. He is put on hold and a particularly frustrating piece of classical guitar music, it might be bloody 'Cavatina', is played back to him. Whatever it is, it is the same endlessly looped piece played to him when he phoned the bloody bank last week.

'Hello, can I help you, Archie?' a woman's voice reaches out to him. It sounds reassuringly reasonable.

'I am at my work, but I have had to say to the head teacher that I am not going to take my classes today,' says Thorn. He realises he is sounding less than sensible. He needs to justify his actions. 'I came into work this morning and there was a big poo on my chair. It has really thrown me. I don't think the principal teacher and the head teacher are taking it seriously.'

'Sorry?' she says, as if she sincerely hasn't heard. 'What did you find? Where?'

'Sorry,' he repeats back to her, 'but when I went into my class this morning, before the bell, there was a huge mound of human excrement on the teacher's chair at the front of the class – on my chair. And I don't think that's acceptable. All the PT and the boss want to do is get it tidied up, so that I can get on with my job.'

'Do you think it was put there intentionally?' the union advisor asks.

'What? What do you mean?' Thorn says, more than a little surprised. 'How do you think it got there? I don't think a very large seagull dropped it, if that's what you mean. It's huge.'

He is now not at all reassured that this person will have any idea of how to help him.

Maybe a question about pensions or conditions of service would have been more up her street. He gathers his thoughts quickly and readdresses the point.

'Yes, I think it was put there intentionally, by a person, who did a shit on my chair. But I really want to know who did it, so that they can be dealt with, and I really want a bit of support from the management team.'

'And you are sure it was human excrement, Archie? You don't mind if I call you Archie, do you?'

'No, I don't mind. Yes, I'm pretty sure. I suppose, though, without scientific analysis, it's pretty hard to tell. But with my past experience of human waste, it certainly smells human and is a sort of brown colour...'

'Okay, Archie, I believe you. And you say you haven't been debriefed or anything? Your managers have not given you time to talk this over?'

'No, well that's the problem. They just want to ignore it and get me back in front of a class as soon as possible and I don't think that's right. I mean, this is a stressful situation. I haven't been debriefed, as you say. They have not shown any interest, as far as I'm concerned. I mean, I thought they had a duty of care to me.'

'Can you give me the name of your head teacher, Archie? I wonder if someone should contact him to discuss the matter?'

'It's a Mrs Butcher and the number for the school is...'

'I have the school number here. Where are you just now, Archie?'

'Outside my classroom door on my mobile. Sorry, I didn't get your name.'

'My name is Sandra Warrender, Archie. If you need to contact me, you can phone back here.'

'Thanks, Sandra. Any advice about what I should do now?'

'You should probably go and sit in the staffroom or something, Archie, so that you are still in school if the head teacher wants to speak with you. You might be well-advised to speak to the union rep too, so that, if there is an interview, you have a witness – just to make sure that no one says anything that they might regret, if you know what I mean.

'So,' says Sandra, 'I'll ring off just now and you can phone me back or I can get back to you on this mobile number, if necessary. Okay? Bye.'

Before he can agree, the call ends.

# Tuesday, 1315

Most lunchtimes, most days, it was as much as Thorn could stand to just sit in his own room.

There was a time, in another school, at a different stage of his career, when to share time with colleagues was an interesting and enjoyable thing to do. In fact, in his first permanent job, there were a few people he enjoyed spending time with.

It was not like that any longer. Now, he worked with colleagues, communicated sufficiently and occasionally shared a thin joke. He did not seek their company and, habitually, they did not choose his.

So, when the lunch bell rang, he sometimes went to the staff base to heat something in the crusty old microwave. Then, as it warmed, he might catch up, briefly, but he never had any intention of spending anything but the minimum amount of time up there.

He needed some solitude to conserve his strength or recharge his batteries – time to switch off.

At lunch break, when he was eating, the last thing he could stomach was the interminable teacher chat. Some thought it endlessly interesting to talk about school life – on and on. The intellect was tuned to low, the verbal taps were turned on and the steady flow of soupy shit – about trivial interactions with miscreant kids – ran on and on.

Not only that, because this was interspersed with the recurring monologues on the tedious minutiae of assessment. Every single mind-numbing element of the national curriculum was gone over – again and again.

That his co-workers found it therapeutic to embrace a collective memory loss and play deaf to the repetition and inanity of their themes was up to them, but Thorn did not wish to hear them deliberate.

If he had thoughts on the teaching of English, which he occasionally allowed, he kept them to himself – for his sanity's sake. He had long ago realised that his role was as a functionary. Regardless of his opinions and of how critical he felt, someone of his lowly status and squandered ambition could not change the course of language and literature teaching.

So, there was no point in pondering it incessantly. All he could do was plod through the routines, ticking off the days on the calendar. Regardless of how fruitless and profoundly futile the teaching activities appeared to him, the reality was that his salary-slave status left him with no fecking option.

So, with last night's veggie curry lukewarmed by the antediluvian microwave, he usually cut back down to his own room and shut the door on the rest of the world – with no regrets.

Back there, the irony was not lost on him that his room – his prison during class time – was his sanctuary at breaks.

And why not? He had spent the morning doing 'education'. And another little measure of him had died. Then he would waste the afternoon doing 'teaching' and more of the dregs of his life would dribble away. The last thing he wanted to do was to fritter time going over it again and again, in agonising detail, with the teacher drones.

No, in his own room, with his door shut, Thorn could drop bits of food in his lap and briefly imagine himself a member of the human race and not merely a subset of the teaching profession.

# Wednesday, 0920

Putting his phone in his pocket, Thorn turns around in the corridor. He sees the genial depute and the less-than-genial head teacher advancing. The female janitor is just behind them, with what looks like a bottle of bleach in her hand. The male assistant janitor is almost jogging along in their wake. The male janitor is the one who does all of the work. He has rubber gloves on and he is carrying a short-handled shovel and a bucket.

Thorn sees them and instantly understands that confrontation is about to ensue. The depute is effectively here as bodyguard, because the boss is not prepared to do the dirty business on her own. The depute's mouth is set in a line, as if he is actually gritting his teeth. The boss churns down the corridor, painful heels pounding on the lino. She has no grace or speed, but she is doughtily determined.

She fires her first salvo from the hip. 'Mr Thorn, you have gone too far with this! It is completely unacceptable. What is an internal school matter should have stayed within the school. How dare you publish that picture on the internet!'

As she comes closer still, Thorn sees that she has fire in her little narrowed eyes. However, when he glances at Depute Honnigan, he thinks he can see something else other than fury.

'Remove it from Facebook this instant, Mr Thorn. That was a completely inappropriate thing to do and you know it.' She is bristling. She is in a stew. Thorn can see full well that his slightly reckless cat is storming around amongst her prized pigeons – and is having a feast of a time.

'I'm sorry, Mrs Butcher,' he says. He always starts with an apology. He has learned to use this strategy in many of his interactions. Sometimes, it can be immediately disarming. He is not sure that it is having that effect just now, but no one can accuse him of being aggressive and unreasonable.

'I'm not sure I can do that at the moment, Mrs Butcher,' he says. He takes out his phone. He looks down at it, presses it on and the screen lights up. He holds his thumb to it. He continues to stare down at the phone. In fact, he takes his time and keeps his eyes on it for another little while.

He can sense the head teacher's eyes boring into him, scrutinising him. He wishes he had brushed his hair. He is not used to being this close to his commanding officer and he can feel her hate rays drilling into his skull. He has always felt her contempt of him.

Apart from anything else, she is a mathematician. She inhabits a parallel universe – of digits and data. She cannot understand English teachers or why literature, never mind literacy, is at the core of the curriculum. She probably struggled to make sense of it at school.

Also, since she was promoted, she cannot fathom how someone of Thorn's age has failed to climb through the ranks. She cannot understand how he can be so lowly and can afford to buy so few shoes, when she is so powerful and significant and has bought so many shoes.

He looks up from the phone. 'I don't seem to have a signal at the moment. I'm sorry,' he says. 'The signal is not always great in the school. It sometimes takes a bit of time to link up.' He looks down again. 'Oh, there it is,' he says and pauses. 'Oh, no, down again. Sorry.'

He looks up at her, careful not to appear smug. 'Sorry.'

'That's not good enough. I want it removed immediately. We have already received some calls from outside of the school. I want it dealt with.'

*This is good*, thinks Thorn, *this is really good*. Never has he seen her so exasperated, flustered and weakened. He wants to milk this moment. Now, he senses a desire within himself to screw up her week and screw it up badly. Strange that he has never felt this willing to agitate before. Had he had this level of leverage, he might have learned to enjoy the taste of power.

But who would have thought that he would ever have had the slightest clout to manipulate the emotions of this stone-hearted manager?

He looks down at his phone again. 'I'll just have another look,' he says. In a moment of madness, or in a moment of genius, he takes his chance. The Facebook post has really riled her. Now he has the opportunity to capture this little fracas for posterity. He has always wanted to do it, during one of the ridiculous exchanges that he experiences in school. Now he has the opportunity to seize something spectacular. He touches camera. He swipes to video. He touches record.

'No, sorry, nothing yet.' He drops his hand to his side. As he does so, he flicks the mobile over in his hand. He hopes that the phone's magical little lens will capture as much of her as possible, just in case he is beyond redemption and has to play hardball.

'Anyway,' he says, 'I wanted to get your attention.'

The depute, who has been standing by good-naturedly, takes it on himself to alleviate some of the pressure of the situation. He does not want to see his head teacher blow her little fuse. He has to live with her. He must defend his position and be seen to do some work. He does not want to suffer her retribution if she is underwhelmed by his performance in this potentially stressful situation. 'Can you make sure you take it down as soon as possible, please, Archie? There have been a number of calls, as Mrs Butcher says, and we really don't want this spiralling. I'm sure we have all got more important things to do just now...'

'I usually get on with my work, most days,' Thorn returns, 'but today there was a great big pile of crap at my workstation, and it wasn't just the usual pile of marking and English jotters – it was a great big pile of human poo. All I asked was that somebody investigate the situation or take it seriously and Mrs Butcher was not even prepared to take a look. For all she knows, I could be making it up...'

'I said no such thing. I said that it should be cleaned up and that you should return...' she begins to fulminate.

'Hang on a minute, please, Mrs Butcher. Again, I am sorry, but you were not prepared to consider my position. In putting that picture on the internet, I virtually guaranteed that you would be able to see what I was shocked to see in my class this morning, when I came in to get on with my work.

'Not only did I have to look at the thing – the great big pile of human faeces – I also had to smell it. And to be honest, it smelled so strong and so filthy, that I think I tasted it too.

'Now, I don't know how you would have reacted, but I think I can honestly say that you would not have had the appetite to face a class of twenty-six pleasant-to-obnoxious kids – especially if you thought the kids had got wind of it and especially if you thought that one of them or some of them could have been responsible.'

If Thorn is going to post this on the internet, he thinks, he wants to make a good job of it. He wants to drop one into the pond and make some far-reaching ripples. He doesn't want it just to sink without trace. He wants to build an audience – give them some drama.

He hopes he has the camera at the right angle to capture the face of the boss, because it is a picture. He cannot hope to get her minions in, but, from their expressions, they cannot countenance what he is saying. They are probably very surprised, having known him for some time, that he has the cojones to bludgeon her like this.

But Thorn is making a play for it. He is a teacher of English, after all. He has practised saying this sort of thing to her so often in his head. So often. Now, he is mindfully aware of the situation and, if the shit is flying, he wants to make some stick.

She is burbling with rage. He can see that she is almost speechless. But not quite. She storms at him. 'Mr Thorn, it is of gravest concern that you have put news of this school on the internet. It is extremely unprofessional. I have never had to speak to any member of staff about something like this before. There is no way that this sort of behaviour can be justified or sanctioned.

'An act of vandalism may have taken place, but my first priority must be the running of this school and the teaching and learning of all of the pupils. That learning is being hampered by your behaviour today. I will be looking very carefully at the steps that I can take in order to make it quite clear to everyone, in this school and beyond, that I will not have the business of this school paraded over Facebook for everyone to see.

'And, for your information, I have already spoken to the director about this matter. He is in complete agreement that you should take down the offending article as soon as possible.'

'The offending article, Mrs Butcher, the offending article!' interjects Thorn, with some fire in him. 'What a ridiculous thing to say! I am sorry, but you are definitely missing a very big point here – the point that I have been trying to make all along. The offending article isn't a picture of the article. The offending article is the big blob of jobby sitting where I usually sit in front of my class. Mrs Butcher, if you had taken the time, in the first instance, to show a bit of empathy or some other human emotion, like distaste or disgust, or to make some little noise to indicate that you identified with some of the feelings that I had this morning, we wouldn't be in this intractable situation.'

Thorn can't believe that he is getting these big speeches in. He needs to be careful and not grandstand too much. He wants her to say something. He wants her to make herself look utterly ridiculous.

'So, I am sorry, Mrs Butcher, but I don't know where we go from here.'

She rails at him. 'I have said to you quite clearly that the absolute priority is to take that ridiculous post off Facebook. Thereafter, I will take advice from the director. This is unprecedented. As soon as I can be assured that the post has been taken down, I would suggest that you go home, because I am not sure that we can resolve this issue today.'

'No, no, hang on a minute,' says Thorn, 'I am not leaving the building until I have spoken to a representative of my union and I am not going to be able to do that just now. Also, if you are going to send me home, or if you have any intention of sending me home, I would like some sort of assurance that my pay will not be affected. I came here to work, prepared for the usual stresses and strains, but not these conditions. So, from my point of view, I am completely dissatisfied with the steps my managers have taken to support me. This is a completely unacceptable working environment, Mrs Butcher, with that enormous big bit of raw sewage in my room, reeking like that and spreading germs. My personal safety and my mental health have been compromised here, possibly by a member of this school community. I am telling you, within the hearing of your colleagues, who are my witnesses, that this has been an extremely distressing morning, and I am concerned that my professional reputation, my health and my emotional well-being are at risk.'

'Maybe we could discuss this downstairs, Archie, or maybe you could speak to your union down there. I don't think we should continue the discussion in the corridor.' This is the young depute breaking in. He can sense the tension, if he has any sort of relationship awareness at all. He is also probably looking out for his head teacher's health. He does not want to suffer the rough edge of her tongue for not becoming involved. He is also thinking that, if he can defuse the situation, it might be useful to the advancement of his career.

# Tuesday, 1355

He peed at 13.55. He always did.

In the coming period, he was downstairs in the Assisted Learning base.

At the start of the year, he was asked to fill space in his timetable with a couple of periods of learning support. Maybe it was obvious to the timetabler that he was tired of classroom teaching and needed a break, or else, he flattered himself to think, he was recognised as a person who had some residual patience with some of the more challenged kids.

Whatever the reason, it tied up some of his time, so he was quite happy. Also, if he was in the support base, he was not in his condemned cell classroom, coping with more comic kiddie capers.

The time was committed to a clunky, computer-based literacy programme. It wasn't difficult to administer, there was no preparation and the kids posed virtually no behavioural obstacle at all.

The class was meant to consist of two wee girls and two wee boys from first year – although one of the girls was giant and one of the boys was tiny. Also, one girl was regularly absent.

Thorn reckoned the bigger girl must be nearly the same weight as him. She was maturing, but it was excessive amounts of cheap food, rather than hormones, that were bulking her up. Not only was she obese, but she was also exceedingly dirty and poorly clothed. She was a wretched thing.

There was an unpleasant smell to her. It was so bad, sometimes, that Thorn had to be careful not to dry boak near her. It was disturbingly awful.

He had now sent notes three times, on email, that she 'appeared to have issues with personal hygiene'. This was a euphemism for *'This girl stinks of pee and other unpleasant stuff. Her hands are mockit and she is developing a very noticeable*

103

*array of blackheads in the dirty folds on either side of her nose. She comes to school with sleep in her eyes and without cleaning her teeth, which are thick with furry, yellowy plaque and obviously rotting. Her shirt, which is meant to be white, is worn day after day and is filthy round the cuffs and collar. She is wearing a skirt that is too small for her, the hem of which has become unstitched at the back. The only shoes she has are very worn and down-at-heel. They are also too small. Please do something about this. It is very difficult to sit close to her. Her peers must have noticed and commented, so she must have difficulty building and maintaining relationships. The likelihood is that she is frequently bullied. It is a terrible, dreadful shame that social and financial poverty produces kids like this. It's not my job to do anything about it, but you have the people skills or the training, so get on with it, please, so that this poor, pitiable girl does not need to suffer anymore from the desperate problems of her parents, her environment and serious inequalities in society.'*

His emails made no difference whatsoever.

A climate of shame continued to hang about her, which impacted on her demeanour. Miserable on a daily basis, her lot was unlikely to improve.

Another small child was just extremely small – the tiniest and most helpless boy in the year group. His learning support file was enormous.

His life was an ongoing battle. He could not organise himself. He could not tell the time. He was not sure what day it was. He had some recall of faces, but less so of names.

Thorn felt sympathy for him, mostly because he was socially isolated – although it was arguable whether the boy noticed that or not.

In scale, he was the opposite of the big lassie – a shilpit thing. He had a ghostlike complexion – big dark eyes and pale-grey skin. His clothes hung from his shoulders like he was a little doll made of wire.

If there was an archetypal 'wee soul', it was him. A draft at the door could have lifted him away. And, sad to admit, he was of so little consequence, that it would be a surprise if anyone missed him.

He was no trouble to teach at all. Any backchat came from a little hardwired hard nut. He smelled badly, too, and did not have a jacket – no matter what the weather. He had won notoriety around the school because he swore at teachers, pushed over desks, threw things and slammed doors.

A staff meeting, held early in the year, raised awareness about this kid's personal plight. It emerged that he was still with his birth mother, as was the younger sister, but social work had been on the case for more than a decade.

On numerous occasions, he and his sister were taken into care, because they were subject to abuse – physical and probably sexual. Often this was attributed to the abject mother's rapid succession of unsuitable partners – from which one could draw any conclusions one wished.

The mother, still only twenty-nine, was ill-prepared for motherhood. Multiple convictions for theft and substance abuse confirmed this.

On occasion, in recent years, the children were found in the home without any bedclothes, hot water, electricity or light bulbs. Frequently, they had no food and sometimes the responsible adults were unconscious on the premises.

It was an absolute bloody disaster and it made Thorn sick to the depths of his soul, if he let it in. But there was nothing he could do about it. He was only mightily relieved to find that this hostile kid was a much more placid animal in this small group.

So, at two o'clock, that was what he contended with. The trio were there when he arrived, just sitting on their typing hairs in front of dark screens. They often needed to be reminded to turn the computers on.

They didn't want to mix with each other. There was no point in trying that as a project. All they did was turn on, log into the spelling programme and work their way through repetitive exercises, intended to diagnose and cure their bad spelling.

The dated and barely interactive programme did virtually nothing to support the kids. Nonetheless, what the time meant to them was a bit of personal attention outside of class. In class meant being bullied, being ignored or arguing with the teacher, so, in Thorn's head, all he had to do was try hard to give them some minor league respect and a semblance of engagement.

105

And, man, oh, man, it was a change which he cherished, because, even though it was only Tuesday, his energies were sapped in his abominable classroom. He was so tired of trying to teach so many kids anything whatsoever about reading or writing, when it appeared to be programmed into their DNA to resist.

# Wednesday 0926

But Thorn feels a little bit of the devil in him. He is still recording. He has done most of the talking. He wants to provoke a bit of action. He wants to record some good footage for later – if at all possible.

'Is there anyone else you would like to speak to?' says the depute. 'I am sure a cup of tea might give you some pause for thought.'

'Pause for thought?' Thorn started, 'Pause for thought? What do you think I have to think about, for goodness sake? You have told me to take down the Facebook post, which I have said I will do as soon as I have signal. I don't really know what else I have to think about. I am really looking for some support from your side. I want to know who is responsible for this monstrous behaviour and I want to see them taken to task and tidying up the mess they have made.

'I was in here at ten to eight this morning. There must have been someone here before that who knows something about it. Have you even asked the cleaners if they saw anyone?

'The other thing you could do is check the CCTV. I am sure you would be able to see anyone lurking about, either late last night or first thing this morning.'

'You are missing the point, Mr Thorn,' says the head. 'I would like you to come downstairs. I accept that this issue could have been better handled. Perhaps, as Mr Honnigan says, a cup of tea would help us to sort things out.'

This is weird, weird, thinks Thorn. Why does she want him downstairs? Sounds as if she might offer him a biscuit too. Is she softening? Weird...

All of a sudden, his phone rings. He looks down at it. It is a number he doesn't recognise, but he wants to break the monotony. Ah, well, he could do with an adventure. He takes the chance to answer it, putting it on speaker as he does.

107

'Hello!' It's a polite voice. 'Hello! Mr Thorn, Archie Thorn?'
'Yes, Thorn speaking.'

'Hello, this is the Daily Report. We got your number from a friend of yours, Bill Watson.'

Thorn's eyes make contact with the head teacher's face. She is suddenly white with alarm and her pupils are darting between Thorn's eyes. This is a scenario she had not envisaged. Social media has done the trick. Within a few minutes the journalists of Scotland are seeking him out to research his end of the story.

The depute tries to break in, whispering, 'Archie, maybe you should say you'll call back. We need to get this sorted out before anyone speaks to the papers.'

'Yes, Bill is an old friend of mine,' says Thorn. 'He used to teach at this school.'

The head is clearly dismayed. She has half turned away. She has been silenced. She knows very clearly that anything she says now could be recorded and used for copy. She is utterly without option. Thorn has her trumped. Unless someone dashes the phone out of his hand at this moment, the call is going ahead and she, the boss, can do nothing, simply zero.

She turns back slightly. 'Maybe you can deal with this, Mr Honnigan,' she mutters behind her hand and turns fully away. Thorn discerns an almost imperceptible stagger, but she quickly regains composure and clicks off down the corridor.

'Can you tell us what happened this morning, please, Mr Thorn? We believe you had a bit of a surprise…'

The depute is still listening. Thorn doesn't feel free to express himself. Also, he is not a fan of the paper. It's a rag – although he does not want to lose the opportunity to drop the boss right in it.

'I'm not at liberty to speak at the moment. I have a senior member of staff here. Can I ask your name?'

'I don't think you should be taking this call on the premises, Archie,' the depute breaks in huskily, 'not given the nature of the problem.'

'I'm sorry, who is that speaking? Is this Archie Thorn?' It's the reporter again.

'Yes, sorry, can I have your name, please?' says Archie.

'This is Lesley McKibben, Mr Thorn. Did you say you couldn't speak just now?'

Thorn can hear the noise of the newsroom behind the phone call. 'Can I just call you back on this number, please? I have the depute head with me just now.'

'Okay, yes, of course, but as soon as possible, please, Mr Thorn. That would be much appreciated.'

The depute is visibly relieved when Thorn hangs up. He has an open hand half out – almost as if he expects to take the phone from him – but Thorn switches it off and sticks it firmly in his pocket.

'What the hell can we do about this now?' asks the depute, anxiously. 'Mrs Butcher doesn't really know how to progress it.'

'I don't know either,' says Thorn, 'but I need to speak to the union or something. There's certainly a bit of a log jam here.'

'I can give you ten minutes, Archie,' Honnigan says, amicable again. 'That's about all. But come down the stairs for a word after that, will you? We don't want this going on all day. Just think carefully about what you are going to do though. We certainly don't want it in the papers. The boss will be pleased to hear that you didn't talk to them, but don't go phoning them back, eh. And that Facebook post needs to be taken down as soon as possible.'

The janitors are still standing around like spare parts. 'Let's go and give Mr Thorn some space for a few minutes, guys,' he says and leads them away down the corridor, shaking his head slightly.

It is only 9.32.

Thorn doesn't know what to do now. Instinctively, he takes his phone out. There are more notifications on the screen. He never usually arouses this amount of interest. Clearly his post is having an effect. He taps the call return. He is through to the *Daily Report* in ten seconds.

'Hullo, Ms McKibben, this is Archie Thorn,' he says curtly. 'I am returning your call. I have a small problem here. I wonder if you can help me?'

'Of course, Mr Thorn, glad you could call back. I have a pen here. Can I just take down a few details? You are in Hopeton High School, is that right?'

A few minutes later, Thorn strides out towards the toilet door fifteen metres away. He has relieved himself, spilling his story to the press and now he must pee.

# Tuesday, 1420

Thorn knew what it was like to be a kid, but he reckoned that he was one of the few teachers who remembered being force-fed half-baked drivel, day in, day out.

He saw 130 kids four or five periods a week, for approximately 200 days of the year.

The educators talked endlessly about teaching methodology, when, in fact, crowd-control skills were really what was needed. Those skills had very little to do with teaching or learning.

Whilst everyone played along with the pretence that activities in school were educationally meaningful – vital to the pupils' intellectual development – school, in Thorn's head, was primarily about containment.

The Victorian model, designed to produce conformist worker drones, was still in place, and, for a hundred years, no one had examined or reframed the fundamentals of the concept.

Stepped away from and looked at, much of 'education' was just cheap childcare. Kids were someone else's problem for seven hours or so a day. They were captive – rendered harmless in a holding cage. Any learning was incidental. In reality, what they learned was how to temper their expectations and to forsake independent thought. Personal development was thwarted, social order was maintained and the status quo was preserved.

It was obvious that many of the able kids were bored rigid in school. But most bided their time and, in due course, the world had options for them – like university or employment opportunities. Those kids kept mum and did not rock the boat.

For the rest – and there were many of them – the whole thing was entirely baffling. So, they often just baulked – especially in moribund English departments, where the currency was close reading and critical essays. Kids were so disappointed not to be doing something more interesting and, when these activities had

111

so little perceived value anywhere else in the world, it was little wonder that they were disinclined.

These activities were the bane of Thorn's threadbare life too. Whenever he set a task – knowing that few would complete it satisfactorily – he gave them detailed plans, exemplar paragraphs and vocabulary lists. He talked them through it, led them, step by step, through the whole thing.

Then, each time he saw the kids' half-baked work, he felt so disappointed with the outcome of his life. Almost every script he lifted was clear evidence that they had not listened or learned one thing.

They did not 'learn'. They just went on producing the same old, largely indecipherable, turgid dross. And the worst of it was that it was Thorn's paid job to read every misspelled word of it.

It never ceased to amaze him that colleagues applied to be markers for the exam board. They received scripts by post, they marked them, sent them back and were paid for their time.

No matter how well paid, Thorn could never endure more of that torment. He would rather take a red-hot ballpoint pen to his eyes, than spend any more time than necessary marking pupil papers.

No amount of money could tempt him to sacrifice one more single evening to the mediocrity of pupil marking. He had aspirations to do something in his spare time which did not constantly remind him about the dreary nature of his work. Hell would freeze solid first.

# Wednesday, 0935

It's just as well he is only peeing for ninety seconds. When he comes out, he sees the janitor wading down the corridor towards him. She is on her own, carrying rubber gloves and a bucket with a bottle of bleach in it. She has a blue roll of industrial cleaning paper under her arm.

She stops short, not wanting to near him or confront him. 'Sorry, I thought you'd gone,' she says, making excuses.

Thorn approaches the door again. He places a hand on the handle and presses, just to reassure himself and the janitor that it is still locked. He is loath to leave it now. There is no closed-circuit television in this corridor – the boss must be cursing herself for not having it installed. She must have watchers at either staircase. The janitor would only have come to clean when she thought he was no longer there.

'I just nipped into the loo,' he tells her. 'It's okay, I can look after it now. If you just leave the bucket, I'll get things sorted.'

He says this to disarm her. He has done the odd favour for her before. He has been polite in issues of maintenance and repair. He is always appreciative of her and her services. He is not in the habit of being unpleasant to anyone.

She doesn't quite believe him, but feels neutralised by his offer. She can't argue. She must accept. In no position to dispute, she places the bucket and paper on the floor near him. 'Will I leave the gloves?' she asks.

'Aye, please,' he says, 'I'm not taking any chances with that thing.'

She hikes up her trousers as she moves away. 'I'll say to Mrs Butcher I left the stuff with you then.'

'Aye, that would be great, Netta,' he agrees. 'Thanks a lot. See you later.'

'Aye, see you later.'

113

*Bastards!* he thinks. As soon as his back is turned or he goes for a wee pee, they are after his evidence.

He has not noticed the noise building in classrooms near at hand. The bell explodes again, not far from his head. Pupils spew into the corridor, making their way to the period two class. He stands aside. Some look down at the bucket, then at him. There is still no discernible evidence of awareness amongst the rabble. To several he nods in recognition.

'All right, Mr Thorn?' an odd one says.

Thorn is sure that no one that he sees is aware of the situation. It won't be long. Although banned in class, the smartphone is in constant use throughout the school – whether it's under the desk, obscured by a bag or under a book. The pupils cannot help themselves. They are so wired into the fug of social media that many can only intermittently disengage from it. Theirs is a techno-present. Their lives no longer exist just within their own vicinity.

Very, very soon, they will get wind of his predicament. In fact, he can guarantee that, right now, thumbs are twitching across screens. It will only be a matter of moments before kids and adults alike become alerted to the shocking presence in his room.

Still he wonders if one of the kids, or a group of them – or even one of the adults – already has that knowledge – the perpetrator.

The corridor does not take long to clear. In the English department, this Wednesday morning, third year come first period and then there is a lull. No further classes come until after the morning interval. At this time in the week, Thorn usually breathes a little sigh of relief. Now is a little different. He wonders if, today, the pause in teaching might initiate some other kind of action.

His nearby colleagues leave their rooms one by one, lock their doors and, mostly without looking at him, walk to the base at the far end of the corridor. They do this without a word. Only Agnes the probationer says anything. She has to walk right past him. 'Hi, Archie,' she says, 'the PT's called us to the base for a meeting. Are you coming?'

Thorn shakes his head. 'I don't think so, Agnes. I didn't hear anything about it,' he says.

Agnes shrugs and walks away.

Then he looks towards the PT's door. She is closing it firmly and locking it. She sees Thorn looking at her, but turns away and walks smartly after Agnes to the English base. She closes that door behind her too.

Almost immediately, the boss and the depute – her witness – enter the corridor. Thorn wonders if they are in liaison with the principal teacher. Her disappearance and their reappearance are almost simultaneous.

The boss looks purposeful. Presumably she has been on the phone to her line manager. She has girded herself up. If she draws herself up to her full height, she will now be able to stare Thorn straight in the chest.

Her able lieutenant, or, at least, her depute, is by her side again – or walking a respectful twenty centimetres behind her. He cannot really be the enforcer, Thorn thinks. He is not that intimidating, but she must have backup. The boss could try to deal with Thorn on her own, but she needs someone to defer to her in this type of situation – especially if it is not going to be Thorn.

Thorn speaks first in an effort to take the heat out of the situation – or at least to delay her. 'Thanks for coming up again. I guess you've come to look at the big steaming jobby on my chair,' he says agreeably.

This aggravates her. It gets right up her nose. He can see it in the lines of her face. But she does not shoot from the hip this time – even if that is her instinct. She has a potential publicity disaster on her hands and classes needing teachers. She has Thorn blocking her progress in addressing that situation.

Maybe she is on the verge of exasperation. This is suggested from her tone as she answers. 'Mr Thorn,' – no first name informality here. That stage has passed. It is now titles and second names. This appears to be for the record. Her demeanour is humourless – it usually is – but there is no measure of tact, diplomacy or even humanity evident here. 'Mr Thorn,' she repeats, 'I have spoken to the Director of Education and Leisure Services about your situation. He is very concerned that you are obstructing the work of the school. He is even more concerned that you are airing your grievances on a public forum. He asked me to instruct you to remove your posts from the internet. He also told me that I should instruct you to allow us into the classroom to clean. He also told me that, if you continue to be obstructive, I should ask you to go home until further notice. When I asked him what to do if you did not do as we instruct, he said that I should call the police and have you removed.

'And, Mr Thorn, just after our conversation, he sent me an email in which he confirmed all of these points.'

Thorn lets her speak, but his mind is whirring. He doesn't even know the name of the Director of Education and... whatever, but he knows there is a good chance that Butcher, the boss, isn't bluffing.

On the other hand, he also knows that his opinion has not necessarily been well represented in Butcher's dialogue with him.

'Has the Director seen my Facebook post?' he asks her. 'Does the Director actually understand my point of view here? I mean, I'm still waiting for my union to return my call, with further advice. I wonder if...'

'Mr Thorn, enough!' She almost barks in interrupting him. Her tone is threatening. 'You will remove the post now and you will take yourself along to your department meeting, or I will have ample cause to start proceedings against you.'

'Hang on a minute,' says Thorn. Then his phone rings. He looks at it. He cancels the call. Probably better that he doesn't take a call from his old school friend just now. 'Sorry about that. You were saying...?'

Up until this point, the depute has been looking on. Now it is his turn. 'Listen, Archie, get the post down, go to the meeting and we can take it from there. Otherwise, we take it to the next stage.' He says this in the faintest of hopes that it might actually work. He has to say something, otherwise he has not earned his considerable crust.

'Sorry,' says Thorn, 'I've not spoken to the union rep yet. And I am not prepared to have any more meetings with you without a witness for my side and some notes taken. Once I've spoken to the rep and she or someone else is with me, we might be able to make progress, otherwise, I am not shifting just now. Sorry.'

The boss is already turning away. The depute gives Thorn another last chance. He attempts to drill him with a stare.

Thorn smiles wryly at him. As he does so, the boss is off. The depute hurries in her wake. 'You have left me very few choices,' she calls, retreating. Then she raises her voice a little. 'I hope you are not going to regret your actions, Mr Thorn.'

'Are you threatening me?' calls Thorn to her turning head. 'That's not very professional. I am staying here until I get a proper investigation.'

She does not turn round.

'I said "a proper investigation". Did you hear me?' he almost shouts.

The head teacher enters the department base at the far end of the corridor. The depute follows her. They are in there for a few moments, then they both leave by the nearby stairs. Only the depute looks back towards Thorn.

Thorn could remove the post. He could go to the base. He could even go home.

But he doesn't really want to do any of these things.

He is getting a bit peckish. Fortunately, he has a muesli bar in his bag. He takes it out and peels the wrapper back. He only has time to enjoy the first bite before the door to the base opens.

Agnes appears in the hallway. She looks small and far away. 'Do you want a cup of tea, Archie?'

'No thanks,' he shouts back along.

'You sure?' she says, sounding a bit pleady.

'Fine just now, thanks, Agnes. I'll give you a shout if I need one.'

She reluctantly returns to the base. This is, perhaps, a last gasp effort on behalf of the English department to move him on. On the other hand, it may have been the head teacher's initiative. Best to leave them to their meeting, Thorn thinks.

117

# Tuesday, 1450

It was the third time in three weeks that Thorn had a 'please take' in art.

A 'please take' was a class where a teacher, who had an extra period of preparation time, was required to cover for a teacher who was absent.

Every morning, Thorn checked the email on his antique classroom computer. After three or four minutes, a grid opened, with a list of the day's absentee teachers and their replacements.

He might have to cover a class anywhere. Generally, it was not a problem for him. As a semi-permanent fixture in the school, most kids knew that he would not take the face off them.

In his early days, a please take was a nightmare. As raw meat, the rougher classes would give any newbie a hellish time. The same could still happen to a probationer or supply teachers. Some idiot kid, thinking it was sport, would wind up an adult until they were white in the face and swallowing swear words.

But this was the third time Thorn had taken this class − a bunch of first years. He suspected a blip in the timetable. Admin were probably short of a real art teacher for a period, but, because art was just art, no parent was going to bother about it.

It didn't matter to Thorn. The room had a better view than his and, Christ sake, it was just art.

His friend was an art teacher. Periodically, it gave him a dose of unrestrained outrage − when he kicked it around in his head. As far as he was concerned, it was a poor joke that there was no job-sizing for main-grade teachers. On paper, he and his friend had worked the same number of years, had the same status and working conditions − and took home the same wage.

But that was where the similarity ended.

For instance, in this class, the kids were making masks. That was their 'work'. Each had an A3 sheet of white paper and there were other sheets with eye shapes reproduced in strong black lines – the work of a teacher. First, the pupil had to trace two eyes, but then it got even less complicated, because they had to use coloured pencils to colour in the eyes. Then this process was repeated for the nose and mouth.

This – tracing and colouring in – was what passed for work in the art department.

As an English teacher, in contrast, Thorn was the member of staff held responsible for the linguistic development of every single child in each of his five classes. In theory, this meant exhaustive teaching and assessment in the skills of listening and talking and, in particular, reading and writing.

Therefore, in terms of marking, Thorn typically had to wade through two to three pages of error-strewn, badly structured, immature writing, from nearly every kid, whilst, in stark contrast, an art teacher cast their eyes over a sketch or clay object, conferred a grade, made fleeting comment and that was it.

Make no mistake, Thorn loved the arcane art of writing ancient symbols on paper. That it transmitted thoughts from writer to reader was almost miraculous – one of mankind's most wondrous achievements. But, during his working day, when the only thoughts he had time to read were those of careless secondary school kids in grudged essays, it gave him a headache just to think of it.

Indeed, to him, the endless stupefaction of an English teacher's marking load felt like a hellish masochism.

And Thorn would never allow himself to be one of those English teacher martyrs who wore their marking burden as a badge of honour. Some – the naïve or the lonely – stoically accepted their lot and believed it their unquestioned duty to red-pen endless pages of interminable tosh. What pish!

Nevertheless, he had a please take in art and, as way of getting paid for half-inched old rope, it was not bad. All he did was sit atop a tall stool and look across the kids, who were colouring in at low-lying, wonky art tables and he could see over trees and industrial buildings towards the hills, where, in the dying light, turbines spun in the steady wind.

He had his notebook to hand as well. He'd taken to carrying it – not that he had anything significant to write – but, it was something of his own in the hostile environment. In it, he could

119

jot down a fleeting thought, a quotation or an item for his 'to do one day' agenda. It was a trivial act of rebellion, but a little something to sustain him and give the impression that, even on company time, he could be something of his own man. If nothing else, the few dog-eared pages were evidence of his existence as an entity in some way distinct from the school.

He would have loved to be a political radical, a writer of meaningful prose – someone who filleted the world's problems with the flourish of a sharp sentence in an archly contrived essay. Would that he could have been that person. But he was not and could never be now. However, even acting in imitation of someone who might have an original idea was something to him.

# Wednesday, 0956

He could go to the base. He could accept the offer of tea. He could sit down. They could talk about the curriculum. They could talk about assessment or parents' night or discipline. They would be happy with that. But would it satisfy him? What Thorn needs at the moment is to feel a sense of justice done. He can't just be walked over. He can't live every minute of his life with a prevailing sense of unfairness. He needs, one day, to make a stand. This may be that day.

Just as he is beginning to feel determined to succeed, he sees a small boy come down the corridor. Even at a distance, Thorn recognises him as Douglas Caldwell, or 'Coddy' for short. He was a blight on Thorn's life in second and third year, but he now seems to feel affinity for Thorn, now that he is in fourth year. He now has a scary teacher – one who has no sense of humour or sense of kinship with people and expects lengthy essays written in double quick time. He now sees that Thorn was not so bad after all.

Coddy has his hands in his pockets and the gait of a footballer – legs tending towards bandy and walking on the outsides of his feet. He is wearing school uniform – white shirt, black jumper and black trousers. The only expression of his individuality are fluorescent orange trainers.

'Awright, sir?' says Coddy, with a nod, when he is close enough.

'Hi, Doug,' Thorn returns. 'I'm fine. You okay?'

'Aye, sir,' says Coddy. 'I hear you had a visitor last night, sir?'

Thorn's antennae twitch. 'Sorry, Coddy, I don't know what you mean.'

Coddy is abreast of him and pauses to look up. Thorn moves in front of the glass panel in the door, so that a view into the room is impossible. He sees Coddy hesitate, move slightly and peer slightly.

'It's all over Facebook, sir. Word's got oot. There's nae hidin it.'

'What's on Facebook?'

'Aw, come on, sir. Somebody seen your post and noo hauf the school's seen it. The big shite on yer chair, sir, whit ye gonny dae aboot it?'

Thorn realises he has nothing to hide. That horse has bolted. He turns to the window himself. The misdemeanour is not clearly visible. He says to Coddy, 'You can't see it just now, Coddy. It's on the chair. It's horrible. Vile.'

'It's terrible, sir. Disgustin. It's no fair that it wis you. If ah wis leavin a shite somewhere, there are other teachers deserve it mair than you.'

'Thanks, Douglas. That's very kind of you to say. Anyway, where are you meant to be?'

'Toilet, sir.'

'Best get off then. You don't want to have an accident or get into trouble.'

'Ha, good one, sir. See you.' And he is away along the corridor, with maybe a bigger swagger in his step.

Thorn now knows that the word is on the street. Little wonder the boss was so incensed.

He knew it would be quick, but this fast – less than an hour. Most of the school will be aware. The kids will be accessing the story under their desks. If teachers aren't on their phones, the kids will mention it to them. His own department certainly knows. Probably they are discussing it now.

He imagines, as well as he can, what's likely to happen.

He could remove the post, but he can't turn back time. Someone will have screenshot it by now. It'll be out there in the world of social media for ever. So, now, whether he removes it or not is of little consequence. All that would mean would be that he has adhered to his head teacher's wishes – and the wishes of the Director of Education. He can think about it.

Downstairs, the boss will be contemplating her next step. She already knows what her plan of action will be. He is clearly not moving from this spot just now. She will be looking at calling

122

the police to have him removed from the building – if he is not prepared to go peacefully.

Perhaps he should call the police himself. His rights are being infringed. Maybe he should call someone else. The union, for which he has paid monthly for the past twenty-two years, has been of no use. He has phoned them several times before – once to change his address and once to change his phone number. The only purpose they have really served is as a recipient of his money – something like nine pounds a month. Over decades, it amounts to a considerable sum. Now, he is in direst need – certainly more significant need than he has ever felt before – and the bloody union seems to have evaporated. He wonders if the union actually exists, or if it is, in fact, just a bank account and a competent secretary, who is good at mimicking a variety of voices.

Just as that thought passes through the front of his head, irony of ironies, the union rep reappears in the hallway. It is almost as if she has been summoned, like a genie. Thorn is surprised that there is no puff of green smoke behind her.

He knows that she disappeared downstairs earlier, when she seemed to be on her way to see him. There is every chance that she is visiting now because she has been in conference with the management.

He is immediately on his toes.

Perhaps she has been in touch with the Edinburgh office. Maybe she has had more luck than him in garnering advice.

She marches smartly along the corridor. The fact that she marches smartly instantly makes Thorn feel guarded. Anyone with so resolute a stride is inherently suspicious.

When she speaks, her phoney bonhomie is nauseating. 'Hi, Archie, how you doing?' she says.

She has never shown him the smallest hint of friendliness in the past. Probably her only motivation for being union rep is so that she can ingratiate herself with management – rather than the rank and file. He thinks that she believes that responsible execution of her role – and not rocking any boats – will facilitate her prospects for promotion.

He has had minimal interaction with her before. He knows that she is a scientist. They are, more often than not, slightly other-worldly. He fully imagines that she is one of the humourless and bureaucratic ones – one of the science teachers who has mastered the theories and data of their field, rather than skills in the field of human communication.

'Hi,' he replies. 'Do you think you can help me out here? I tried to contact head office, but I've not heard back from them yet. I don't think I am being fairly treated.'

Her veneer remains. 'I'm not sure what I can do to help, Archie. I did speak to head office, but they referred me to the area rep and I've not been able to get a hold of him yet. Mrs Butcher would like to get the problem sorted as soon as possible though.'

'Aye,' he replies, 'that's all very well, but she hasn't given me any assurance that she is going to do anything about it. It's ridiculous. I'm not coming to my work to be abused like this. It's terrible. I can't work in these conditions and I've had no support at all.'

'I don't know what you expect, Archie. Mrs Butcher wants things to get back to normal as soon as possible.'

'Aye, but what's happened in here is some kind of vandalism and it was clearly aimed at me and it's disgusting and I want something done. I want someone's arse in a sling for this. Anybody who's ever seen a police drama knows that you don't disturb anything at the scene of a crime until the investigators have done their work. So, basically, I'm not happy to have anybody clean the thing up until I can be sure that we can find the culprit.'

'But, Archie…' she starts to say.

'Don't "But, Archie" me. I'm getting sick and tired of this. I want an investigation and I want to be consulted and I want progress made in finding the miscreant and, if that is not going to happen, I'm going to continue to be blooming difficult, because that is my right and I am the blooming victim here.

'So, if you or the boss or her deputes or the Head of Service cannot give me any reassurance that my demands will be met, I am going to make myself objectionable. So, you can take that message to her. Go on, take it to her now and tell her to stick it in her pipe.

'And, as far as the union is concerned, I want to speak to that area rep as soon as possible. And if that's not possible in the next hour, you can contact the union and tell them I will cancel my membership at the earliest opportunity, because, in this situation – the only time I have actually needed them for anything in my bloody life – they have been as much use as an effing chocolate teapot.'

She doesn't say a word or wait for anything else. She gives her hair a shake, backs off and beetles down the corridor – no doubt heading straight to the boss's office, so that she can brown-nose and leave her career prospects undamaged, by not rocking the bloody boat.

# Tuesday, 1648

Every parents' night was a humdinger of a drag for Thorn.

One advantage at this place, at least, was that the event was held straight after the school day. He could tidy, have a coffee to perk himself up, straighten his tie, clean his teeth, organise chairs in the corridor and print out a copy of the marks. Then, at the back of five, the first parents arrived, tentatively stepping out along the corridor, accompanied by their casually dressed child, Dylan or Amber, who was ostentatiously wielding a mobile phone out of school hours.

Most nights, parents came and went. Thorn smiled, was civil and complimentary. Every small criticism was tempered with some sweet praise and some generalisation about the subject not being a 'walk in the park'.

Many of the parents in this post-industrial neck of the woods were fairly genial and easy to please. Thorn's easy-going manner was usually an advantage on these occasions and he affected to be a reassuringly substantial presence.

Many of the parents were native, too, and had been through the same schooling themselves. Commonly, what they wanted to know was that their kid was not at risk of abject failure.

But, of course, this was the parents' night for his blinking Higher class.

During the early part of the year, knowing that many of them would struggle, he tried to buoy the kids up – keep it light and positive. He hoped that they would grow in confidence during the year. He didn't want to knock the stuffing out of them too early.

But now they were twitchy. It was a big year. The pressure was building. And, for kids that age, everything was always someone else's fault. They always looked elsewhere, because it saved them looking to themselves.

And that was just how it was. Thorn knew never to trust a kid. Some were nice. There was no doubt about that, but many had side to them and did not have a scruple, when it came to saving their own skins.

So, not long after this parents' night began, Thorn sensed teenage pre-exam paranoia stalking.

One mother – tall, well-dressed, tanned, articulate and professional – said that there was some concern in the class.

Thorn was unsure what this meant, but said that there should be some concern in the class. Higher was a challenging course, the prelim results were disappointing and pupils had to put considerable work in to have a chance of success.

The mother looked hard at him, through her clean, stylish spectacles. She told him that her son was struggling to understand what he could do to improve his chances of passing. She worried that he had not done well in a close reading internal assessment. He had always done well before. What was the problem this year?

Thus, she insinuated that the problem was Thorn.

Thorn asked her if it would help to have some other resources, so that her son could do some extra work at home. Did she know that there were links on the class blog to a number of resources online? He suggested that he was available at lunchtimes or after school if the son had any questions or if he needed any particular help.

She was not pleased, but she was mollified – he had gone some considerable distance to placate her.

What he really wanted to tell her was that her son was nice, but that he was not cut out to study language. He had seen it so often before. The lad sailed through maths, biology, chemistry, and technical drawing, but he could not perceive why English was such a bloody big bugbear.

What Thorn wanted was to see it written down on a sheet of paper, signed by the principal teacher and handed out as a letter to parents. He wanted the fact of it to appear on the school website, in big, bold letters. He wanted a formal declaration that the study of language and literature was not the same as the study of one of these STEM courses. Language skills evolved over years. They had to be purposefully nurtured, in a rich linguistic environment. They were not accrued at the Xbox, on the PlayStation, playing football or on the various social media.

In English, the pupils had to be sensitive and imaginative. They were compelled to write interesting and original pieces of work, both creative and discursive. They had to read and respond to samples of text, which, significantly, they had never seen before. Then, they had to write thoughtful responses to literature, under pressure of time.

This was hard work for a literate pupil. For a kid who had not read a book, a newspaper or a magazine in the past five years, it was going to be hell of a difficult to complete with any degree of competence.

But, no matter, the mother left and Thorn breathed again.

He couldn't be bothered with that sort of misdirected pressure. It was ludicrous. A few months he had known these children for. They spent a few hours a week in his company, amongst a class of twenty-eight. Since they entered the school gates, the majority had not made the slightest effort to improve their reading or writing. Many had not read anything more intellectually challenging than *Diary of a Wimpy Kid* in primary seven – despite repeated urgings. How could Thorn be expected to have some transformative effect, when he was not qualified in alchemy?

# Wednesday, 1008

Thorn takes stock again. He realises that he should not have become so angry and that the 'union rep' was probably not the person on whom he should have vented his wrath. On the other hand, what the hell, he needs to have a go at somebody, because he has spoken plenty, but nobody seems to have heard a word that he has said.

He looks at his watch. There are twenty-two minutes until interval. Then, again, the corridor will fill with pupils. He anticipates that, by that time, everyone will be aware of the situation – pupils, teachers, support staff. He cannot begin to imagine what will happen next.

What does happen surprises him – as if he hadn't been surprised enough already. As if by magic, two police officers appear in the corridor. He is not quite sure why this has happened so quickly. Certainly, he does not think it is in response to his request for an investigation. He suspects that they have been called to remove him.

Both approach him and his classroom door in a disarming manner. There is no suggestion of aggression about them. Clearly, they have been trained to defuse potentially confrontational situations – situations such as this.

There is a tall officer, a woman, and a small officer, a man. Both have their hats in their hands. They also have their stab-proof vests on and all the other necessary accoutrements of their job. The shorter officer has a clearly marked camera on his lapel. It does not appear to be switched on.

'Mr Thorn,' says the taller officer, 'Mr Archie Thorn?'

'Yes, officer, can I help you?' he responds amiably.

'Eh, yes, I think so. This is Constable White and I am Constable Constance.'

Strange, Thorn thinks, that White should have such black hair.

'I'm surprised to see you in the school,' says Thorn.

'You're right,' she says. 'We're not often called to deal with situations in school, but Mrs Butcher called. She said that there was a situation here that needed sorting, so I hope that you'll be able to help us.'

There is the sound of the door at the end of the corridor being opened and the head teacher appears. She just stands. Her expression, as far as Thorn can see it, is set.

Almost at the same time, her depute, Honnigan, comes through the door at the other end of the corridor.

They both look on with interest.

Thorn suspects that they are cutting off his options. He decides that, if he makes a run for it, he will probably run towards the head teacher. She is unlikely to rugby tackle him. Big Honnigan, on the other hand...

'Well,' says Thorn, 'I'm sorry Mrs Butcher felt she had to call you. I'll certainly help you if I can.'

The shorter officer straightens himself up and hitches his thumbs in the armholes of his vest.

The taller officer continues. 'The head teacher tells us that you have refused to move from the corridor and to carry out your professional duties. She also tells us that you have behaved inappropriately on social media and brought the school into disrepute. She would like you to go home and contact the school when you are ready to be reasonable, but she is concerned that you are unwilling to co-operate.

'As I said,' she goes on, 'we're not usually called to schools, but we've spoken to our senior officer. He tells us that if you're being obstructive and not doing as the head teacher asks, we've sufficient reason to remove you and charge you with obstruction and breach of the peace.'

'I see,' says Thorn, 'I see. I didn't think this would happen. Just give me a minute to sort things out in my head, please.

'By the way, did Mrs Butcher say why I was upset? Did she tell you what the problem was? Or did she show you the Facebook post?'

Neither police officer responds immediately. They look at each other.

Constable Constance then says, 'Mr Thorn, we suggest you go home and have a rest. It would be best if we could accompany you from the building. Then you and your head teacher can take it from there.'

'And if I don't accompany you from the building, you will arrest me, is that it?' Thorn responds. He is feeling rather a lot of pressure to conform, even though it is in his nature to question every new initiative and to examine the motives for it. He is thinking hard. 'Can you just give me a minute, please?' he says.

He turns away from them for a moment. He takes his phone from his pocket and looks at the screen. He has a number of notifications. At the top is another message from Polly. *Call me now, please. xx*, it reads. He will need to get back to her as soon as possible.

He returns his gaze to the police officers. As he looks from one to the other, he runs his hand through his hair and scratches his head. 'I've just got to get one or two things from my filing cabinet and then I will be right with you. Is that okay?'

'Don't be long then,' says Constable White.

As he lifts his bag and coat and turns towards the door, the officers turn away from him, as if they are going to converse.

He unlocks the door, enters the room and a waft of shitesmell rushes past him. He narrows his eyes. The automatic closer sweeps the heavy door shut behind him. He appears to walk towards the filing cabinet.

But he has the room key in his hand. In an instant he turns, slips it into the keyhole and locks the door.

Then, just for a moment, there is silence.

# Tuesday, 1728

Another few parents came and went. Then, after consulting his list, Thorn went to the door and invited Lindsay Harper's parents in.

Notably, Lindsay was not with them.

Her uncomfortably overweight mother was wearing a Barbour jacket – in expensive artificial fibre, but black and greasy round the edges. What Thorn took to be Harper's father was wearing a shiny grey suit, about a size too small. He had cheap, pointy, sharky shoes, of the type that pinch the wearer's feet and look stretched and scruffy very quickly.

'Come on in,' said Thorn. 'Nice to see you. Have a seat. Sit down over here, please.'

The woman glanced at her partner. There was hesitation before they sat and it was very unusual – as if they might want to fight him standing up. Their momentary reluctance put Thorn on his guard. On parents' night, he usually controlled this space and his time.

They slowly took their seats.

Jeez, he thought, as he sat down opposite them, it was easy to see where Lindsay Harper got her sniffy attitude from. Just as she had a good conceit of herself and a very low opinion of him, so he did not sense a gram of goodwill from her parents.

She had a rather florid face – probably a consequence of too many evenings on the vino. He was large and meaty-looking, with a belligerent air about him.

Thorn suspected that the father was used to taking issue with people. He was heavier than Thorn, but Thorn knew that he could take him, unless he was a black belt Karate expert – which looked unlikely. He was big and ugly, but he was saft-looking.

'So, I think you got the report yesterday, it that right?' said Thorn brightly, keen to take the lead. Then he remembered Lindsay was not in yesterday and she did not ask for the report today. 'Oh, no,' said Thorn, 'you may not have received it. Lindsay was ill yesterday, wasn't she? And then, today, she…'

But the mother ignored his questions. She was angry. Thorn could see that now. The blotchy redness of her complexion, spreading down her neck, was the result of her unexpressed wrath. 'Lindsay would have come tonight, but she is not happy in this class,' she said, staring straight through Thorn. 'And we're not happy either…'

'I'm very sorry to hear that,' said Thorn, instantly apologetic and on the defensive, but keeping it as light as possible – to avoid conflict. 'I know we had a bit of a fall-out a few weeks ago, but I thought we were beginning to get things back on track. I said I would give her any help she needed.'

'I don't think things are back on track,' the father broke in and stopped. He sat forward in his seat and put his elbow on the desk between them.

Thorn was already sitting forward. This guy was accustomed to using his bulk to intimidate and he was moving into Thorn's space.

'I'm sorry you think that,' said Thorn, not conceding anything, but squaring his shoulders to this guy and looking him in the face – letting him know that he wasn't easily squashable.

'I don't think you realise that Lindsay needs her Higher English to get into her course at the art school. And I don't think you are doing anything to help her,' the mother said crossly.

Thorn let that hang there for a bit. In his own mind, he reviewed her claim.

Higher English was not beyond Lindsay, but she could not complete the course by turning up two or three days a week, not handing in work and, apart from anything else, looking to all the world as if she didn't give a flying fuck about anything he said.

Also, Lindsay did not have 'her' course at the art school. She had nothing other than a desire to go there. This woman made it sound like Thorn was denying the girl the fantastic future to which she was entitled, when, at the moment, a place at any institution of tertiary education was fanciful – without some considerable change in Lindsay's work habits.

As far as help was concerned, Thorn did what he could, but, if he presented the materials, set the deadlines, marked the work, spoke to individual pupils regularly and offered support at every stage, that was about all he could do.

The reason this shit was hitting the turbocharger was that he had sent a letter home to these parents, informing them that their Lindsay was tardy with her written work.

Lindsay, in turn, had then gone into psycho hyperdrive – spinning yarns to her folks and shifting the blame for her negligence and immaturity onto him.

She had clearly found a receptive audience.

How could it be, he wondered, how was it that so many parents were willing to side with their offspring in disputes with staff? What made them so willing to believe their own children?

Thorn knew, as a former pupil, a parent and as teacher, that kids fibbed. For god sake, so many people did it at school – they lied about homework, pretended they had lost stuff. It was commonplace. Why in hell had today's parents obliterated from their memories that they were scheming, duplicitous little brats too?

'Well, I am sorry you think that,' he replied. 'I have said to the whole class that I am here before school, at lunchtime and after school, if any of them needs help.'

Thorn said this because it was true. He repeated this quite often. He knew that there was little or no chance that a kid would come to see him – certainly before school or during their precious lunchtimes, but it was a good line to use in situations like this.

'Also, I sent a letter to you the other week because Lindsay had not completed her folio work. I know that was something that she had a problem with, but it is a necessary piece of work.'

'I spoke to the principal teacher about that,' the bloody ruddy-faced mother snapped, even more huffily. 'Lindsay did try to complete the work, but she said that you did not give her enough help with it.'

'Well, I spent time in class speaking to each of the pupils about their choices for writing. I gave them input on writing style and I showed them some examples of successful writing. I also made myself available to help, as I said, even after the deadline had passed...'

Thorn was beginning to get his nose ahead. He got really pissed when kids who did sweet Fanny Alice in class got credibility at home. This woman must be looking for a battle, he thought. She must have a sad, empty life, with nothing in it. Or else it was a rear-guard action – she had been neglectful for years and now she was looking to scapegoat anyone she could.

'And the other thing is,' Thorn told her, with some assurance, 'it's meant to be the student's own work. You can find the arrangements documents online at the SQA website. It tells you that the teacher shouldn't provide too much support for the student. In fact, there was a teacher hauled up and disciplined recently because she was helping a student too much last year.'

The father figure sat forward again to interrupt. He had a mad, mental 'Haud me back!' look in his eye. He had already had enough of listening to this shit at home –without having to listen to any of Thorn's pertinent answers. 'What we're saying is we are not happy with the situation in your class and we've spoken to the head teacher. Our daughter needs her Higher English this year and it's your job and you're failing.'

He turned slightly, not used to being interrupted, as his wife broke in, 'And we spoke to some other parents outside and they are not happy and they are going to the head teacher as well... And it's because of your attitude to your pupils!'

Thorn wanted to keep his cool, but he also wanted to tell them to *FUCK RIGHT OFF*! and tell them that they could not begin to imagine what it was like to try to lead a disinterested group of sixteen and seventeen-year-olds through an academic course, when they had neither natural aptitude nor the vaguest interest.

'I'm not sure that there is anything else to say just now,' said Thorn, briskly. 'I would have said that you should go to the principal teacher, if you had any concerns, but you've done that.' He started to stand up.

'This isn't finished,' said the father. He was still sitting, but turned round to watch Thorn move. 'You're going to hear more about this,' he muttered.

'If you can excuse me just now, please,' said Thorn, holding his hand out in the direction of the door, 'I have other parents to speak to.'

The unpleasant couple grunted as they rose and shifted their weight in the direction of the door. Thorn reached it first and opened it in front of them. He gave a smirk into space as they left. A breath of her sweat and old perfume and his stale cigarette smoke assaulted his tubes as they lumbered past.

*Happy days*, he thought, closing the door purposefully behind them.

Going back to his desk, he picked up the visitor list. He still had eight parents to see. His chest was hammering. He was not one for confrontational situations, if he could help it. That sort of thing he abhorred.

It was all he could do to stay in the building.

He knew he wasn't some omni-talented teaching god. He knew he had plenty of weaknesses and one or two strengths, but he didn't need to be reminded of it by the careless parents of some conniving schoolgirl. His head immediately kicked into an anxiety-related downward spiral.

It was an effing joke – a symptom of the consumer society. People used to complaining about goods and services wanted to complain about school as well. They could not see that it was not the same thing.

However, he was as pleasant as any professional when he stuck his head around the door again. As it turned out, thereafter, there was little to worry him. Much more like normal.

Nonetheless, before long, his napper began to bounce. And, when his last client left, he sat heavily in his chair and swung from side to side, staring up to the back of the room. Those arseholes had stirred things up by complaining to the Heidie.

*Bastards!*

# Wednesday, 1012

Now Constable Constance is visible in the window. She is holding the handle and waggling it. She finds the door locked. Her call is muffled by the stout wood and the thick, wired glass panel. 'Mr Thorn! Mr Thorn!' she calls, her voice rising. 'Open this door, please! Open it now!'

But Thorn is not listening. He has turned his attention elsewhere.

He scans the room immediately. Beside the door is a tall bookcase. He starts shoving it towards the door. This is a race against time. There are other people with keys to the room.

He stops, thinks, takes his key from his pocket again and, from a position out of sight beside the door frame, reaches across. Placing the key in the lock again, he turns it slightly. Now, nobody on the other side can readily insert a matching key to gain access.

The police officer pounds on the door when she sees his hand again. 'Mr Thorn, you are running out of options!' she shouts aggressively.

*So are you*, he thinks, as he places his shoulder against the bookcase again and shoves it across the carpet. It spills some books, but it moves. It is sufficiently tall to obscure the glass panel and the angry face of the thwarted constable.

Thorn now has the bit between his crowns and fillings. He is sick and tired of all the crap. He is making a stand. What the hell! Why not?

He is intent on barricading himself inside the room. Let them shout and bang on the door. Let them rant! There is no way he is being arrested because someone shat in his room. At least, there is no way he is going to be arrested without putting up a bit of a fight.

He fills the bookcase with more books – piles of them from the countertop. Now he ponders. He does not want to destroy the place, but, if he can move some more furniture, he can make it more difficult for them to enter. In fact, if he can move some of the bigger furniture, it should be impossible to push the door open. He can use the filing cabinets. They are heavy in themselves. Filled with paper, they must weigh sixty or seventy kilos each.

But he soon discovers that friction is a problem. The filing cabinets are enormously heavy and the carpet is worn and loose. He finds that he cannot shift one of them by pushing it along the floor. If he does manage to shift it, a wrinkle in the carpet prevents him from moving it more than a few centimetres.

He is stuck. The filing cabinets are stuck. He needs a solution. He needs a trolley or castors. He needs a sled.

Then, he sees the answer.

When the school was refurbished ten years ago, shelves were removed from his walls. The steel uprights, which were previously fixed to the wall, have lain undisturbed in his room ever since. On a number of occasions, he has asked the janitor to remove them. Several times he has thought about moving them himself, but he too has left the job undone. Just as well. He can use them as track.

Now he fetches two of the steel strips. He places them parallel on the floor, with their ends next to the filing cabinet. As he tilts the filing cabinet slightly, he gently kicks the end of each runner under the edge of the base.

After some strong-armed jostling, the incredibly heavy steel box, filled to bursting with meaningless mounds of paper, is sitting atop the steel runners. Now, the steel strip is immoveable on the carpet and the filing cabinet is almost free of friction. Thorn finds that, as he lends his weight to the back of the cabinet, he can push it slowly towards the door.

The cabinet reaches the end of the steel strips and he quickly retrieves another pair from the back of the room. He begins to feel empathy with the builders of the pyramids – although his construction will probably not be as impressive or take as long to build.

Never did he think that these filing cabinets, filled with recycling never done, would come in useful. If he can move all of the cabinets to the door, they will provide an insurmountable barrier to his opponents – unless they have a bulldozer.

He slides the filing cabinet until he is almost at the door. There, as he manoeuvres it off the rails, it falls with a thud against the bookcase.

Another brick in the wall.

There is another banging at the door. This time it is far more muffled.

Thorn decides that, given his position – barricaded in a classroom – he is not going to speak to them just now. They have given him enough hassle. Let them sweat it out for a while.

He continues to sweat as he heaves the other filing cabinets, using the same method, from the other side of the room. He relishes his task. He has been inert and helpless and grumbling for too long.

Once his fortification is complete, he looks around.

He realises quite quickly, but perhaps too late, that he is not in a very strong position. He has his phone and his charging cable and some data left, so he can communicate, but, as siege situations go – even as self-induced siege situations go – he is not in a commanding strategic situation. He has no water and little food. In fact, by rights, it is nearly coffee time – and there is no chance of boiling water today.

Also, he is trapped with one helluva smelly shite. Maybe in a bit of time he will become accustomed to it, but, meantime, the bouquet still catches his throat.

What he doesn't want to do is spend all of his time sitting looking at it. That just wouldn't be healthy.

Maybe, he muses, as time goes on, he can do a bit of work or some writing. Or he could compose some more content for Facebook. He could address his audience in the outside world...

On the other hand, how long can he be in here – realistically?

He is cornered, but he is here to draw attention and make a valid point. What the hell! He can't just allow himself to be walked over, day in, day out. That has gone on for long enough.

He takes a seat at the back of the room. It is the chair furthest from the crime scene. He wants to clear his head and to think a little, before the next phase.

He doesn't have much time, because the bell rings. It is interval time. His head tells him it is time for a caffeine hit. His bladder tells him it will soon be time for another pit stop... although, he reflects, he can always use the plastic bin and throw it out of the window.

He wonders what will happen now.

The interval bell rings. Going by the timetable, after break, in fifteen minutes, the corridor will again be filled with pupils coming to class.

*How are they going to manage that?* he thinks.

The place will be in uproar downstairs. The business manager will be rushing round trying to find alternative rooms. They can't have classes coming through the corridor when his door is under police guard. The boss will be doing her dinger.

They'll need to block off the corridor. Any kid who didn't know will soon know. There can't be police in the school without the kids having something to say about it. Jeez, some of the kids hate the police.

Just then, there is a noise at the outside window. Then another one. It sounds like small stones.

He stands up and walks over to the windows. Before the windows, for most of the room's length, is a large sloping roof. Covered in plastic membrane, it has several vents and chimneys on it and four large transparent plastic domes, which allow light into the kitchen below. Adjoining this roof, to one side, is the dining hall, which has a much bigger, but slightly lower roof, dotted with six see-through plastic pyramids.

However, on the other side from the dining hall, he has a view of the ground, where there is a patch of weedy tarmac, strewn with litter. It is a dead zone between school extensions.

Sometimes there is a rubbish skip in this space of puddles and swirling rubbish. Today, there is a group of three boys. One of them is Coddy, the boy he spoke to a short time ago in the corridor, before the police arrived.

'Y'awright up there, sir? They've closed off the corridor,' Thorn hears through the open window.

Now, it is as Thorn wished. The police are treating it like a crime scene. The corridor has been cordoned off. The only problem with this is that the real evidence, the real crime scene, is inside the room and they cannot investigate that when he is locked in here.

But they have given him no choice. He was in an emotionally challenging situation. They will have to consider that, before they discipline him. Where is their sense of natural justice? What he says to the boys is, 'Yeah, lads, I'm fine. I had to lock the door. Mrs Butcher asked the police to come and remove me from the school. And I've not done anything wrong. It's not fair.'

The boys seem to be listening, but he doesn't know if they have heard what he is saying. Coddy speaks up. He is the ringleader. 'Are you a hostage then, sir?' he calls up.

'Yes,' says Thorn, speaking before he can fully think things through, 'you could say that. A hostage to fortune.'

The boys are immediately in conference. Then one of them has his phone out. He is photographing the window, with Thorn in it. He must be posting to social media.

Thorn realises he does not really care about what message is getting out. But a message is being broadcast and, however his case is represented on social media, surely, if these are his fifteen minutes in the spotlight, then he deserves as many people as possible to know about his conflict with the authorities.

'Do you need anythin, sir?' Coddy calls out.

Thorn shakes his head. 'No, I'm fine, thanks. Just don't get into trouble on my account, lads,' he says, only half meaning it.

It is still interval and, within a minute or two, as he stands at the window, he sees that the group of three is swelling in size. Kids come rushing round the corner – first in twos and threes and then by the half dozen. They are all looking up and shouting out in recognition and laughing.

He acknowledges them with a wave – but immediately understands the instantaneous and very effective pull of social media. There is a flash mob outside his window.

Realising this, he also recognises that he has only made one post to Facebook himself. If he is going to draw other people into this story, in which he is a main player, he will need to take up the baton again and fire out an update. Without another episode, the story will lose currency and readers. His followers will lose interest.

And he needs to make some running before the other side does. He has to set the agenda, as a matter of priority, because he is in a unique position to do so and he will never be availed of this opportunity again.

He takes out his phone. The battery is getting low. He quickly checks his bag for the cable, plugs in and switches on.

Again, he reverts to Facebook. It may not be the platform of the times – he knows the kids prefer Instagram or Snapchat – but it is what he is most comfortable with. And it was effective the last time.

But the kids do like pictures and, surely, the news media will need photos. Here, on his phone, he has the means to furnish them.

He quickly takes an artificially smiling selfie. Then he takes a shot of his obstructing heap of furniture.

Then he starts drafting.

# Tuesday, 1843

He switched off the computer, which had been humming in the background. He had been up since ten past six in the morning. He spent the day in school with bloody classes and assorted shit and now he had major head-nip because a couple of cranky parents had taken their inadequacies out on him. He was getting rapidly pissed off.

Situations like this he absolutely loathed. They made him despise the school, hate the kids, abhor the parents and, worst of all, thoroughly detest himself.

It bored into his brain, like a non-stop dentist's drill – the old-fashioned kind, with all the strings and pulleys and whirring noises. It bit into the centre of him and opened him up – like someone wanted to expose his nerves and insecurities and parade them around in front of his bosses.

He would surely be better when he was on the road home...

Having changed from his collar and tie into his damp bikewear, he reached the foyer, rolling his bike alongside him. There was a scattering of sixth-year pupils, looking their smartest in braided blazers. The head teacher stood with one of her female deputes. She muttered something behind her hand to the junior colleague when she saw Thorn coming.

'Eh, sorry to interrupt,' said Thorn, as he approached them at the front doors, 'could I have a word, please? Sorry to interrupt.'

'No, that's okay,' said the head teacher, making no eye contact. 'Come through into my office.'

He rested his bike against the wall and took his bag with him.

Thorn seldom saw inside the heidie's office. This was about the third time. The first time was when he was interviewed. The second time, he made the mistake of expressing interest in a temporary job within the school. On that occasion, he realised that his application was being dealt with as a formality. The heidie had a preferred candidate and, since, nine times out of ten, she appointed women, Thorn's wedding tackle was an impediment.

'Sit down, please,' she said, almost before he was in the door. Thorn noticed that the depute came in behind him.

He was appreciative of the seat, but he did not feel comfortable. With his lycra on, he held his bag in front of himself, defensively. The heidie sat down too, above him, at her desk, but the depute stood guard near the door.

'I've never had a parents' night like that!' said Thorn. 'Never.' He was exasperated and getting it off his chest. He wanted some consolation. He was shaking his head and still clutching his bag awkwardly on his lap. 'I spoke to Lindsay Harper's parents. They didn't seem very pleased. They said they had spoken to you. I think they've got things all out of proportion.'

'Yes, they did come to speak to me,' said the boss. There was a slight suggestion of smugness in her look – as if she was already enjoying the exchange. 'They were concerned about Lindsay's progress with her Higher English. They said she needs it for her course at the art school.'

Thorn did not feel the love or the respect or any degree of support. What he felt was regurgitation and disapproval. Something was beginning to stink.

'I had Pupil Support send a homework letter a few weeks ago,' he said. 'Her mum contacted the school to find out what Lindsay still had to do. I sent an email to say that her essay was not finished and that her poor attendance would soon impact on her performance.'

The head teacher heard him out and then punched back. 'But the parents were talking about close reading as well. Lindsay doesn't feel she is getting any better at close reading and she said you refused to mark her work.'

Thorn reeled. Not only had he just heard a load of undistilled merde from the parents, now he was hearing it replayed by someone intended to be his leader. No questions, no investigation, no curiosity – just reiteration of their point.

He was fed up. He wanted to get up. He wanted to get out. He wanted to get home.

But he continued, because he could not just let go. 'I am sorry, but that is not what happened. What happened was that Lindsay turned up late to class and we were already going over the marking as a class. She had missed the start of the lesson and was about fifteen minutes late, so she had missed the first few questions –'

'But you didn't mark her work when she asked,' the boss interrupted.

Thorn looked askance at her. She didn't care to register what he was saying. She did not have the slightest interest in his point of view. She had made up her mind about him some time ago. She now felt obliged to fight the parents' corner. No, in fact, she was relishing joining this dispute with him. He was faced with a manipulative manager, who was quite content to pin him to a wooden cross in full public view – at the end of a long and exhausting day.

All he wanted was to get himself home and to clear the accumulated detritus of the job from his mind for a few hours, before submitting himself to it the next day. He did not want this.

'It wasn't like that,' Thorn protested weakly, with a growing sense of futility. 'She missed the start of the period. I said I would give her the marking scheme, so that she could check her answers and ask me if there was anything she couldn't understand. It's what I usually do in situations like that.

'She wasn't very happy. I could see that, but the rest of the class was waiting and I couldn't spend time arguing with her, so I cut her short. She clearly wasn't pleased with that either.'

'No,' the boss said curtly, 'she wasn't. And she said that the class has not done many practice close reading passages yet?'

*For fuck's sake, the girl is hardly there and does virtually nothing!* Thorn thought. He did not have the energy left for this sort of slaughtering.

'No, I did a formal one just before Christmas and then there was the prelim, but I don't think it always helps them to improve, doing a whole paper, if they have not practised the different types of questions and are just failing all of the time.'

'Well, that sounds like an admission,' the head teacher said, with a tone of satisfaction. 'We will discuss this again tomorrow. Can we make a priority of that, please, Ms O'Brien?'

145

'I'll put it in the diary, Mrs Butcher,' the depute said, rather obnoxiously.

Thorn was now completely pissed off – immensely so. She didn't have a piddly little clue about the pedestrian progress that the pupils in his class were making. The kids struggled to engage with any printed text.

'Yes,' he said, standing up and self-consciously pulling down the front of his bike jacket. Now, he just wanted out. He was suffocating in that room with those people. There was nothing more to say.

Before resentment bubbled over, he left and walked down the management corridor, past the framed sixth-year photos. He had a bad taste in his mouth. He wanted to spit it out onto the shiny linoleum. He resisted the temptation and breenged through the double doors to the foyer.

'See you tomorrow, Mr Thorn,' one of the nice sixth years said as he walked past.

'Oh, yes,' said Thorn, swinging his helmet onto his head, 'looking forward to it.'

He retrieved his bike, pressed the button and the sliding door opened with a rush of cold air. He didn't want ever to enter by those doors again. He hated the place. He hated its mealy-mouthed, stupid atmosphere, where every bloody thing had to be done, where every tiny portion of his time was accounted for – completing or half-completing fruitless tasks.

That person – his head teacher, his manager – hadn't offered him a murmur of solace or reassurance. Why should he be surprised? She had no reputation for compassion.

He rolled his bike out of the doors and headed for home. It was over for one evening. The plain truth was, if he could swing it, he would leave and never, ever go back.

# Wednesday, 1040

*'I am Archie Thorn and I am hostage to my situation,'* he types.
*'As you may have read earlier, my place of work has been vandalised and defaced. Since I discovered this, I have received no help or support from my management team, particularly Mrs Butcher, the head teacher. In addition, my union, the RTSA, has been of no use whatsoever.*

*Now, Mrs Butcher, with the connivance of the local authority, has asked the police to remove me from my place of work.*

*For this reason, I have locked myself in the room, which is the scene of the crime. It is only by so doing that I can protect the evidence and ensure that it is not tampered with.*

*I have done nothing wrong. I have suffered abuse in my workplace. A great pile of human excrement has been left on my chair. Until a proper investigation is launched and until I receive guarantees that I will be treated with the professional respect and courtesy which I am due, I will stay here.*

*Here and now, I am making a stand. If this had happened to the head teacher, I am sure that she would have been incandescent with rage and determined to find the culprit.*

*I am not prepared, therefore, to be the victim of her double standards. Until she has scrutinised every bit of evidence, from CCTV footage to interviews with possible witnesses, I will not be satisfied. I do not come to school to suffer indignity and humiliation, I come here to teach. I cannot do this without the full support of the management team and the council.'*

Quickly, he rereads his words. It's always important, he tells the kids, to write, then edit. He makes a few amendments and posts with his pictures. *What the hell!* he thinks.

He returns to the window. Now, there is a bigger crowd. He can hear them. They are quite rowdy. His cause has obviously struck a chord with them. They have something of the mob about

147

them. They should not be at the back of the school. They should not be so close to someone who is revolting.

Then, when they see him at the window, a cheer goes up.

'Mis-ter Thorn, Mis-ter Thorn!' some begin to cry. The chant builds.

Thorn waves back to them. He is tempted to raise a clenched fist, but he is not sure that is an appropriate reaction or symbol. After all, someone just shat in his room. This is not class or race war or anything. Just now, he is just a single teacher, making a stand against authority – albeit an authority which is widely seen as unsympathetic and, within these walls, some might say, totalitarian.

He lifts his clenched fist to the window. He looks down on the upturned faces of the growing number outside. A new cheer goes up and some members of the rally raise their fists in salute.

Just at this moment, a janitor appears. He must have seen the pupils siphoning around the corner towards the back of the school, which is strictly off limits. His pale-blue, council-issue V-neck is very apparent amongst the rank-and-file pupils, with their largely black uniforms.

He looks up at Thorn's classroom window, but Thorn averts his gaze. Then he starts to chivvy and chase the pupils away – back to where they belong.

But the kids are having none of it. They laugh. A few begin to move, but very slowly.

Thorn sees the janitor – quite a young lad – talking into his radio. He must be alerting the other janitors and the management team that there is an unruly gathering round the back of the building.

Just then, the bell rings for the end of interval.

Looking down from the window, Thorn can see some of the kids moving off to their classes – but not many. A substantial number, maybe thirty, stay where they are.

They see that he is looking out of the window again. They cheer. They give him the clenched fist salute.

*Oh, no!* Thorn thinks and hopes that they are not going to get into trouble.

Another moment and the big depute head comes round the corner into the dead zone between the two buildings. He is clearly on the warpath. Given his size, his suit and his narrow tie, there is something of the Basil Fawlty about him. He has no moustache, but he is awkward and ungainly.

Rashly, he shouts, before he is within reach of the children. Mostly boys, they know how easy it is to avoid an awkward adult. They show a clean pair of heels before he has any of them – running off in the opposite direction to that from which he came.

The janitor and depute confer briefly, then follow.

Thorn can see them as they disappear round the far end of the admin block. They will be captured by the globe of the CCTV camera, which is suspended from the fitting on the corner. Most of the boys will not care – not one bit. They will enjoy giving the management team the runaround – especially this big fella, Mr Honnigan.

Sorry to see the last of them, Thorn turns again to his phone – his only real means of communication with outside. He has a number of messages. The one that catches his eye is from Polly.

It is a text: '*What the hell have you done? How is this stupidity going to help pay the mortgage? What on earth are you going to do, sleep in your classroom? What will you do for food? I can't believe it. But keep in touch, please.*'

*Fuck sake*, he thinks, *that's a bad sign. No kiss, kiss.* He is in real trouble now.

He feels a surging wave of doubt and negativity rush through him from his stomach to his head and back to his chest. It's almost overwhelming. He sits on the edge of a desk facing the window.

It is soon gone. Quelling his doubt, he tells himself he cannot afford to buy into these feelings of negativity. He must act with confidence and be self-assured.

A few minutes later, he hears movement again below the window.

A handful of his mirthful supporters have appeared again. Within a minute, there are a dozen more.

All boys, except for one girl, they have circumnavigated the school – probably misleading their pursuers into thinking that they disappeared back to their classrooms. They have continued through the school buildings, probably exiting through a fire door, and they have arrived back where they started.

They are laughing and out of breath. One or two of them are on their phones, presumably spreading news of their latest exploit.

Moments later, climbing up over the far edge of the kitchen roof, Thorn sees Coddy, the lad he spoke to earlier in the corridor. He manages to get one fluorescent trainer onto the roof, then hauls himself onto the plastic surface and dodges across towards the windows. He has an unexplained bag over his shoulders. He never has a school bag.

He hesitates, until Thorn shouts, 'Over here!' and taps on the window.

'Oh, sir, sorry, I couldnae see you wi the reflection on the windae. You okay, sir?'

'Aye, I'm okay. Just a bit tired.'

'Nae bother, sir,' says Coddy, as he unhitches the bag from his shoulders. 'I've got some supplies for you here, sir. We just nicked intae the vendies. Here you go.'

He unloads two bottles of water, two cans of Coke, two rolls and cheese, three packets of crisps and one pancake with a margarine portion heat-sealed into a plastic bag. He makes a pile on the roof, then passes the delivery in several handfuls through the narrow gap at the lower edge of the window.

Thorn is overwhelmed. He was feeling the outsider, the renegade, the outcast. Now, the kids' thoughtfulness gives him a small sense of being appreciated. It is gratifying that some people are not condemning his behaviour out of hand – even if it is just a bunch of daft boys.

'Can I give you some money?' Thorn asks Coddy.

'Naw, nae bother, sir. Happy tae help.'

'Well, thanks. Don't make trouble for yourself now, not on my account, please.'

'Naw, you're fine, sir. Nae probs. Just let us know if you need anythin else. See you.'

As Coddy walks off across the roof, Thorn looks after him. He's just a wee lad, a wee, undersized town boy, but he has a big heart.

Thorn makes a pile of the goodies on the table at the back of the room. There is nothing he really wants just now, but he might be hungry later. Good of the kids to think of him and take the risk of buying him provisions. The vending machines are off limits during class time.

Then he sits down, drained already. It must be the emotional and rebellious energy he has been expending. Maybe he should have some caffeine, some Coke. He doesn't usually drink it – he despises multinationals – but it might perk him up, allow him to think through the next phase. He should be getting some more calls and messages soon.

Briefly, he puts his head in his hands. This could mean that he is thinking hard – or that he is tired and wanting sleep.

'Ya dirty big bastard!' he hears – the words breaking violently into his momentary silence.

# Tuesday, 1926

When he turned down from Henry Street onto the cycle track – just at the point when he ought to be relishing the easy run through the railway cutting, sheltered by sycamores – he was ambushed and very nearly overwhelmed by a colossal sense of futility.

His mind had been racing until then – motoring over and over the events of the difficult day – replaying everything. His senses were aflame.

But, as he rolled down the ramp from the main road, his bike suddenly became heavy – like a brake pad was stuck – like he was cycling through sand. Any freewheel speed from the slope, which usually turned into pedal speed, was lost. Each turn of the cranks took unbearable effort.

He became beset with his growing mass. Gravity had doubled…trebled. His legs were leaden. His energy level flatlined.

In that dip in the ground, at that low point, he dropped like a stone into a trough of self-revulsion.

Worn out, half-demented and hungry, he was deadbeat and six kilometres short of an energy fix.

He had never felt it so bad. As an existential crisis, it was a big belter. It was so grim, he was running out of will to go home.

Bred to be determined, optimistic, energetic, he could no longer claim to be any of those things. Embittered, disappointed and bored shitless, his continued existence weighed on his conscience and he resented it.

The rancid toxins of his working life seeped through him and ate away at his insides. He was dangerously depleted and ready for change – any change.

He knew, for certain, that he and his career could not travel much further along the same road together.

At times like this, if he disappeared magically in a puff of smoke, or if someone flicked a switch to teleport him back to the Enterprise, he would not have given one toss about it.

# Wednesday, 1107

He looks up.

There is no one at the window.

The barricade at the door is still intact.

Maybe he is hearing things.

'Dirty big shite!'

No, there is no mistaking those words. If anything, they are a bit louder. They appear to be directed at him.

But he cannot make out where they are from. He stands up and quietly steps over to the door. He puts his ear as close as possible, but hears no movement or noise whatsoever. There might be any number of people in the corridor – or maybe there are only one or two and some keeping an eye on the other points of access – but none of them is making a sound.

'You're a dirty big shite!' the voice hisses.

Thorn looks down at his mobile. Maybe someone is remotely controlling Siri, the man who speaks in the phone. Or perhaps he has pressed the Siri button by mistake.

However, there is nothing on the screen – no sign of action and no wobbling wavy line to indicate that Siri is listening or about to speak. He turns the sound down and clicks the phone off.

Pocketing the phone, he looks round the door frame. Surely nothing has been inserted through the doorway – a camera or a microphone or a loudspeaker.

There is nothing that he can see, so he explores the roof with his eyes. The next most obvious place in the room is the suspended ceiling. It is held up by wires of about a metre in length, which are tethered to the steel-reinforced concrete floor above. It may be that there is crawl space or an opening between his and neighbouring rooms. From here he cannot detect anything amiss. And surely twenty minutes or so is not long enough for the authorities – the management team and the police – to have investigated this possibility, found the space and passed a speaker through.

154

Anyway, why would they be calling him a 'big shite'?

He continues to wander round and look at the roof anyway. He can see no sign anywhere that the white-painted, compressed paper tiles have been disturbed.

There is no indication anywhere of any sort of intrusion into his locked space.

'You're so ignorant!' the voice says. 'What have you done?' He walks around, all around the room. He peers through the windows – looking from side to side, up and down. He cannot locate the source. But he definitely heard it. Didn't he?

There is something familiar about the voice, like it is a colleague or a friend. But the computer has not been switched on and his phone is turned off. In fact, just in case, he pulls it out again, flicks it on, places it next to his ear.

'It's not the phone, ya daftie,' the voice says – and not from inside the phone. 'Think, for God's sake, think!'

He rams the phone deep into his pocket.

There is a recognisable timbre to the voice. It's very recognisable, like hearing his father or his brother on the phone. He just can't work it out.

He scouts round the hard edges of the room again – at the shelves, the worktop, the network trunking, the chipped skirting board. There is no sign of any sort of penetration. All of the plaster, the paint, the woodwork is intact. He is entirely mystified. Not since Peter Pan flew over the audience in the pantomime when he was five has he been so perplexed.

He sticks his head into the gap of an open window and tries to peer down onto the roofing. Again, there is nothing there. A discarded textbook, some puddles, some rubbish, leaves and weeds, but nothing capable of using the local vernacular to address him.

He is standing near the window when he hears the voice again and is able to ascertain its source.

'There's one place you haven't looked, Archie boy,' it says.

He heads towards his desk. He often takes a phone from a pupil and places it in his desk drawer. It must be one of those, forgotten at the end of a period yesterday. Yes, that must be it.

'You're getting warmer. I'm right here!'

155

# Tuesday, 1950

All Thorn wanted to do was to survive his working days and make as few waves as possible. He didn't do inspirational or life-changing lessons. He'd never experienced any himself. That was *Dead Poets'* fiction.

There was novelty in teaching for the first couple of years – perhaps, when he thought he might build something – when he had furnished himself with a motivating narrative about the social value of the job. He could affect to have a social conscience.

Then what struck him, like a big shovel across the face, was that it was an all-consuming, unmanageable task and that, if he continued, every iota of his energy was going to be sucked into the black hole of English teaching.

He had no time for anything else, other than living on his nerves, on the margins of a big sump of angst and debasement.

Now, at this stage in his 'career', he had met every type of kid, every condition, every degree of behaviour.

He was plagued by pointless deadlines. There was always something – jotter checks, pupil reports, internal assessments, tracking, marking... And he detested the overbearing scrutiny.

Nothing about his practice made him proud. With negligible resources, more than a hundred pupils and a yawning gap between what the kids needed and what they actually got, everything he did felt half-baked and mediocre. Even as a moderately capable bipedal being, all he did was firefight. It drove him screwy.

These days, as time roared on, he was agonisingly aware of the pressing vastness of wasted opportunity.

It made him desperate to jack it all in. He had waited long enough.

It was clear that significant change would not happen in his lifetime. Too many people were blindly invested in a Sisyphean system, which only perpetuated itself. What he sorely needed was a big lottery win. What a life he could have with a few grand a month in the bank! He'd load up the bike and be off. Thirty-five thousand kilometres, riding east – one loop of the planet. Surely that would preoccupy him for long enough to purge himself of this pernicious preoccupation with school.

# Wednesday, 1111

Astonished, gobsmacked and seriously confounded, Thorn realises that the voice is coming from the direction of his chair. He narrows his eyes in suspicion and opens them wide again. 'Found me at last, ya daftie. Who did you think it was?'

The voice is emanating from his chair and, as he listens and looks more carefully, he sees that the jobby, when it speaks, moves a little.

'I'm here. Look!' it says. 'Say 'Hullo!''

Thorn moves a little closer. He can see that a small mouth has opened, near the top end of the shiny brown heap of excrement. There are tiny lips and Thorn thinks he sees miniscule brownish teeth, when the mouth articulates the sounds. A suggestion of a chin protrudes slightly.

'Say 'Hullo', Archie. Where are your manners, sunshine? Speak when you're spoken to, for god sake!'

However, Thorn is beyond words. He has spoken to plenty of wee shites in the past – plenty of nasty wee kids who didn't know how to behave and who had given him considerable grief – but he has never spoken to an actual faecal shite – one that appears to be addressing him.

'Archie, Archie! Hullo!' The jobby raises its voice. It is beginning to sound infuriated, as if it does not like to be ignored.

Thorn is now sitting down on the edge of a desk. He rubs his eyes. He gapes. He is exasperated and utterly, utterly bewildered. He decides that he is not going to speak to a jobby. He is not going to sink to that level, surely...? Surely?

As he stares at the jobby, the jobby opens its mouth again and shouts, 'Archie! I'm the only bit of fucking company you've got at the moment. You can't afford to bloody ignore me. You've cut yourself off from the rest of the world and piled filing cabinets up in front of the door. Even your Mrs has taken the huff with you, by the looks of things. What the hell, man? What the hell?'

Archie thinks he must be going off his trolley. Maybe he is getting hungry. It's a good while since he had anything substantial to eat. Or is he dehydrated? He must be hallucinating. Maybe he has food poisoning. Maybe he is having a stroke – or some kind of fit...

This is a living nightmare – not just a hallucination. He has isolated himself and, before he can even begin to think out some sort of strategy, he's not seeing wee green men, but, instead, talking turds.

'I'm not talking to you,' he mutters to himself. 'You do not exist and I am not talking to you!'

'Ha!' shouts the jobby, with a grin, 'caught you out. I thought you said you weren't talking to me, ya daft bastard. Caught you out!'

'Jesus Christ!' says Thorn, this time to himself. He perambulates away from the front of the class, takes a few steps round the desks and heads towards the rear of the room.

'Where are you going, ya daftie? You cannae go up there. I need you here so's we can have a wee heart to heart – a blether.'

'I'm not saying a word,' Thorn mutters. 'I'm not saying a word,' he says to himself.

'Ha! I heard you,' the jobby shouts to him. It is easily loud enough for Thorn to hear, but he ignores it and does not turn round.

'I heard you, I heard you,' the jobby says with a laugh.

Thorn is losing it, he thinks. He is hearing voices in his head. He is imagining sounds.

Maybe there is something wrong with his ears. Has he got an ear infection? Could someone be playing tricks? It could be some police device employed in hostage situations.

And yet... he saw the jobby's mouth move. Surely his eyes aren't deceiving him as well...? Surely?

He turns back to the front of the room and marches down between the desks. He is intent on confronting his fears, his imagination, his tormentor.

The jobby is on his chair, sitting proud on the fabric. It still has a good deal of lustre to it and, as he nears, he realises with horror that, as well as a mouth, it has now opened little shining eyes. Then it looks at him and, with a flash of recognition, it laughs out loud again, its whole form shaking with mirth.

'I knew you'd come back to look. I knew you would. Haha! You couldn't believe it, could you? I knew it. You heard the voice and you told yourself it wasn't real. But it is real. I'm fucking real and I am talking to you and now I can even see you.'

Thorn can see himself that this is true, but he isn't going to acknowledge it straightaway – and play into its hands.

He can now see, even with his own disbelieving and cynical eyes, the little lids, the brown irises, the tiny black pupils. He can also clearly hear the giggling sound issuing from the little mouth, but he is trying as hard as possible not to engage, because to actually talk to the terrifyingly animated jobby would mean some kind of submission – a submission to god only knows what!

He stands open-mouthed for a moment or two. He is shaking his head with incredulity.

Now he peers at the door to make sure that no one is taking advantage of his preoccupation with the miraculous and lively turd, by pushing their way past his barricade.

But the corridor is still silent. He assumes they are in conference, deciding on the next step.

He looks back to the jobby. It has its little eyebrows arched curiously.

'So what are you going to do next, maestro?' it says, chortling quite obnoxiously. 'What's the next phase in your plan to defeat the forces of evil oppression? Haha!'

'Just shut your mouth!' Thorn reacts, muttering angrily, 'and fuck off!'

The jobby only laughs uproariously again. 'What the hell do you think you're saying, ya cheeky big bastard? Don't think you can speak to me like that, ya big eejit. You're the one who's shut himself up in his bloody classroom. Hardly a genius move that, was it?

'What do you think you're going to do, start an effing revolution from here, ya loony? Don't think so.'

Now, bizarrely, Thorn has it in his mind to deal a blow to the big jobby. He is so angry, he wants to thump it for its cheek. He wants to shut it up for good. He doesn't need any smart-alecky excrement getting ideas above its station.

160

But he has no gloves and he does not want to lay an uncovered finger on the little shit. Neither does he have a big lump of wood with which to batter it into next week.

'Come on, ya nutter, say something. You can't just stand there all day. What the hell's going to happen now? You're making your big stand against injustice. Big deal. What are you going to do? Your bosses are out there and the police. Are you just going to sit tight until something happens? Jeezo, what a fine fucking mess you've got yourself into!'

Thorn leans against a desk again. He puts his hand to the side of his head. He must be imagining this. He must be losing his marbles fair and square. But he is captivated by the vision of an eloquent jobby sitting on the seat in front of him – trying to bloody engage him in conversation.

'Oh, Christ!' he exclaims to the ceiling.

'What the hell has religion got to do with it, ya big prick? You're the one who's got yourself into this state. You're the only one. Just you.' Then there is the cackling laughter again.

Thorn levels his unblinking gaze at the jobby. He looks straight into its twinkling eyes. 'Just shut the fuck up, will you?' he fumes.

'Heh, haha, ya total prick! You spoke to me. You're talking to a fucking jobby, ya nutter! Haha!' And again, the chiding chuckle.

'Right, shut it! I heard you and I see you, but I don't want to hear another word out of you. All right?!'

'What the hell are you talking about? I could have been cleaned up and flushed down the toilet by now – swimming off to freedom to re-enter the food chain. Instead, you've chosen to lock yourself into a room with me. It's your bloody fault. It was you that wanted to keep me. You shut and locked the bloody door. I was your evidence. Nobody else in the place wanted me here, only you. Don't give me any of your bloody grief, madman!'

Thorn wants to fulminate and rage, but, sometimes, when he feels like he might be exposed or embarrassed – like when he is in a shop picking his nose – he always looks round to check for CCTV, because he doesn't want to appear on one of those TV shows as that person in a shop pulling a bogie from his nose. He always looks, just in case.

And, really, he has that sense of being massively set up just now. Surely to hell he is being set up. How the hell can this not be a set-up? Surely to hell this is a big joke and he is going to be…

# Tuesday, 2003

At school, the unending seconds became everlasting minutes, which formed the limitless hours of each interminable working day.

Then, he never had any goal other than to get to the end of the afternoon and return to the comfort of his home.

When the final bell rang, he just breathed a heavy sigh, because another epochal shift at the whiteboard was over and he was free to leave.

If there was some other distraction – like a full staff development meeting or a parents' night – it felt like slow death.

Home was largely a safe space. Within his own four walls – or the mortgage company's four walls – he was at liberty. Not at liberty to do anything in particular, but at least free from the soul-stifling obligation of his contract.

That night, when he rolled up to the door, having made the distance from school to home in record time – taking a hell of a lot longer than usual – no one was home. He sighed as he fished in his back pocket for the key. No matter, he thought, he needed time to sluice away the shame and grime of the school and gather his frazzled head together.

He wheeled his bike through the house and, after flicking the switch on the kettle and hanging his jacket to dry, he climbed the wooden hill, peeling layers as he went.

Within ten minutes, he was downstairs, showered, clean, ready for the evening.

Another three minutes saw him sitting on the couch with a mug of decaf on the coffee table and a couple of biscuits in his hand.

Fourteen minutes later, he came to. Or sort of. Like Rip Van Winkle, he felt as if he had been out cold for twenty years. He could barely lift his head from the back of the chair. He had been sucker-punched by gravity.

His brain failed to find focus. His eyes struggled in the effort to reopen. It felt like the groggy process of wakening might last for hours, rather than seconds. More like concussion than school-induced fatigue, he knew it for what it was – the after-effects from the battering about the brainbox that he had soaked up earlier.

That wee horror, the boss, had stunned him. Yes, she had. She had dented him deeply and injured him sorely.

School had been his routine for a score of years. He was no saint, but he was no shirker either. He had tried at every turn to toe the party line. He was always there – always in the room, in front of the kids. He didn't do duvet days when he had a bad cold. The kids came, the periods were ticked off, no one got hurt and they all went home.

All he ever wanted was to go to work, keep a low profile and get out. But now, even that wasn't possible.

As he revisited his degradation, his head started to spin. He felt the rapid thud of his heart in his ears and realised that one of the stress responses to this shit blizzard was palpitations.

It was an utter betrayal. She showed zero managerial nous. The parents' point of view was given total fucking primacy – and they were solely informed by their bleating kid.

She might have allowed him the courtesy of listening to his side of the story. It was a grievous farce. Obviously, the professional and personal humiliation of an English hack was of no consequence to her.

As a sentient being, he was exactly the type of person who needed a bit of the old softly-softly. What he didn't need was being taken to task in front of a sycophantic depute witness – to be toed in the ging-gangs and then birled around and booted up the arse.

But now, despite his efforts, the heidie had suddenly become his judge, his jury and his executioner. That obviously gave her kicks. And that thought raced round, whirling in the middle of his noggin and his heart thrashed like it wanted to run away, because it was his neck that was on her chopping block.

# Wednesday, 1115

'What the hell are you looking about for, dipshit? Talk to me. Give me your abuse. I'm over here, loser.'

Thorn goes and sits down in a pupil's chair at a desk near to his own. He is nearing his wits' end. Surely it is not a talking jobby? It must be voices in his head. Must be. It's all been too much. Surely?

He places his forearms on the tabletop and places his forehead on them, letting out a deep sigh. He is silent for a moment, letting his head still.

The jobby sits quietly too, letting him relax.

Thorn now lifts his head. In his heart of hearts, he is hoping that there is nothing but a turd sitting on the seat before him – not a budding personality.

He stares for a moment. The jobby stares back. Then it winks at him.

'For god's sake, I don't know what you think is so bloody funny!' Thorn snarls.

The jobby can't conceal another grin. 'Well,' it says, 'you've got to admit, this is one hell of an unusual situation you've gotten yourself into here, don't you think?'

'Oh, Christ,' says Thorn, shaking his head, 'you're right. How on earth did I get myself into this mess? And how the hell am I going to get myself out of it?'

He drops his head to the desk again. He is not liking the situation. It seemed a sensible thing to do – to preserve the evidence. Effectively, though, he has backed himself into an unpromising corner. It is hard to see how he might extricate himself.

'To ask a reasonable question,' says the jobby, 'have you had a difficult time recently? Maybe the stress has built up. Have you had issues at home? Sometimes people just snap for no obvious reason. Has something been getting you down?'

165

'Getting me down, getting me down, for fuck's sake!' Thorn is beginning to shout. 'I'm meant to be bloody teaching. It always gets me down. But that's what I do. I'm here to teach the little fuckers to read and write, not sit locked in here.'

Then the jobby says, 'But think back, Archie, has anything happened that might have made you a bit snarky? Did you have a big fall-out with someone or something, mate? You don't mind if I call you 'mate', do you? I don't want to be overfamiliar.'

'No, no,' Thorn snaps back, 'you are being over-fucking-familiar. You're a fucking jobby. I am a human being. There is no way that I am or ever will be your bloody mate.

'And no, I didn't fall out with anyone. All I did today was come to my work. Then, when I found you here and raised a perfectly valid objection, nobody took the slightest interest. Now, because, unlike the other adults in this building, I have acted on principle, I find myself locked in here. Hell's bells, I can't just surrender. I would hardly be going down in a Butch and Sundance hail of bullets, would I? I'm trying to make a point. Fuck sake!'

The jobby has been sitting attentively and is inclining one of his tiny ears towards him thoughtfully. 'You are in a bit of a hole here,' he says, nodding. 'I don't like to say it, but it's hard to imagine a satisfactory solution to this. I mean, I know you've been badly treated, I've witnessed some of that, but, you're right, it's hardly the Alamo…'

Thorn is repeatedly shaking his head, like he has some twitch or something. He is on a serious downer now. He can't imagine anything to lift his spirits.

'I need to… think outside the box,' he says, rather forlornly. 'I can't stay in here for ever. I can't stay in here overnight, even. How the hell would that look? I mean, I'm going to need the toilet sometime. I can't live on crisps and Coke, for goodness' sake. I need to think outside the box.'

'And how's the missus going to feel about it, buddy?' says the jobby.

'She's going to be bloody furious – if she ever speaks to me again. I could have burnt my boats there, shit!'

166

'And it's all over social media too,' says Thorn. 'That could have been a major strategic error. I mean, why the hell did I think that would be a good idea?'

Jobby chimes in, helpfully, 'Listen, bud, the boss had you under the cosh. She wasn't treating your complaint seriously. Jesus, she can't expect you to work in these conditions.'

'Oh, I know,' replies Thorn, 'I just didn't expect a fix like this. I mean, I spend my life trying to avoid any confrontation. I don't know why I needed to snap today. Shit, what a mess!'

'Listen, Archie, it's clearly been building up for some time, man. I expect you snapped because something inside told you that things had gone far enough and there was no way they could continue.

'You know, there are some people who just trudge along for ever, same thing every day – day in, day out – until they finally fall off the perch and that's it. At least with you, when the final reckoning comes, maybe you'll be able to say, 'I am Archie Thorn and one day I made a stand against authority and refused to be pushed around'.

'And not only that, Archie, there will be people out there who will remember you for what happened today. I'd put money on it. I bet, in years to come, people on the surface of this planet will say to each other, 'Do you remember that day when Archie Thorn locked himself in his classroom because he wanted to make a stand against bullies in authority?' And Archie, I suggest that the person listening will say, 'Yes, I remember Archie Thorn and I remember he stood against injustice.' And do you know what, Archie, do you know what?'

# Tuesday, 2047

He wondered if this was what it felt like to have high blood pressure. His wee heart was going and he knew his colour was rising. It was as if his blood was bubbling furiously in his body, ready to burst out.

He lay back against the cushions. Mazy ideas were swimming in his head. He could not pin any of them down. One thing after another was floating past him.

In one way, he cared that he had been hopelessly emasculated. In another, he would happily relinquish the responsibility for that damned class…

Now he felt a surge of relief. Then it was a wave of shame. The two conflicting emotions swept back and forth and he sank down and down into the trough of self-pity.

Polly would soon be back. She would be hungry, but it was as much as he could do to just sit on the couch, where the heaving to and fro of his emotions made him feel quite sick.

Sure, he had experienced many shitty days – many homecomings when he wanted never to go back. But, man alive, the day just passed had one or two cherry-on-top moments. Then the deplorable meeting with a disgraceful head teacher had put sugar frosting on top of that cherry.

For how many more years could he drag his reluctant carcase back to that place? How many more days did he need to be up before the larks, driving himself towards that gloomy building, only to be demeaned and derided when he got there – and not just by the lousy kids?

He wasn't fit for purpose and, anyway, he no longer had any wish to fit the template. The job no longer held any interest, appeal or inducement to him and he was in over his head in the quagmire of teenage disdain and adult alienation.

To get the hell out, whilst he could still kick – however feebly – against the system, was all he wanted. Otherwise, every last bit of his character and every shred of scepticism would be wrung out of him.

Without decisive action, he was going to be left, just a wrinkled old skin of retired teacher – a wizened old fuckwit with a tedious tendency to tell stories about crazy classroom capers in days of yore.

Something had to force his hand. Something had to give him licence to pack it in. And this might be it. There was nothing to be gained from hanging around – nothing, other than the salary...

The way he felt, the head teacher might just as well have taken his teaching certificate, slapped him about the face with it, ripped it up and flushed it down the toilet.

He wished to hell she had just tied him to a lamp post and ordered her minions to throw rotten turnips and stale eggs at him. That would have been more dignified.

# Wednesday, 1119

'What?' asks Thorn.

'I think,' answers the jobby, 'that many people, in this neighbourhood, will laugh and think back on this day as one of the more interesting days that they have lived through during their lives – certainly one of the more unusual.'

'I'd like to think that's true,' says Thorn. 'I'd like to agree with you, Jobby. You don't mind if I call you 'Jobby', do you?'

'No, that's fine,' says Jobby.

'I just can't help thinking,' continues Thorn, 'that while you are painting things in a positive and constructive light, there might be some other people thinking, 'Oh, yeah, that arsehole, Archie Thorn. I remember him. He took a hissy fit when he found a shit in his room. Then he locked himself up in the room with the shit, because no one else thought it was a big deal.'

'Aw, come on, Archie, surely it's not as bad as all that? You might be banged up here with me, but at least you've got someone to talk to. And you've some supplies and a mobile and some supporters outside.'

Thorn goes to the window. The handful of kids is still outside. One of them sees him looking and they give a quiet cheer. They are hard at work on their phones. He wishes he knew what they were typing or texting.

He looks back at Jobby.

'Everything okay?' says Jobby. 'Are they still there?'

'Aye,' says Thorn, 'half a dozen of them.'

Just as he has uttered these words, another four kids come around the corner to join the original gang. Then another two appear.

Thorn wonders how they have arrived here again. He puts his head to the gap in the window and says down to the boys in a loud whisper, 'How did you boys get out? Should you not be in class?'

'It's all right, Mr Thorn,' Coddy shouts up, 'we're startin a demonstration. We're puttin the word out on Insta and Snapchat. It's no fair that you've been picked on by the heidie. We're goin to get as many folk as possible, Mr Thorn. Don't worry. This is goin to be big news!'

'Are you sure that's a good idea, lads? I don't want you getting into trouble. You've got your lessons...'

'Listen, Mr Thorn,' said another of the boys, shouting – an even smaller lad with thick black hair the colour of his school jumper – 'it's no just you that wee Butcher picks on. She had my parents in the other week because ah tellt her she was talkin shite. As soon as ma da got me hame, he says that, as soon as she opened her mooth, he knew that she wis full ae shite. Ah tell ye, sir, it's no just you she's picked on.'

'Well, just take care, boys. Don't do anything dangerous or daft.' It's what Thorn often says to kids as they leave his classroom for the weekend. He usually says it without much of a thought. This time he really means it. He's not in a strong bargaining position, as things stand. He doesn't want anything to befall one of his young hangers-on, because they have been drawn into his act of rebellion. He doesn't want anyone else's blood on his hands.

He is just about to step back from the window, when he sees another couple of kids come round the corner, then another. This time it's a couple of girls. He recognises them from last year's S4 class. They see him, too, and wave up, shouting, 'All right, Mr T?'

They are quickly hushed up by the rest of the crowd and are absorbed in their number. Presumably, Thorn realises, they don't want to attract more attention than necessary at this stage.

'What do you see?' asks Jobby from behind the desk.

'There are some more kids gathering. I don't know what they're planning,' he replies.

'Maybe you're best to leave them to it,' says Jobby. 'You don't want to be accused of leading them on – you know, making the natives restless and that sort of thing. You can't be held responsible for their behaviour, if they come out in sympathy. On the other hand, if you encourage them to leave their classes, you'd be breaking the law, probably. And you might have done enough of that already.'

'You are quite right, Jobby boy. We're thinking along the same lines. The boss will get her knickers in a twist if the kids are swarming round the place. Bad enough that they've had to cordon off the corridor. Thanks, Jobby, it's good to have another pair of eyes and an ally in a situation like this.'

'Aye, no problem,' says Jobby, looking quite pleased with himself.

'I need to play my own game, you're right. I must set the agenda. I can't just wait for the cops to break the door down or something.'

Just then, Thorn's phone rings. He does not recognise the number, but he answers. It might be the union. It could be someone at the county buildings. He does not know until they speak.

# Tuesday, 2052

His head and his heart were still bouncing along together when Polly came to the door. The bell rang. With everything banging and jangling about inside him, he hadn't heard her car draw up. She often rang the bell when her hands were full of bags and she couldn't find her key.

He forced himself up from the settee with an anguished groan – mostly real – and staggered through to the front of the house. He reached for the latch and a shaft of pain pierced his skull. He leant against the door jamb as Polly brushed past him.

'What on earth's wrong with you?' she said, dumping her bags down in the usual heap on the floor.

He knew she was surprised, getting no answer, because, without taking her coat off, she followed him through to the sitting room.

'Have you not made the dinner?' she asked, which was not an unusual question, even before she asked how his day had been.

Thorn was collapsed on the couch already, rigid and unwell – the nasty pain in his head continued.

'No,' he said through a cough.

Then she asked him about his day. It was their ongoing charade.

He didn't look at her. 'Fine,' he said.

This was a classic tactic. Polly knew he didn't like the job, the place, the classes. He had spoken wistfully about career change. He dreamed of a time, in the not-too-distant future, when he might drop a day or two, go part-time and still pay something into the measly little pension pot – without the habitual crap of the five-day week to contend with.

What 'Fine' meant, in this case, was entirely different to what it meant in other circumstances. In this instance, it was a euphemism for 'I have tried to explain to you before how completely demoralising my experience at work is. Here is a one-word answer, which will have to satisfy you. Do not ask me any more probing questions –unless you are able to wave a magic wand and change the circumstances of my life beyond recognition.'

It was an answer which left Polly to interpret, from his tone and body language, what kind of *Fine* he meant – whether it signified a 'just bearable' *Fine* or, as in this case, a 'really shit and I never, I mean never, want to go back' kind of *Fine.*

'What is it? Are you not well or something?'

Thorn wasn't sure how to react. Generally, he was quite well. He had the odd cold or a tickly cough through the night, but he was normally physically well.

The trouble here was that, whilst he had some inclination to answer, he was expending a lot of energy fighting the nasty pain as it ran around, or, more precisely, battered about inside his head. With his heart still thumping in his ears, reacting to rather obvious questions was not at the top of his list.

When she said, 'Did you already have dinner?' he knew that he had to get something out in response.

But he was in pain – quite a lot of pain – so he was not at his most diplomatic.

'Did I fuck!' he whispered.

'What did you just say to me?' Polly raged, before marching back through to the kitchen and slamming the door.

# Wednesday, 1126

It is a call from Smelter Street, where the council has its offices. Clearly they think that intervention is necessary to break the stalemate. Perhaps it is.

'Mr Thorn, this is the Depute Head of Education and Leisure Services, Myra McGoogan. I got your number from Mrs Butcher, your head teacher.'

'Yes,' replies Thorn, 'how can I help you?'

Rather taken aback by his tone, McGoogan says, 'At the moment, Mr Thorn, you seem to be the one in need of help. Mrs Butcher tells me that you have barricaded yourself in your room. Am I right?'

'Yes,' says Thorn, tersely, 'and your point, please?'

'Well, Mr Thorn, you were asked to vacate the premises and you have not done that. In fact, you have occupied the room and locked yourself in. The thing is, I'm not sure your actions are conducive to good relations in the school.'

'I'm sorry, Ms McGoogan, but I am not sure if you understand what relations are actually like in the school.' Thorn is trying to be direct here. 'It's your assumption that, if you have not heard anything to the contrary, management has the respect of the staff and things must be going along swimmingly. I'm afraid things aren't as hunky-dory as that.'

'Sorry,' says McGoogan, 'I'm not sure I know what you mean, Mr Thorn. Could you elaborate, please?'

'Well,' replies Thorn, 'you assume that Mrs Butcher is running the place like a professional, but, the truth is, there are many people who are dissatisfied with the way she runs the place. Many staff know how unpleasant she is. The kids barely hear a supportive word from her. She appears to think that the way to run a school is in an atmosphere of fear and intimidation.

'And I know I am in a silly situation – at the moment. I mean, I have blockaded myself inside my own room, but, you see, I was feeling troubled, because of Mrs Butcher's complete lack of empathy. I think you will find, if you are prepared to talk to other members of the school staff, that she finds it difficult to interact on a human level with lesser beings.

'For example, if you pass her in the corridor, which is a rarity, because she seldom ventures outwith the management block, she is unlikely to even acknowledge you. Now, I don't know what kind of people you work with or how you were brought up, but I consider that poor manners, if not quite insulting.

'Now, it may be that good manners are not fundamental to good management. Frankly, I do not know. What I do know is that, if she'd shown the slightest bit of sensitivity or compassion to me this morning, when I came into work and found this pollution in my working environment, I would not have been forced into this situation.'

'I'm not sure I can see your point, Mr Thorn,' interjects the McGoogan. 'What you're telling me is that it's the head teacher's fault that you locked yourself in your room. You don't expect me to believe that, do you?'

'Well,' says Thorn, talking right back, 'I would expect you to stand by her, because you are in management too. Or perhaps you played a part in her appointment. I don't know–'

'I don't know what you are talking about, Mr Thorn, I really don't,' interrupts McGoogan, a bit testily. 'Mrs Butcher was in the post before I was, but that's not the point. We have an issue now, because you are obstructing the normal business of the school. I'm phoning to resolve that issue. I really can't stand by and do nothing, especially when you are being so critical on social media. We really must address this situation and I am only phoning you now to discuss a solution – not anything else.'

Thorn is thinking, all of the time that he is on the phone, that the boss, Mrs Butcher, and this so-and-so from the council are in cahoots. Now that he thinks of it, he wouldn't be surprised if Mrs Butcher is in on this call.

But, truth be told, he senses a whiff of power. He has the Depute Head of Education and Leisure Services willing to discuss solutions. He has dug his heels in over a principle. She mentioned the issue of social media. Perhaps he has a stronger negotiating position than he imagined, when he was speaking to Jobby only a few moments ago.

He immediately switches his own phone to speaker and turns round to Jobby. He flicks his eyes at the phone, as if to say, 'Listen to this.' He needs a second opinion. He needs to bring another analytical mind to bear on the problem.

'I'm not sure that I can imagine what kind of solution you have in mind,' says Thorn. 'At the moment, nothing has really changed for me. I'm stuck in this room – fair enough, because I blockaded the door – but, really, the head teacher left me very short of options.

'She insisted that I should do as I was told and then she called in the police. In no way did I get a fair hearing from her. She could never be called a diplomat. I am sure there are many staff who would agree with me. She's not one of those head teachers who wins respect. If anything, it's as if she wants to make herself hard-nosed and unapproachable. I wouldn't be missing the mark if I said that her management style went out with...

'All right, Mr Thorn,' interrupts McGoogan, 'you don't need to go overboard with your insults. Mrs Butcher did not react as you expected, but she has a school to run and children's needs to meet. That's her responsibility.'

'What?' snapped back Thorn, 'without the slightest thought for her fellow professionals? You've got to be kidding. It's meant to be a team effort in here – not just her against the rest of us. She must have left the classroom at least fifteen years ago. I think she's lost any appreciation of what sort of obligation is involved.

'I admit it, I was feeling agitated this morning, when I was speaking to her. But she didn't have enough insight to do anything other than brush me off. Jesus Christ, I have been working in that room for more than ten years non-stop. It's my domain, my habitat, my theatre – well, that sounds rather dramatic. But for me, until this morning, my workspace was relatively unsullied and untarnished.

'Then, as you can see on the World Wide Web, I found myself face to face,' he says, winking at Jobby, 'face to face, with a seriously insulting act of vandalism. It was a terrible situation and, to be honest, Mrs Butcher clearly did not have the faintest notion of how to deal with it. All she could do was employ loutish strong-arm tactics. As a manager, she is a disgrace.'

'I'm not sure we're going to get much further, if you are going to be so insulting about your colleague,' McGoogan says, not sounding very happy. 'I suggest that we resolve the situation now. If you are not going to be more constructive, Mr Thorn, then we will need to finish the phone call.'

Thorn detected a hint of bemusement in their original exchange. Now he realises that there are good reasons why people are promoted to this sort of post. Often it is because they are able to close people like him down – without compunction and with little or no conscience.

'I'm quite happy to hear your suggestions,' says Thorn, positively. 'You called. Did you have anything in mind?'

'At the moment, Mr Thorn, the ball is in your court. You have already tried your hardest to rubbish the reputation of the school and the head teacher. I accept that things could have been done differently, but it would be useful, before you do any more damage to the standing of this council, to remove your internet posts. That would be a good starting point for us, if you are wanting to improve the situation.'

'Okay,' says Thorn, looking round at Jobby, who is grimacing and seeming to shrug his little brown shoulders, 'if I did that, what would you be able to offer in return? Would I be able to go home without being escorted from the school? Would I be charged, or what?'

'I think we would need to discuss the next stage, Mr Thorn. After the fuss you have caused, you couldn't expect to get off scot-free, I don't think. We would need to discuss that. We would certainly need to think about some disciplinary action.'

'Really?' says Thorn.

'Well, I mean, you have disrupted the work of the school. We would need to deter other members of staff from taking the law into their own hands –'

'Listen, listen! Hang on a minute!' Thorn interrupts. 'I'll have to have a wee think about what I am going to do. I'm not sure about the discipline thing. I don't know if that's fair. Would it be possible for you to phone back in a bit – maybe in an hour? I have to think first and make a priority of speaking with the union too. A person doesn't find themselves in this sort of circumstance very often. Of course, I do appreciate you phoning and I'm sorry you've been called away from your other duties just for me.'

There is a bit more steel in her voice as the Depute Head of Services responds. 'I'm sorry, Mr Thorn, I can't give you an hour to think it over. You have half an hour – thirty minutes max – to speak to your union and come to a decision. I'll phone you back then. If you don't agree to remove your posts and to come out of your room, we will need to take things to the next stage, which might not be agreeable to you.

'I will phone back in half an hour. Goodbye.'

# Tuesday, 2058

This was one of the problems – one of the perennials. Thorn spent so long telling Polly that things were '*Fine*' that, when it was obvious to him that they were not, she could not tell. And her sensitivity was not finely tuned when she came crawling in the door after an exhausting day.

So far, his communication had got him nowhere. He was at home, where he wanted to be, but Polly had no idea that he was in no fit state to make dinner. Basically, he was in no condition to do anything. All he wanted to do was roll round the couch and groan.

His headache was intense. He wasn't accustomed to that and, when it gripped his skull fiercely and made opening his eyes near impossible and standing upright out of the question, he was uncharacteristically thrown.

Now, on top of that, Polly wasn't talking to him. Lack of clarity was an issue of long-standing in their coming-home-time communication. Now, he had alienated her – not only because he was struggling to be frank with her, but also because she was tired and in no mood to deal with his cantankerous side.

However, at that moment, all he could do was loll on the couch and hope against hope that she might hear his faint moaning and come and ask him what was up.

Several minutes passed before she slowly opened the door. She must have realised that his reaction was unusual – exceptionally so.

'Is there something wrong?' she said. 'You really shouldn't swear at me like that.'

Completely appreciative that she was showing some renewed interest, all he could say, through painfully gritted teeth, was that he was sorry and had a really bad headache.

'How bad is it?' she asked, her curiosity ignited – she often had a headache after a long day. 'Is it a sharp one or a dull one? Where is it on a scale from one to ten?'

'It's a sodding thirteen,' he spluttered.

'It can't be a thirteen,' she replied, with a touch of pique. 'The scale only goes up to ten.'

'It's the worst headache I've ever had.' When he raised his voice, it made his head hurt more. The end of the sentence was very muted.

'Have you had some paracetamol?'

'No, I've no…'

'That's what I take.'

'I know.'

'Will I get you some? I think I've got some in my bag.'

Finally, he seemed to be getting through to her. At this time of night, during the long, depleting days of winter, they could lapse into the 'I can only bear to think about myself' mode, when all they could do was focus on self-preservation. This often meant attack as the best form of defence.

A generous and considerate Polly brought him tablets and a glass of water. 'You're sure you're that bad?' she said.

If he had any strength left – if he had been something other than an incoherent body attached to a bouncing, bashing brain, he might have done something else other than growl, 'It's bad,' before he turned his head away.

He might have marched off or sworn again or thrown something.

This was when he missed his mum. Just now, Polly should have been sitting down beside him, asking what he wanted, running her hand through his hair and giving him the peck on the cheek he needed to feel loved. That's what she would do if one of their grown kids was back in the house and ill or down in the dumps. Instead, having passed him the pills, she stood with her coat still on, phone in hand, likely looking at an item of clothing for sale on the internet.

Sometimes, she just didn't get it.

He was done in. He had not felt pole-axed like this since, as a spotty fifteen year-old, pished on a quarter bottle of gin at a school friend's house party, he crawled into a darkened room to the security of a similar sofa.

After twenty minutes, maybe with the paracetamol kicking in, he relaxed slightly. The tension in his back and shoulders lessened and there was a gradual ebbing of the ice-pick stabbing in his head. It gave way to a focused ball-peen hammer thumping.

This easing allowed him to edge away from the threshold of pain and closer to conscious awareness.

Not that the awareness was pleasant. All he began to regain was a heightened sense of indignation at the blunderbuss management style of his leaderene.

Polly had, by this time, taken herself off to the kitchen cupboards. From somewhere, he summoned up the energy to follow her.

A chocolate biscuit had revived her and, when she looked up from her phone, he saw a faint glimmer of alarm in her reaction.

'Do you need a hand?' he offered, leaning against the countertop.

'I think you should just go back to the couch and sit down. I'll get it. You don't look too good.'

This told him that he must look terrible. He often looked haggard at this time of night, so his appearance must have been pretty shocking for her to turn him away without an expectation that he would help.

'I'll empty the dishwasher later,' he said, with a stagger, hoping she didn't hear him or that she would feel so sorry for him that she would be reminded to do it herself.

He felt his way back through and dropped onto the couch. He couldn't do anything else. At least he was lying down. It gave him a chance to take some stock.

His head was hurting. He was aching all over. And he was mightily pissed off. That was about the sum of it.

# Wednesday, 1133

She hangs up before Thorn has the chance to respond. Clearly Myra McGoogan is no pushover – that's the reason why she is Depute Head of Education and Leisure Services.

'No messing about at that end, Jobby, eh?' says Thorn. He is left wondering what to do. Immediately the phone call ends, he feels time beginning to press on him.

Jobby is pensive. 'What's the plan, then, Arch? Looks like the clock's ticking.'

'Oh, come on, Jobby. She might phone back in half an hour, but she's not going to send in a SWAT team with smoke grenades and automatic weapons raised in thirty-one minutes. I'm sure I've got a bit more time than that.

'But let's try and think it through and be methodical, all the same. I don't want to be backed into a corner without thinking this through. So, let's get started here, Jobby. Give us a hand, will you?'

He rises, takes a cloth and red board marker from his desk drawer and goes to the whiteboard. He cleans a section of it.

'Right, mind map. Sorry, Jobby, can you see?' He quickly moves the computer monitor and cautiously turns his revolving chair by a few degrees so that Jobby gets a better view of the board.

He writes 'options' in the centre of the board in quite small letters. 'Right, give me a hand here, Jobby,' he says, looking over at him.

Jobby doesn't respond. Maybe mind maps are not his thing. He moves on, like he might do with any reluctant student.

He circles the word and puts several lines radiating from it. At the end of one line he writes **1 - walk out**. From this word he draws several other lines.

Then, on another radiating line he writes **2 - break out**. Again, he makes several lines radiate from this.

183

**3 - they break in** is the last phrase.

He goes back round the options, adding ideas.

Next to **1 – walk out**, he writes – 'peaceful, desired, might get home, police involvement unlikely, return to work conceivable'.

Radiating from **2 – break out**, he notes – 'physical damage (window), could get hurt jumping from roof, could be captured on camera, might be pursued, could be caught, legal action possible, return to work less likely'.

Beside number **3 – they break in**, he jots down – 'dramatic, would make good social media story, could get hurt, would be caught, legal action likely, return to work unlikely'.

He takes a step back and looks over at Jobby. 'What do you think?' he says.

Jobby is non-committal. 'It's really up to you, Arch. I think you have to look at the wider picture too. There are your fellow staff members. What about the family – your wife, the kids? What will they think, for god sake? Going down in a big blaze of glory might seem like a romantic way to go, but do you really want to spend the rest of your life as the guy who sacrificed everything for a wee keech on his seat?'

'Hey, hey,' says Thorn, 'enough of the "wee", Jobby. You are one mighty big jobby and, apart from anything else, it's the principle. I don't know how many times I have to say that.'

'Aye, I know,' replies Jobby, 'but there are some principles worth fighting for and others not. Is this really a full-scale, very wide, red-line issue, Archie, is it, really? Or is it just a wee red-line issue?'

'Och, I don't know, Job, I really don't know. On the great jaggy horns of a dreadful dilemma, I am carefully perched.'

Just at that second, there is a cheering noise from outside. Surprised – having temporarily forgotten about the goings-on in the playground – Thorn goes to the window.

He is astonished to see that quite a crowd has gathered. It is swelling in size as he looks. He can see towards the back gate. There are kids coming through it – about thirty kids wearing the uniform of the Roman Catholic school down the road. They are marching towards the crowd below his window. It must have been their appearance at the gate which raised the volley of noise.

There must be nearly a hundred kids out there now. They must have come out of their classes.

Amongst them, Thorn sees the depute, Honnigan. He is standing in their midst, but very much alone. He is remonstrating with some pupils, but they are mostly laughing at him. He is completely unmanned by the situation. With a motley bunch in such numbers, he has no hope of exercising control.

The head teacher is nowhere to be seen. She would get lost in a scrum like that.

As Thorn looks down, one of the police officers, the shorter one, appears round a corner. He walks into the midst of the pupils as well, but someone reaches up from behind him and knocks his hat off. As he bends to retrieve it, another one kicks it away and, humiliatingly, he has to scramble to get it back. It doesn't look as if he is going to have much luck placating what is now quite a rowdy crowd.

Someone sees Thorn at the window. A cheer goes up, which quickly turns into a chanted, 'Mis-ter Thorn! Mis-ter Thorn!'

He ducks down again. He has no wish to be seen orchestrating some kind of insurrection.

Just as he is thinking this, another cry rings out. He sneaks his head above the parapet and, this time, his face goes unnoticed, because the pupils have momentarily forgotten him. They are looking back towards the gate.

Where the gate meets the main road, Thorn sees that a Scottish Television van has stopped. It is one of the large vans with a huge collapsible satellite dish on the roof. As he watches, several people get out of a car parked behind the TV van. They open the side door of the van and start retrieving equipment, including what looks like a TV camera. He sees a long camel coat and a shock of unnaturally red hair and suspects a reporter from the news programme.

'TV crew! TV crew!' the kids start to chant – in wont of something more original to shout. Many of them have smartphones and are pointing their cameras in the direction of the truck.

Thorn slinks away from the window again and keeps his head down all the way to the middle of the room. He has no wish to appear on teatime television news.

'Right, Jobby, help me out here. Things aren't getting any quieter. Come on, help me. We need a plan A, or I am going to be shat on from a great height. Oh, eh, sorry, I didn't mean to be insulting.'

There is something amiss with Jobby. He seems to have taken a step back. He is not the lively, animated object he was when he first spoke to Thorn.

'Are you okay, Jobby?' asks Thorn, concerned. 'Are you a bit off colour? You were a lot perkier-looking earlier on.'

# Tuesday, 2107

He could just stay on the couch. He could be that guy. He had a headache. He thought Polly almost believed him. He could give up for seventy-two hours. He could lie around, do sod all and he might feel a whole lot better by the end of the weekend.

On the other hand, it might then look as if he was guilty – as if he was hiding something or hiding from something.

Added to that was the fact that he had not been seen ill at school. No one had noticed him ailing. A handful of people had just seen him at the wrong end of a meeting with the head teacher.

He could phone the doctor and make a strong case for stress. People went off with stress every bloody day. It was a modern plague. Why so much perverse resilience? Why not succumb?

Yet, what he couldn't do, shouldn't do, didn't want to do, was make it look as if he was weakened, embarrassed or humbled.

God sake, he had some vestigial pride to think about. Hell, he was not a complete washout as a human being or as a teacher, was he?

It wasn't his style to stay off. He showed up. They paid him. He didn't want anything to interfere with that tawdry transaction. He needed the money.

However, now, in this precise moment, he was sick to breaking point with the whole thing.

Every day, every single day, he was stretched, scrutinised and beset by the very conundrum of teaching. Now, the day-by-day, week-by-week reality had become an insuperable obstacle.

He was an average guy, with some intellectual capacity, some people-management skills, a reasonable work ethic and a range of interests, but in no way was he ever tooled up to be a bloody secondary English teacher. Nobody was.

He was monumentally tired and, after today's sick circus, he knew he never again wanted to return home feeling like he had 'guilty' stamped in big letters all over him. The nasty wee pupil and her shyster parents wanted his balls on a plate. The bigger issue was that his head teacher was keen to serve them up, malevolently tenderised and copiously smeared with hot chilli sauce.

He was queasy and deflated by the whole exercise. With no faith in the system and no power to change anything, all he saw was his life being pissed away – slowly and painfully.

All of the school-related experiences he had ever needed, he had. Every child was special – every child unique – but the whole world of education had become drearily overfamiliar.

It crushed him. It took the little zest that he had and squashed it to nothing. What little spark he had was extinguished time after time. His soul was being smothered.

If he was not decisive, it would all be over. Shit, anything would improve his situation. Staying at home and keeping house would make his heart soar. Compared to what he endured on a daily basis, jobs which were once menial now kindled in him bright images of contentment and satisfaction.

A functionary – a mere plodder – that was him.

He was well and truly cowed.

His get-up-and-go had all gone.

All he had was a chronic teaching habit.

Besieged from all sides, there was no way he could last until retirement. No way.

Another single year was a stretch too far.

But what could he do?

# Wednesday, 1144

Jobby is not looking himself. He is rather shrunken. His eyes have lost some of their lustre. 'I'm just feeling a bit out of sorts,' he says. 'Tell me what you saw outside, bud. Take my mind off it.'

'It's pretty mental out there just now, Jobby. There are loads of kids and the TV cameras have turned up. Looks like we could be making the national news, you and me.'

'Whoa, hold on a minute, Archie, I'm not in on this with you. This is your baby, fella. It's really got nothing to do with me, nothing to do with me at all. The limelight's all yours, dude.'

Thorn is a little taken aback at this. He remembers Jobby's high spirits earlier.

Jobby continues, 'Listen, I am feeling a bit faint, mate. Could you give me a bit of water or something, please?'

Thorn fetches a bottle. 'Where do you want me to stick it, Jobby? It's too big for your mouth.'

'I know, I know,' says Jobby, 'just drip a little over my head to freshen me up a bit. The pressure in here is getting to me.'

Thorn gently tilts the bottle over the seat of the chair and lets a few big drops splash over Jobby's face. Some of it dribbles into his mouth and he licks his lips.

'Thanks a lot, Archie, that's much better. I should be okay for another while now.'

Looking at Jobby, Thorn sees that he has brightened a bit. He's looking refreshed. And, to be fair, the stench, which was originally so revolting, is now beginning to die down – either that or Thorn is getting used to it.

'But tell me, Arch, what's the plan? You've not got long left, mate. That boss woman is going to phone back and you need to have a plan of action.'

Thorn sits down opposite his wee buddy again and, chin in hands, he looks rather miserable. 'I only wish I could think of something, Jobby – something clever. I made a fuss about the situation, but I do not know where to go from here. It's all a bit of a mess.'

Jobby pulls himself up and stares back at Thorn. 'You know, you're right. You've persuaded me. It is a bit of a mess. Maybe you should have thought of that before you shat on your own chair.'

Thorn's head snaps up. 'What the hell are you talking about?' he barks angrily.

'You don't need to sound off, Archie,' Jobby replies indignantly. 'I don't know why you're acting surprised.'

'What do you mean, surprised? I came into the class first thing and there was a crap on my chair. End of story.'

'Naw, naw, you're missing something,' Jobby says, quite forcefully. 'What happened, as I remember, is that you came in, dropped your pants, held your cheeks apart, squeezed down hard and then, with some precision, dropped a big steamy one on this chair. For fuck sake, I should know, because I am that turd – the turd talking to you right now.

'Then, without looking back, you wheeched up your breeks, headed for the door, checked that there was no one in the corridor, walked away a bit, then walked back…'

'What the fuck are you talking about, Jobby? Have you lost the fucking plot, ya dirty wee bastard?' shouts Thorn. He almost spits with fury.

But Jobby replies, 'Listen, dickhead, it's not me who's lost the plot. You got yourself into this. Maybe you've forgotten, but, if that's the case, you can't blame me for taking time to remind you of the truth. Where do you think this great big talking jobby came from – other than inside of you?

'You are not the victim of some prank,' he continues. 'There are no evil kids out there, placing poos in your classroom and wreaking vengeance on you for failing to get them through their exams. The bloody truth, whether you like it or not, is that I am your dump. You left me on your own seat, probably because, deep down in your twisted, convoluted, miserable little mind, you wanted to sabotage your own classroom to make it insanitary and unusable. Apart from anything else, it's probably because it's the room you've been banged up in for the past ten years, period after period, day after day, with loads of disinterested children.

'Your bizarre subconscious had to fabricate some excuse to prevent you from facing up to that crazy S4 class. And you had to give yourself a reason for not sharing a space with that horrible S5 kid, whose parents gave you such a roasting last night.'

'No, no, no, no! No! I will not accept that,' hisses Thorn, frantically. He is holding his head together – a hand on each side, just above his ears. He also feels a piercing pain beginning in the base of his skull. It's as if someone is inserting a long screwdriver and driving it upwards into the centre of his brain-space.

# Tuesday, 2128

Lolling on the couch was probably not going to cut it with Polly. It never did. He rolled onto the floor on all fours and pushed upwards to his feet.

'Is your head any better?' she asked him, as he started to unload the dishwasher.

'A bit,' he replied.

'The paracetamol must have helped. If we get to bed early, that will help too.'

By the time he had finished unloading the dishes and had set a tray, the dinner was good to go.

She plumped the cushions on the settee and he laid the tray on the low table.

He let her find something she wanted to watch on the TV – to make her more amenable to listening to anything he had to say.

After she had noisily munched and swallowed several forks of food, he spoke. 'I had a shit day at school, really shit.'

'Can you not see I'm trying to watch this?' she said.

He wasn't sure if she realised what she had done. Probably she didn't mean to be rude.

Nonetheless, his rage started burbling. He stopped eating and laid down his knife and fork.

'What's wrong?' she asked. 'I'll speak to you once this is finished.'

He was not fit to pick up his knife and fork again. His hands were shaking. He felt blood rush to his face. He could not bear to listen to the crunch of her jaws and watch her intellectually degrading television programme about ballroom dancing any longer. He took his plate and went through to the kitchen.

By the time he arrived there, he had realised that she had no idea that he was in crisis.

Quite naturally, she was focused on her immediate problems – her hard day, her fatigue, her hunger. She was unable to offer him any sympathy.

She could not know that what he was coping with was a completely new intensity of pedagogical stress. Her point of view was elsewhere.

Thorn realised that he had to avoid any crisis. He could not afford to alienate her. He couldn't handle that. At that moment, even living through his pain, what he did not want to do was to escalate things and fall out unnecessarily.

He took some tomato sauce from the fridge and lathered his dinner with it. He trudged back in and sat down.

'Sorry,' he said, 'I meant to get tommy k.'

'Oh,' she said, chewing animatedly, her eyes still fixed on the complete crap on the screen. 'I thought you were annoyed.'

'No,' he said, 'don't be daft.'

By the time the programme finished, she had forgotten about his stress. 'What was it you were saying earlier?' she said.

'Doesn't matter,' he lied.

'Is your head better then?' she asked.

'Not really,' he said.

'Maybe you should make an appointment with the doctor, if it doesn't get any better.'

'That's an idea,' he agreed.

He knew that he was on to plums. She didn't recognise his mood. She didn't understand. She was too knackered to be interested.

He wasn't rolling around in agony, so she thought the issue had gone away. She didn't know the half of it.

She loved her teaching job, as much as he hated his. Thorn suspected that she thought that the flaw lay with him. She never understood why his experience of school was in complete contrast to her own.

In her place of work, she led her primary classes with panache and pleasure through an endless variety of topics and themes. She engaged in outdoor learning, art and music. On a never-ending voyage of intellectual discovery, she sculpted impressionable minds, enhanced experiences and fuelled imaginations. The management practically left her to her own devices and she

193

found delightful new methods for the children to explore the magic of their environment.

It was quite the opposite for him – shut in a room, keyed into a curriculum of someone else's choosing, implementing mind-numbing policies in which he had no belief.

Often, he was jealous of her – her enthusiasm, her engagement, her willing. It was just so contrary to his own experience. So different.

He couldn't blame her, but that was why his misery barely made an appearance on her event horizon. She was so preoccupied and so switched on. She could not conceive that anyone so close to her could be so utterly disinterested and switched off.

'You're not really yourself,' she said to him, not even looking. 'What's wrong?'

'I'll be fine,' he lied. 'I'm just suffering from this headache. I'll get to my bed early and I should be fine.'

'Maybe you should take some ibuprofen as well,' she suggested.

'Aye, maybe,' he said.

He was wasted now, truly wasted. He couldn't just go back to work and do it again and again and again. It stymied him. He feared being stuck at the bottom of the big dark hole, helpless to get out and hopeless that he ever would.

Unless he changed the pattern of his days…

A recognition began to dawn, filtering through his aching skull – a recognition that rebellion was in the wind.

By Christ, he was no radical. If anything, he was born and bred for conformity – narrow, conservative conformity, with a Presbyterian tinge. He was ill-prepared for any kind of confrontation or challenge. Instinctively, he was more mouse than man.

But, man, his remaining sensibilities were numb from the battering they received day after day. His youthful resilience was gone. Without acting independently, he was going to be knocked down – not for a count of ten, but for the count to eternity. He was going to be completely and permanently rubber-ducked.

But to hatch a plan, jeez, at such short notice – especially with a beast of a headache – was difficult. Stuck on the couch next to his wife, Polly, it was impossible. She had no conception of how much his life honked. He knew that, rather naively, she still held onto a slender hope that he would see the light, commit the remainder of his life to teaching and rise to the impossibly heady heights of principal teacher...

'Do you want a cup of tea?' he asked Polly, by way of finding an excuse to leave the room. She nodded.

Once in the kitchen, he laid down the tray, filled the kettle and went straight upstairs to the toilet to have a serious think and to void his bowels.

As he sat, in the smallest room, elbows on his knees, staring at the roll of recycled paper hanging on the back of the door, he considered his options.

Then, just then, in that quiet and contemplative cell, he had a kernel, a little nugget of an idea.

In double quick time, he pulled up his breeks and was on his way to bed. A cursory brush of the teeth saw him stripped and there, duvet pulled to his chin.

And, as he lay, longing for the half-death of sleep, with thudding heart and booming skull, his dark and empty soul told him that the time had come. He was going to place a decisive stick in the spokes of his career in secondary education, because it had blighted his existence for far too long.

# Wednesday, 1156

He stands up. 'No! You are not going to lay that at my door, you little shite! No way!' He flings his hand out at the moist jobby. 'That is really unkind of you.' He points and, as he is doing so, he narrows his eyes. 'Aargh, for god's sake. Aargh!' The shiny, incisive tip of that screwdriver is rising to the top of his head, making his brain scream as it goes. 'Aargh! That is a fucking lie, you wee bastard. Fuck you, you jobby! Why, why on earth would I?? Aargh!'

He still has his finger pointing at the jobby when he reels back and collapses to the seat in agony. He furiously massages his temples. He drives his thumbs into the little hollows to the side of his eyes. Usually this gives him some relief. It does so now. Just a bit. Just enough to let him shout again, raging with anger, 'Liar! How could you? I have never, ever been insulted in this way. You, you…'

The jobby is just sitting there. Thorn cannot understand why on earth he is not saying anything. He does not know how the jobby can just sit motionless, at a time like this. It has something like a smug grin on its face, as if somehow pleased with itself – pleased to be, not an ally, but a horrible, preposterous and venomous little enemy. What a loathsome article! What an ugly and shameful piece of human accumulation!

'Why don't you say something?' he mutters. 'Say something!' he shouts. 'You could have been flushed down the toilet hours ago. But I saved you. I protected you. And now, now you turn on me with your lies. You fucking maniac!'

He is breathing heavily now and the piercing pain is thrusting through the pulp of his understanding. He is so sick and tired. So tired. All of this rebellion is draining him, squeezing him.

Lying back in his seat, he is in shreds. He has nothing left to fight with.

Momentarily, he blacks out…

196

* * *

He is aware of coming to on the floor. He has been woken by a noise, a thrumming drone. It gets louder, turning into a roar. It sounds like a helicopter.

Slowly, he pushes himself up from the grubby carpet and goes to the window. He can see the police helicopter, yellow and black. It is hovering, lights flashing, high above the crowd of kids at the back of the school. The number of people has swelled again and the arrival of the helicopter has energised the participants. They are shouting and jumping up and down and waving into the sky. Thorn can see upwards of two hundred upturned faces.

Around them is a cordon of about fifteen police officers and ten teachers. One senior officer, silver braiding on the peak of his hat, has a loudhailer – a grey megaphone – which he lifts up to his mouth. As Thorn watches, the megaphone makes a shrieking sound. The volume must be turned to maximum. In short staccato sentences, with the helicopter still hovering menacingly overhead, he addresses the crowd.

Even above the thrumming roar, the officer's voice can be clearly heard. 'This is Inspector Holmes, of Police Scotland. Safety is our first priority. We respectfully ask that you leave the school grounds and go home. The school is now closed for the day. Your parents and carers have been informed by text message. Please make your way home safely. Thank you.'

He repeats the end of the message.

The school is closed!

Reluctantly at first, a few of the kids on the periphery of the crowd allow themselves to be ushered away by the teachers.

A shower of fine rain has come on. It is smearing across the panes of the windows, making it more difficult for Thorn to see faces. He moves a little closer.

He is spotted by one of the kids. A taller boy with red hair shouts recognition and, for a few seconds, this halts the dispersal of the assembly.

But not for long. Now the police and the teachers are moving freely amongst the kids. Now that the rain is on, the kids are glad they are able to go home. With closure of the school, they have won a small victory against the establishment.

Thorn turns his attention back to his own predicament. With the short-lived diversion of what is happening outside, his headache has dwindled a bit. He still feels it, but not the penetrating torture of a few minutes ago.

Looking at his phone and then at the whiteboard, he realises that he has not yet come up with an answer for the Depute Head of Services, should she phone.

Then he looks over to the source of his protest.

He immediately has a strange and jarring sense of having been elsewhere. He is now emerging on the other side. He is back home. He recognises, for the first time, the truth of what Jobby was saying to him, when he was in his animated state.

It is very obvious now. Thorn has been misleading himself. It is, it must be his own big brown jobby. He now recognises that it belongs to him. He senses, just by looking and smelling, that it was once at one with his person.

It is still a significant size – although age and central heating have shrunken it somewhat, from what it was a couple of hours ago. As something extruded from his own blessed sphincter, it is truly a substantial and scary specimen.

But the water has failed to revive it much. There is a moist area of fabric around it on the seat, but the upright and towering presence of earlier has dwindled. Now, in sorry contrast, it is lifeless and lustreless.

He hears the hum of the helicopter rotor as it wheels away into the distance.

Then, Thorn has immediate recognition of the need to think quickly. He is in a potentially catastrophic pickle. Without question, he realises, what he does not wish to do is to provoke anyone or to make his precarious situation any more awkward.

There is his wife to think about. What about the kids?

He doesn't care about his colleagues. They care nothing for him.

The head teacher he detests. Though he is not the only one.

How is he going to make amends, to resolve the situation?

What if he comes out with his hands up?

What concessions can he win by confessing?

Should he stick to his original story?

What can he gain by being hostile?

He is on rocky territory. His previous social predicaments have involved bumping someone else's car or coming home half an hour later than he said he would. This is of an entirely different scale. In fact, in terms of its capacity to impact on his future, this is king size.

*Shit, Shit, Shit!* he is thinking.

# Wednesday, 1217

Then his phone rings.

Alarmed, he picks it up from the table and clicks it on. It is his mother.

'Archie, you're not in class, are you? I hope you can talk.'

'What is it, Mum? I am a bit busy.'

'I was wondering if you could do a message for me and take a parcel down to the post office. I would do it myself, but it's a bit heavy. It's books. I'm sending them to Auntie Jean. Would that be okay? Be sure and tell me how much the...'

'That'll be fine, Mum. I've got a class coming. I'll need to go. Bye.'

He ends the call. Immediately, the phone rings again. His mother is forgotten. It is an unidentified number. The police, the press or the local authority, he thinks.

He answers. 'Hullo,' he says.

'Hi, Mr Thorn, this is BBC Scotland News. My name's Billy Hunter. I wonder if I could ask you a few questions? Mr Thorn?'

But Thorn is not taking any more calls from the media. He thinks quickly and responds. 'I really don't have anything to say, thanks. There has been a bit of a mix-up. Everything is getting back to normal soon. I have nothing more to say. Thanks for phoning. Goodbye.'

That is the end of the media story, he hopes. Going over to the window, he sees that the news van is still outside the school. There is a policeman being interviewed on camera. Thorn thinks it's the cop who was shouting through the megaphone. Yes, it is.

Putting the phone down, he goes over to the door and starts to heave the filing cabinets away.

Very quickly he realises that he is not feeling nearly as strong as earlier. It's even difficult to prise the edge of the first cabinet off the carpet. In the end, frustrated, he pulls the first one towards

200

him, and jumps away when it topples and booms onto the carpeted concrete floor.

The others are as heavy, but he is better able to move them. Again, he uses the shelving strips to slide them a little way from the door. He finds some relief in the activity. Thinking about his predicament has filled his mind for too long.

He leaves the bookcase upright at the door. It's obscuring the glass. He has not fully decided to leave the room. He is coming to that conclusion, but he does not yet wish to see what lies on the other side.

A sense of his own wrongdoing is not yet fully formed. His mind is only beginning to digest the events of earlier.

Really, literally, he has no recollection of anything other than his utter indignation that the dreaded object should have appeared in his workspace.

What should he do? He made the fuss. He cast the aspersions. He proclaimed someone else guilty. He needs to be careful though. If anyone begins to think it is his misdemeanour, he will be in some amount of trouble.

Shit, what can he do? Can he pin it on someone else? How could he do that? Can he blame a kid?

And another thing, more importantly, is he going off his head? Was the jobby an inner voice? Maybe it was his inner voice, his subconscious, wanting him to be disciplined, to be sacked. Maybe his subconscious wanted him to find another life, another, less hassle-ridden, less stressful thing to do…

Would it be any wonder, jeez?

When the phone rings, he is halfway through these thoughts. He has not come to any conclusion. He does not know where he is going to go with it, so it's with some trepidation that he looks at the number and suspects, this time, that it is the Depute Head of Education and Leisure Services.

'Hullo,' he says obligingly, as he answers.

'Mr Thorn, it's Myra McGoogan again. We spoke half an hour ago.'

'Yes,' says Thorn, 'I remember.'

'Yes, Mr Thorn, you may have heard the noise outside your window. I'm afraid we had to send the pupils home today. With all of the disruption, there wasn't any point in holding onto them.'

'I hope you're not blaming me for the disruption?' Thorn replies, again sounding a little more confrontational than he usually does when speaking to a senior member of staff.

'We're not blaming anyone at the moment, Mr Thorn. We just want to get things sorted out as soon as possible.'

'I'm sorry it has come to this,' says Thorn – an apology is always welcome, whether he means it or not. 'I would like to get things sorted out soon. I'm not sure I was right in taking things so far. Maybe I overreacted…'

'Well, then,' replies the Depute Head of Services, 'perhaps we can get things moving then. You have trapped yourself in the room. Is that right?'

'Yeah, well, I was a bit worried that nobody was taking my concerns seriously. I'm not in the habit of this kind of thing, you know.'

'Oh, I know, Mr Thorn, I have Mrs Butcher right here. She has been telling me that you are always very punctual and very seldom absent.'

At the thought of Mrs Butcher, Thorn stiffens. He does not want to proceed with the conversation if his nemesis is party to it. It was that horrible little person who escalated this problem. He does not want to engage in dialogue when she is in the background making faces. He can see her in his mind's eye now, the old toad.

But, on the other hand, he can't spit his dummy – even at the thought of that little Nurse Ratched of a woman. He has to appear calm, at this stage. He has to be docile, contemplative and reasonable. He will never win Butcher over with his charm, but he may be able to sweet talk this Myra McGoogan.

'I'm glad you've had the chance to chat with Mrs Butcher, but I wonder if it would be more suitable if I spoke to you alone. I want to remain as positive as possible, but, if you speak to some of my other colleagues, they will share my view that Mrs Butcher can have a deleterious effect on many interactions…'

He imagines Butcher's face at this stage, assuming the call is on speaker, which, judging by the tinny reverb noise he is hearing, it could be.

She will be incensed. So what? She needs to hear a bit of backchat. He wants to be reasonable with McGoogan, but he does not want to do or say anything which might give Butcher any sense of satisfaction.

'Mrs Butcher is not the subject of our conversation here, Mr Thorn. She is your head teacher and I will listen to her point of view for balance.'

'I was just saying,' replies Thorn quietly, 'but, if Mrs Butcher is still there, will you please apologise and say it's nothing personal.'

This is a blatant misrepresentation. It's entirely personal. Even though he tries damn hard not to hate anyone, he is close to loathing the head teacher. Though he wants to move forward and put the morning's events behind him, he would be much more ready for that without the image of her sneering mug at the other end of the line.

He hears the Depute Head of Services' voice again. At least, he assumes it is her. He is not a criminal mastermind or anything. He doesn't think that the police have passed over control of the affair to some devious, psy-ops, anti-terrorist, secret-service operative, surely?

'So, Mr Thorn, you'll need to take the initiative.'

'Well, to be honest,' says Thorn, 'there's really not much I want to hang about here for.

'By the way, are you any further on in finding who the culprit is?'

With this question, Thorn is starting the fightback. He knows he is not going to make any confession. There is no reason why anyone else should be party to his guilt.

'Because I'm still not happy that no one took my concerns more seriously.'

'I believe that you were upset, Mr Thorn. I think you made that clear. I'm just not sure that some of your actions helped your argument.'

'I know, I'm sorry,' replies Thorn – happy to get another apology in. 'I will remove the posts from social media as soon as I can. I was just so angry about the situation. I was taking it too personally.'

'You must have been upset, Mr Thorn, but you understand that Mrs Butcher's first priority was to get the school back in order.'

'I know, but I felt so degraded,' says Thorn. 'It was as if someone was just having a big laugh at my expense. I just hoped that Mrs Butcher would see that it was an issue for me and get to grips with the problem.'

Myra McGoogan, the Depute Head of Education and Leisure Services replies, 'Well, someone else might have handled it differently, Mr Thorn.'

Boom! A score for Thorn. He is delighted. Outside of this room there exists a small degree of sympathy for him. Perhaps not for his actions, but this person he is speaking to knows that Mrs Butcher is not perfect. It surprises him. He thought that all promoted people were in cahoots.

'I mean, she wasn't even prepared to look at the evidence. It just didn't seem very professional. And as I said to her, if someone had done it to Mrs Butcher…'

McGoogan interrupts, 'That's as may be, Mr Thorn, but you have provoked a crisis here.

'From our point of view, your behaviour has been very challenging. And, having spoken to the police about it, they're surprised that we have allowed you so much freedom. In fact, they were talking about charges that they could bring, if the situation isn't resolved immediately.'

'What? Really? You mean charges against me? Ha! You've got to be kidding!'

This does give Thorn something to think about and quickly. He does not need a police record – certainly not involving charges brought against him in the precincts of the school.

That would be his 'career' up in smoke. He has his family to think about, his mortgage, his pension. *Shit.*

'Well,' Thorn replies, 'I'm sorry about that. I didn't think the school would be shut. I thought there was enough room elsewhere in the building. I never thought there would be a protest outside…'

'I think the protest has been dispersed, Mr Thorn. You can see, however, that the situation did spiral out of control.'

He is on the defensive now. 'I did nothing to encourage the protest, for goodness' sake. Your observers can tell you that. I am innocent, innocent of everything, except wanting my workplace to be clean at the start of the day.'

'But are we going to sort this out, Mr Thorn? Are you going to leave the room or not?'

He can feel that she is firming up her approach. He can't hold off.

'Of course I want to come out. The smell is disgusting in here. I am completely out of air freshener too. It's vile.'

'Okay, Mr Thorn, we will await your exit, but we need to get you out and get you home. As I say, the police are very willing to become involved. They've had staff tied up here for several hours already and they have many more pressing matters to attend to.

'First of all, remove your posts from social media and then come out. After that, we can have a quick meeting – I'm actually in the school just now – and then you can go home.'

This is music to his ears. He can't wait to get out of this shitey mess. Jesus, he tells himself, he only wanted to do a day's work, make as few waves as possible and get the hell out of there and home.

Or did he? Was it the ridiculous reality that his alter ego sabotaged the day to force this bust-up and bugger up his career? He can almost remember…

But he can also make a decided effort to forget. And that is what he is going to do. He's certainly not going to own up to it. That would be an act of self-harm. Much better to dissemble.

It is one of those secrets that he will need to keep to himself. There are not many of those. He is largely honest. As a dreadful liar, it's by far the easiest option.

He will need to be canny and avoid any unlikely fabrication. He can only sustain a simple story. The more complexity, the bigger the chance that the threads of the lie would be unpicked.

Put quite simply – he found the shit on his chair. He does not know where it came from.

He tells the Depute Head of Services that, of course, he will remove the Facebook posts, which have brought the school into disrepute and he will not speak to anyone else from the press about the incident. Yes, that is not a problem.

He also says that he will unlock the door and emerge shortly. There is nothing to be gained from prolonging the process. He will be happy to speak to her and then go home.

# Wednesday, 1231

After editing his Facebook page – removing the controversial articles – Thorn returns the phone to his pocket.

Then he stands to survey the room. It has housed him during his working hours for over a decade now. It has been a difficult shift here, with the clatter of chairs and the screech of children – labouring in the shadow of the gloriously extravagant fallacy that school is education.

He looks at his chair. There is a dirty little turd pile on it. He cannot believe the fuss. Somehow, it no longer seems as offensive or as noxious as it did earlier. He wants to lift it up and hurl it somewhere. He wants to get rid of it – out of the window, perhaps.

He sets about looking for a suitable receptacle.

In one of the filing cabinets – the one currently lying on its back on the carpet – he has a pile of paper towels stolen from the cleaners' cupboard. He finds the drawer and, pulling it upwards, props it open with a book. Reaching in, he retrieves the paper towels.

Then he realises that a plastic bag would be useful too. In the same drawer he finds a Tesco bag.

Before he lifts the offending object, he studies it again.

Scrutinising it from a short distance, he sees what he thinks may be a sesame seed – like those in the seed mix he sometimes sprinkles on his muesli. No surprise there, then. He does not see anything else discernible. The consistency is fairly even.

He puts his hand inside the plastic bag, using the same technique as dog owners – who use those small black bags, before they knot them and hang them on trees.

But the bag has vent holes in the bottom. Not wishing to soil his fingers, he places a paper towel between his hand and the bottom of the bag. He does not want poo on his hands. That kind of nasty stuff smells, even after you have washed your hands twice with soap and hot water.

Reaching out, he lifts the turd from the chair. It does not come away as cleanly as he had hoped. He remembers that he freshened it up with water a while back. That's why it is so gungy.

Placing it down again, he uses his other hand to retrieve a plastic ruler from the desk drawer.

Now, holding the poo through the bag in his right hand, he uses the ruler in his left hand to scrape the remaining gobs from the loose weave of the cheap chair.

Lifting the thing has broken its drying skin and a fresh waft of faecal odour rises. He coughs briefly, but resists the urge to cover his mouth, because in one hand he is holding a toalie and in the other he is holding a toalie-covered ruler.

He holds up the object in his plastic-covered hand and gradually pulls the bag up round about it. He is very wary not to touch the ruler on anything. Then, when the bag is more or less upright, he places the ruler, dirty end down, in the bag too. Taking the handles, he lets the weight of the poo and the ruler drop.

He now he has the thing where he wants it – out of sight.

There is still a sticky brown stain on his seat. He remembers the hand sanitiser he has in his filing cabinet – in the same drawer where he found the paper towels. Usually, he uses this gel before he eats anything, to save washing his hands. Allegedly, it kills ninety-nine per cent of germs.

He places the plastic shopping bag on a desk and retrieves the bottle of sanitiser. It is family size, and nearly full.

He squirts gel over the stain, so that it is thoroughly covered. With a handful of paper towels, he wipes the chair, lifting most of the mess, then disposes of the paper in his plastic bag. He repeats this process several times.

When he is finished, there is little more than a damp stain on his chair. The fabric is very inexpensive and coarse and there may still be some matter stuck there, but the damp stain should dry. He doesn't intend to sit on it anyway.

Just to make sure the germs are well and truly killed off, he gives it another squirt with gel. It evaporates very quickly and has an artificial lemony sort of smell. He is not a big fan of the fragrance, but it's better than shit.

Hopefully, those in authority will see his cleaning as a goodwill gesture – as an attempt to help them return the school to its normal everyday function – rather than as a devious effort to tamper with the evidence at the scene of his crime.

Thorn ties the bag with the handles and looks in another one of his drawers. There, he has several black bin bags. They were left over when he was tidying his room and never finished the job. He takes two.

He opens one black bag and drops his Tesco bag down to the bottom. He gathers the black plastic and ties it tightly. After dropping this parcel into the second bag, he rolls the top down and folds the ends round the package. Using the dispenser from his desk drawer, he begins to sellotape. In fact, to guard against leakage, he removes the tape from the dispenser and continues to wind it around the bundle until it is almost completely covered with another layer of plastic.

He bites the tape off from the roll, puts the package down and places the sellotape back in the dispenser.

Taking the unevenly shaped package over to his bag, he tucks it inside, then closes the top and fastens it with the plastic clip. He is happy that the poo is completely confined. There is virtually no chance that any of it will ooze out – unless someone takes his bag and jumps up and down on it. Or unless he is involved in a road accident – in which case it doesn't matter.

Looking back at his chair, he sees that the damp patch has spread a little, but the gel is disappearing. There will hardly be anything left, when it has dried out completely.

He doesn't want to use the seat again, but, feasibly, in a couple of days, someone else, who doesn't know its history, might use it without so much as a second thought. Much of the school furniture is stained or has chewing gum stuck to it. It will probably be recycled within the school and will reappear in another room. If Thorn is still about, he will keep an eye out for it. There is a spot of Tippex on the right of the seat, which will help to identify it.

All he has to do now is return the rest of the room to its original state.

With a new vigour, he humphs the filing cabinets back. There is nothing else for it. He manhandles them. They are heavy and the repeated noisy lifting and shoving makes him sweat.

Outside the room they must hear him. They will know he is either preparing to leave or building the barricade higher.

In order to disavow them of that thought, he slides the bookcase away from the door.

He is surprised to see that there is no one there. He suspected that there would be a police guard or a janitor. Even when he moves close to the window and looks on either side, there is nobody.

He picks up his bag and his jacket. He cannot come back for them later.

His key is still in the lock. He moves it slowly. Momentarily, the key sticks. Then, after a bit of a shoogle, the lock opens.

He places a hand on the lever and it clicks free. He is able to pull the door towards him and to exit the room.

# Wednesday, 1245

His head pops out first. He looks up and down the corridor. As he suspected, there is no one there. All he can see, at the end of the hallway, just before the double doors, is a tripod, holding what must be a small camera. There is no noise anywhere. He moves down the corridor towards the tripod and the stairway. He is not alarmed that he cannot see anyone, only surprised that he appears to be the only person on the floor.

Just before he reaches the door into the stairwell, which is wedged open, he meets a woman he vaguely recognises coming through it. He guesses that it is the Depute Head of Education and Leisure Services, Myra McGoogan. She is wearing a smartish artificial-fibre suit, as expected. Just behind her is the polis – perhaps one of the policeman Thorn saw earlier in the crowd. He is wearing his cap. He has his hands clenched and his arms slightly bent. He does not look warm or cuddly.

'Mr Thorn!' she says, reaching out her hand to point to the camera, 'we saw you in the corridor. I'm Myra McGoogan. We were just having a cup of tea downstairs. Will you join us?'

Thorn meekly shakes her proffered hand, but is taken aback. This is too much positive psychology too soon. He had expected some irritation, some anger, some exasperation. It is rather suspicious. But possibly they are concerned that he could still return to the room. Yes, that's it. They want to secure the room themselves. They want to separate him from his room. Get him out of the building.

Maybe they are right. They must have talked it over. They must have prioritised. They will also want to know where his phone is and that he's not using it to besmirch the council's reputation any further.

'Sure thing,' he says, as if it is the easiest thing in the world. 'That sounds like a good idea.' And in some ways it is. He is on autopilot. He can't really imagine what will happen now or who

211

will be involved. He hopes to see Polly, to initiate the healing process with her, but, as for the rest of it, he just does not know – or much care. So, a cup of tea would be nice.

He has that vaguely surreal, out of body and out of time sensation, as he walks downstairs under guard, between the Depute Head of Services and the bobby.

Feeling incredibly docile – responding well to the kid glove treatment – Thorn immediately falls into step.

There is something distinctly awkward about the situation, but he is all for a return to relative normality. Better just to do as he is asked. If he makes too much of a fuss, he will draw attention to himself. He has probably done enough of that.

What he needs to concentrate on, in the immediate future at least, is to avoid drawing fire. There is no way he wants to have folk sniffing around any longer than necessary. Better to eat pie with some humility.

'We're downstairs, at the moment,' says McGoogan. 'Mrs Butcher lent us her office. You'll need to direct me. I'm always getting lost in other people's schools.'

The place is quiet for the time in the day. Thorn suspects teachers are in their departments. They have probably been given development tasks to do – some bullshit jobs, claimed to be crucial to teaching and attainment.

All he wants to do now is escape. He has no wish to tarry any longer than necessary, but he had better not make a run for it just yet.

At the head teacher's door in the management corridor, he hesitates. It's less than twenty-four hours since he last crossed this threshold. He has no real wish to cross it again until he can be one hundred per cent sure that she, his boss, his head teacher, is not there. The place does not have pleasant memories.

He does not see her, but, immediately more concerning is the presence of another policeman. Thorn saw him earlier – the one speaking to the crowd through his megaphone. He is also wearing his hat – the one with the silvery braiding on the peak. It must signify status. He is seated and sitting very upright. Both of his large hands are on his knees. They appear to be gripping tightly. His huge boots have a perfect shine.

His body language does not comfort Thorn in any way. This guy obviously has something to learn about soft-soaping from the Depute Head of Services.

He does not stand up. He does not give Thorn anything more than a quick once-over with his eyes.

'Mr Thorn,' says McGoogan, 'this is Inspector Holmes. I asked him to come in for our chat.'

The Inspector doesn't look amused at having to spend time with Thorn. He is probably much more accustomed to dealing with car-jackers, rapists and murderers. Teachers starting dirty protests and causing educational havoc are probably not his bag.

Thorn is ushered to a low seat and he sits down with his bag between his legs – in virtually the same position he was in last night when he was admonished by the head teacher.

He is similarly wary now. He's not wanting to let down his guard – particularly with the polis there.

McGoogan moves towards the table with tea and coffee on it – several cups and saucers, an assortment of sachets, some plastic milk portions. She lifts the kettle to check for water, but, just as she turns to ask Thorn what he would like, he breaks in…

'Can I just start by saying how sorry I am to have caused so much trouble.'

There is no response from the copper. He has taken out a notebook and has begun to scribble with a pen.

The Depute Head of Services turns from the tea table and sits down carefully too. She is perched very close to the edge of the low chair opposite. She is a slight person, but capable-looking. Thorn worries that she has misjudged her centre of balance and that she may slip off the front of the chair at any moment.

'It does help when you say that, Mr Thorn, or Archie, but this incident has been a bit of a challenge today. I think you can appreciate that. We will need to try and move things on.

'Mrs Butcher was wanting to be here, but I suggested it better if I dealt with you just now.'

Thorn moves uneasily in his seat and asks, 'Are you going to take any action?' He says this to both, really. He doesn't know if the cop is there to charge him or if he is just there as a witness.

'I think you should have at least a few days at home, until we discuss things at this end and decide on the best course of action.

213

The whole thing has been unsettling for the school community. The place will need time to get back to normal.'

*Oh, ya beauty*! Thorn thinks, but he answers in a professional manner – or at least he tries to give that appearance. 'But what about my classes?' he asks. 'They have exams coming up.'

'Well, we'll need to have a think about that. There's probably something that the principal teacher can organise so that they aren't disadvantaged. There are absences all the time across the authority. I don't think you need to worry yourself about that just now. Maybe the principal teacher will contact you directly if she needs any help. I expect she will speak to the classes as well.'

Thorn doesn't want to appear delighted. Amongst his classes, particularly the fourth and fifth year, there are one or two kids he feels a bit sorry for and one or two isolated kids his heart bleeds for. But, largely, he is surrounded by a bunch of bothersome brats, who think the subject stinks and want to make life difficult for any council employee standing in front of them. Therefore, because he knows that a good whack of them don't give a toss, he finds it very hard to give a toss about them.

He suppresses an urge to laugh. To walk away now, to be liberated from this tiresome toil, to be freed from the never-ending trial of standing guard over apathetic kids, well, that would be fantastic.

'I'll send the PT an email,' he says – still pretending that he has the slightest interest – when he does not.

At the front of his mind is the fact that this Depute Head of Services and the Inspector need to hear that he is willing to co-operate. He has no wish to bring the full force of the law down on himself. He has no wish to stir anything up. All he wants to do is to appear to be interested, to pretend to be apologetic and to lead everyone and his dog to believe that, when he locked himself inside the room, it was a foolish overreaction. He certainly wants to convince them that it is all over and that he has learned his lesson.

'I would like to apologise to Mrs Butcher, if that's possible,' he says, after a moment's pause. This idea comes quite spontaneously to him and, in saying it, he lies so completely that he almost shocks himself. However, he can see that he must humiliate himself, because he knows that he needs to deflect scrutiny. He must undermine the head teacher's wrath by leading everyone else to believe that he is repentant, even if she is not convinced and even though it really grates with him to grovel. Thus, there is nothing else for him to do other than prostrate himself before her mightiness and allow any witness to admit the possibility that he has some professional respect for her.

'I don't see why that should be a problem,' says McGoogan, smiling slightly. 'No, I can't see how there could be a problem with that,' she repeats, possibly to reassure herself. 'Let's think of it as a restorative meeting. What do you think? You have those in this school, don't you?'

Without stopping to reconsider – maybe imagining that an apology will start the ball rolling, in terms of reconciliation – she leaves the room smiling. Thorn is left in silence, in the uncomfortable presence of the senior policeman.

Less than ninety seconds later, Thorn hears both McGoogan and the head teacher coming down the corridor chatting. They both sound remarkably relaxed.

But that is not the impression he gets when Butcher wheels into the room.

She looks ten years older than she did during their meeting last night. Perhaps it is the harsh light.

Clearly, she has put on a show of good nature for the Depute Head of Services, but it is patently obvious to Thorn that she is absolutely bloody furious with him. He can sense her ire. When she is radiating so much ill nature, he would not be in the least surprised if she burst Hulk-like from her clothing.

Meantime, she will just need to swallow her rage. Thorn wonders if she is conscious of how little time has passed since she diminished him at the end of parents' evening the night before. She must have considered it – although he certainly doesn't want to rouse her anger or make her think that he has been anything other than a victim of today's dirty trick. He wonders if she has considered him as instigator. It's possible that she has. He must go out of his way to lead her off the scent.

Before she has the chance to make any utterance, Thorn is on the offensive. He almost leaps out of his chair, taking the policeman by surprise – so much so that he looks up from his notebook.

'Mrs Butcher,' he says, in his most honeyed and cloying manner. 'I hoped I would see you before I go. I just wanted to apologise.'

'Let's all sit down first, will we?' the Depute Head of Services interposes.

Thorn suspects that she thinks that there is less likelihood of a traumatic engagement if Butcher is encouraged to take the weight off her feet. Given the extremely pointy toes of Butcher's expensive-looking shoes, she may be correct. Such mass concentrated on such a small area is a sophisticated form of torture.

Encouraged to sit on a low chair, Mrs Butcher struggles to appear comfortable. She looks warm as well – her barely contained fury is turning her an unusual shade of puce.

McGoogan takes a seat on Mrs Butcher's side of the divide.

Now, they are facing each other across sixty centimetres of brown formica. He can't help it, but something in Thorn encourages him to think that he is in a far stronger position than last night. He has had a chance to speak his mind to the head teacher. He has shat in her school. He has wrecked her day and, with luck, he has made a significant dent in her professional reputation.

He doesn't want to admit the possibility yet, but, if this goes well, there is a good chance that he will have accomplished something pretty big and noticeable, without anything much happening – other than him getting a flea in the ear and being told never to darken the doorway of the school again. From that point of view, he could consider it an honourable victory – a quite considerable moral triumph – especially when he reminds himself what a bloody hard ticket the woman is and what little consideration she has for the people who aren't as hard-nosed as her.

Perhaps, in terms of her professional reputation, Thorn's little intervention will be enough to nudge her towards retirement or towards a job in the county buildings. If either of those things happened, he is certain that she would be in no way missed by anyone who had the misfortune to be subject to her in this command – her very own shite-run tip.

Rather than looking at Thorn, which she probably finds insufferable, she has turned her dark little eyes on the Depute Head of Services, as if she is waiting for her to help with some ice breaking.

But Thorn jumps right in again. He would rather appear keen and make a clean breast of it than hang around for someone else to do the preliminaries.

'Can I just tell you how sorry I am, Mrs Butcher, for the inconvenience that I have caused today. I didn't think things would escalate so much. I think there is a lesson for all of us in this.'

He is speaking almost to the side of her face and, as he utters his words, he notices that a small muscle, high on her right cheek, just beneath her eye, begins to tic.

She must be conscious of it herself, but, in order to look as if she doesn't care about what he is saying, she turns her head towards him. The look which she levels at him is utterly hostile. Seldom have they been so close when he and she are so still. He looks into her narrowed eyes. He has never seen anything like it. They seem, at first, to be rather insignificant and partly submerged in the tissue of her cheeks, but he can't believe how deep and dreadful they appear close up. It feels, for all the world, as if he is looking into a deep and dreadful abyss. All he can see is darkness – a bottomless pit of fury and hatred. He can almost sense her rage-rays radiating towards him.

But he can't allow himself to be distracted. He has to ignore her reaction – even though, in this moment, he strongly suspects that she is determinedly trying to put a curse on him.

He knows that she has nothing but utter contempt for him. That was evident last night. What is more clear now is that she thinks he has bested her in some way – probably because he has contrived to close the school. He has upstaged her and embarrassed her and let her know that, whilst she wields some power about the place, there are some things which even a low life like Thorn can do to make her life difficult. Maybe, he thinks, she is concerned that this will only be the first event which draws attention to her deficiencies as a leader. She may be anxious that she will be exposed to further challenges from below.

He still sees her twitch, so he keeps going. He wants to punish her. He wants her to feel shit – even if it is not as shit as he felt last night.

'I am sorry that I drew attention to the vandalism with social media. It was the wrong thing to do and it did not set the pupils a good example. I would hate to think that they were going to make any posts which showed the school in a bad light. I would hate that. I am so very sorry.

'And, if I could just say that my anger was quite out of character. I was wrong to speak to you the way I did and I am so sorry about that too. I don't expect you will forgive me and I couldn't blame you, but I hope…' And here he is going to say, out of badness, that he hopes her face will stop twitching soon. But he can't do that. All he can say, rather disappointingly, is, 'we'll be able to put this behind us.'

But, now, Mrs Butcher appears to be in something approaching a trance-like state, sending thundering hate-waves straight at him – via what is now an unswerving stare.

'Mrs Butcher,' the Depute Head of Services says, by way of breaking the silence. 'Mrs Butcher!' – a little more loudly.

'Sorry, yes,' Mrs Butcher mutters, shaking her head a little and turning back to McGoogan. It is as if so much energy has been channelled into her loathing that her brain has almost disengaged from the unfolding events.

'Yes, I hear you, Mr Thorn,' says Butcher, still looking at the Depute Head of Services. 'I hear your apology. I am sure that Ms McGoogan, here, told you that this was the best thing to do.'

The Depute Head Services is looking curiously at Mrs Butcher. She can sense her hostility. Maybe she is becoming more aware of her potential for spontaneous combustion. Maybe McGoogan is beginning to see why Butcher found it difficult to engage with Thorn's concerns in the morning.

Maybe, Thorn thinks, he should push her a bit more and try and flick her little anger switch. She has had a long and exacting day, just like him, and she has not been entirely in the driving seat. In fact, his posts on social media have shaped her day in a manner radically different from usual. And she will not be best pleased with that.

218

'I said I am sorry and I am,' Thorn says more forcibly. 'I wasn't wanting the school to be closed. But it just goes to show you...'

He does not have time to say anything else. The head teacher explodes upwards. She towers forty-five centimetres above him. She speaks through pursed lips, neither in Thorn's direction, nor towards Myra McGoogan. 'I am sorry too. I am sorry that I came in to listen to this!'

The policeman has since looked up again from his notebook. He probably thought he was here to keep an eye on Thorn, but, by the way the head teacher starts fulminating, it looks as if he might first need to step in on her account.

'You have done nothing but drag the reputation of this school through the muck, Mr Thorn. What you did today was absolutely despicable. You have undone so much of the good work achieved by other members of staff. You have made the school a laughingstock and I...'

At this point McGoogan actually stands up and interposes herself between Thorn and Butcher. She puts her arm between them, saying, 'I'm sorry, Mrs Butcher, I shouldn't have asked you to come in. I'm sorry. I thought it might help to clear the air.'

Now she reaches out and gently guides Butcher by the arm – Butcher, who was so strident and unhelpful and unsupportive, not only in the morning, but last night after parents' night too.

Then, amidst this bluster from the head teacher, Thorn realises, as pressure builds quickly, that he has at his disposal the wherewithal to comment on Butcher and her horrible behaviour in a quite fitting manner.

She did it to him last night. She pushed him to his edge. She was horrible and heartless and unthinking, when she was strenuous in defence of Thorn's silly pupil and her half-baked parents and she was grossly offensive to him. Without a moment's pause, she made him demented, downcast and depressed.

But now he has the chance to sling some muck at her. He has the chance to say what he thinks about her by entirely appropriate means.

Therefore, just at the moment when she is ushered away from him by the Depute Head of Services and just as she is passing

219

her desk on the way towards her own office door. Yes, just as she is being shown out of her own office, yes, just then – just when the timing is perfect – he purposefully lifts his left buttock from the vinyl chair, clenches his core muscles and lets fly.

It is a terrific fart. It is very clearly his and vibrantly audible to everyone in the office – and, he briefly suspects, anyone in the corridor or in neighbouring rooms as well.

It is a significant report – a big belter. He realises that it has been cooking for a while – a quite normal symptom for him in stressful situations.

He would usually retain it until he was outside in the fresh air – until he was outwith the confines of space and company. But, now, when he is in the position to cause maximum offence, it is as good a time as any to throw his customary caution to the wind and to liberate the grotesque and vengeful blast of flatulence, sending it ripping through time and space.

At any other time, in any other company, he would have been mortified. He would never have let it slip. He would have stifled any temptation. It is – one hundred and twenty per cent – an infantile deed, a classroom classic, a pupil prank. But, what the hell! At least he has learned something about the power to shock in his thirty-plus years of educational incarceration. He is on his way out of the door anyway. His coat is on a shoogly peg and, though he tries not to harbour ill will, he despises this toxic leader with a passion. Therefore, there is no doubt in his mind that this vulgarity, this vehement discharge, is pertinent, pithy and necessary. Indeed, it is his conviction that, in the current circumstances, it would have been niggardly – and uncomfortable – to contain and compress it – only for it to be squandered out of doors.

There is a moment, a fraction of time, when complete silence reigns. But there is no mistaking what has happened and no mistaking the source. The policeman looks awestruck. The Depute Head of Education and Leisure Services swings her head round, aghast. And Mrs Butcher acts.

In a fit of immediate and venomous fury, she grabs the grey steel stapler from her desk and, with an angry yelp of effort and what seems well-practised technique, pitches the hefty gadget directly at Thorn.

Though surprised (and, simultaneously, delighted at this reaction) Thorn shifts his head to the side. The projectile glances off his temple and there is quite a clatter, as the stapler deflects, hits the table, breaks open and spills its staples.

In the aftermath, Thorn quickly assesses the damage. His head barely hurts and he has avoided a nasty injury. Having kept both of his eyes, he immediately hopes that blood will be forthcoming. He puts his hands to his head and affects to groan.

Having failed to prevent an assault on a member of the public, the policeman – the Inspector – can do nothing but intervene. He immediately places himself between Butcher and Thorn – ostensibly and very ironically to protect Thorn from further assault by Butcher.

He gesticulates and barks at Butcher to leave the room. Then, with a furious glance toward Thorn, he escorts her out and actually takes her by the arm.

Thorn imagines that McGoogan, the Depute Head of Education and Leisure Services, has never heard or seen anything like it. Her previously confident manner has evaporated. She looks astounded as Butcher retreats. Then she turns her attention to Thorn. She is dumbstruck.

No one else has to say anything. Thorn's release of bowel exhaust has adequately described everything that he thought about the situation. Butcher's response has made her feelings quite clear.

# Wednesday, 1302

As Butcher leaves, Thorn feels a trickle down his forehead close to his eye. He brushes it away with the back of his hand. It is bloody red. *Yes!* he thinks. He reaches over to the box of tissues on the narrow coffee table and helps himself to several. He noticed them last night. He assumed that they were there so that anyone given a verbal beating by the head teacher could cry copiously. He did not realise that they were there in case a visitor to the room was injured by the head teacher throwing heavy metal objects.

He sits back on the low chair, holding the tissues to the side of his head. He is trying to look stunned by the development. In actual fact, he can feel the blow a little bit, but his head is not hurting nearly as much as it was the previous night, when the head teacher gave him his emotional duffing up after parents' evening.

Relishing the moment, the moment when he was assaulted by Mrs Butcher in her own office, in front of two reasonable and responsible adults, he tries to imagine what might happen to him now.

He was concerned, latterly, when he was stuck in his room, that he had pushed too far. He was worried for himself. But now there is very clear proof, if any was needed, that Mrs Butcher is not the high-flying, calmly competent and consummate professional others assumed her to be. She has now made it clear that she is far more volatile than is desirable in her line of work. Now, with this outburst, she has behaved in a way similar to one of her more challenging pupils.

Thus, he reflects on the piquant nature of the moment – this turning point in her career path.

*Jeez*, it was one turbo-charged fart – a schoolboy's dream of a fart. Not so great that he hadn't heard one like that before – but not recently from his own anus. His guts must have been charging themselves up for some time and, by chance, rather than by design, he got the angle perfectly right to make it reverberate through the steel springs and framework of the chair. When he let flee, it just tore out of him with a defiance and resonance which was beautiful, simply beautiful.

He'd be rather surprised if he hasn't blown a blast hole in the seat of his pants – given that it exited with such a violently sonorous flourish.

It was just the ticket. He knew from her thousand-yard stare, as she gazed at him. He saw, not just the bleakness of her soul, but that she only needed one little push, to send her star-fishing into another state of consciousness. It was a stroke of impromptu genius to drop one. Nothing else that he could have said or done would have stirred her into such fervent response.

In any other circumstance, it would not have been an option. Most times, under such stress, he would have let it bleed slowly out. It would have seeped, rather than trumpeted.

He just knew when he looked at her. He knew from the experience of years – of goading his younger brothers, of interacting with kids, of working with insanely sensitive colleagues, of being married to a sometimes complex wife – that one more small push would do it.

He had nothing else to say to her. The only effective contribution he could make – pertinent and to the point – was with his arse. Appropriate really, because it was the next best thing – short of telling her to kiss it.

And now, with this spur-of-the-moment stroke of fundamental genius, she was on the ropes. Rather than Thorn being huckled off down the corridor – in disgrace, away from the head teacher's office – she, the head teacher, is being escorted away, by a policeman, no less. Meantime, Thorn sits, enthroned, in her very own room.

It is such a euphoric and exquisite moment.

*Oh, oh, oh!* it makes him so glad he came in today.

After the disappointment of yesterday. After running headlong into the buffers last night. Even after the trials and tribulations of the morning, he is finally achieving some sort of fulfilment.

It's not a glorious or romantic victory. It has been a far from noble fight, but, *Oh, oh, oh!* he's so glad there has been resolution – a satisfactory denouement.

Having seen the head teacher out of the room, the Myra McGoogan bustles back in. She is now quite flushed. It won't be every day that she witnesses a senior member of staff in complete mental breakdown mode.

There is still a faint but foosty fug of fart lingering in the atmosphere. Thorn at once jumps up to disarm her, before she has any opportunity to take charge of the narrative.

'I am so sorry,' he says quickly. 'I never do that in public. It was so unexpected. I'm really embarrassed, really sorry. It must be my nerves. It's been such a stressful day.' He pitches his tone towards ingratiating. He doesn't want to overdo it or ham it up, or she will think it was a pre-planned and spiteful action. He must quell any hint or suggestion that his shameful outburst was intended to provoke.

'I hope Mrs Butcher is okay…'

Unsurprisingly, the Depute Head of Services has never had a situation like this to deal with. No one has ever written or presented a course for education managers on strategies to implement in the event of malicious farting.

All that she can do is say, rather breathlessly, 'And your head, Mr Thorn, is your head all right?'

'It's bleeding a bit,' he tells her and removes the paper tissues, so that she can see the collected blood on them, if not the cut, 'but it was just a glancing blow. It's not too bad. I'll be fine.'

She actually gasps. Maybe she wasn't sure that the stapler had hit the mark. She probably hoped that the sound that she heard, as she looked, horrified, at Butcher, was just the noise as it rattled off the table.

'It's okay,' Thorn thinks quickly, ruthlessly wanting to press for any advantage. 'It's okay, I don't think I'll press charges.'

*Oh, oh, oh!* he thinks. It came to him just in that minute. A policeman, two witnesses, a crime… *Oh, oh!* This could run and run. He could be in the papers many, many times. Maybe he could nail her, professionally, for bullying. Maybe he could get her in the courts for assault. He could ruin her. Ruin her. He takes a tiny moment to let that sink in.

But no, he thinks, almost immediately, maybe he should just check his ambition. One reason for this is the look of foreboding that the Depute Head of Services has on her face. And, whilst he recognises the power that he has in this moment, he also quickly realises that he has a responsibility to himself, his kids and, of course, to Polly.

This isn't just about revenge. It's not just a vendetta. And it is certainly not about seeking publicity for himself. It's about more than that. It's about taking the opportunity to make a break with her poisonous leadership, about instigating change – a change in the gloomy parade of his working days.

'Can I get you a first-aider?' says McGoogan, anxiously. 'You're sure you're going to be okay? Your head, I mean?' She moves towards him, lifting the box of tissues upwards. The undoubted complexity of the situation is etching itself deeply across her face. Thorn doesn't know who she is accountable to, other than the Head of Education and Leisure Services, but he guesses that she does not want to end up in court – describing what she witnessed and condemning the head teacher to professional oblivion, or lying to save Butcher's very flawed hide.

'I don't know,' he says, 'how bad does it look?' As he removes the tissue again, he furrows his brow – to look anxious and to squeeze out some more blood.

'Oh no,' she responds nervously, 'I'll need to get you a plaster or something.'

'Is there a mirror somewhere, so that I can look at it myself?' he says.

McGoogan indicates a door which Thorn had not registered before. He makes to stand, slowly, to give the impression that he is properly injured and in a weakened state.

'Do you need a hand?' she says. She is still standing very close to him, as if she wants to reach out. It must be the native nurturer in her.

'I think I'll be okay.' Thorn plays her like a pro. 'I just stood up too quickly.'

Placing a hand on the head teacher's desk for support, he makes his way unsteadily to the door. Pushing it open, he realises that he is in the head teacher's private toilet facility.

He closes the door behind him. The mirror is behind the door, over the washbasin. Putting on the light, he has a look at the small cut on his temple, just a wee bit up from his eye. The skin is quite thin there and the sharpish edge of the stapler, thrown with such force and accuracy, has left a cut about a centimetre long.

It's not much. Back in the day, playing rugby, he was often cut around the eyes. The ridges, the thin skin, there was no protection when he came into contact with another head or a flailing fist or boot.

The cut is nothing. The skin is scarred already. It will stop bleeding very soon, if it has not already stopped. Any trace will disappear in a few days.

It is trivial, in the scheme of things.

But it is an assault. Yes, very definitely, it is evidence of an assault.

He puts the lid of the toilet pan down and sits. He wants a minute to take stock. How often, he thinks, has the head teacher hidden in here to think things over?

Some of the head teacher's personal accoutrements are laid on a shelf under the mirror. There is a hairbrush, a bottle of perfume and some tweezers. Thorn is unsurprised to see that the perfume, in an expensive-looking purple bottle, is called Poison.

There is also a blue electric toothbrush, a cylindrical dispenser of Advanced Whitening toothpaste and an amber bottle of Listerine Ultraclean mouthwash.

As much as Thorn wants to give the head teacher an even bigger headache, he decides not to touch her stuff. Everyone would know it was him.

What he has to do is to make some strategic decisions.

Firstly, he has some leverage. Foremost in his mind is that he has been injured.

Standing at the mirror again, before he takes a selfie picture, he pulls at his cut to open it up again and to prevent it from healing. It bleeds a little. He smears the blood, dabbing it with his finger. He knocks the cut again with his knuckle.

He is absolutely sure that he does not want the wound to look any better when he leaves the toilet.

He rinses his hands under the cold tap. There is a white cotton hand towel, but he chooses toilet paper to dry his hands and flushes it away.

What he does want the Depute Head of Services to do is pity him. But he can't ham it up too much. He does not want her to have reason to think that he is anything other than a bit sensitive, a bit outspoken at times – even a bit peculiar.

To see him bleed after Mrs Butcher's assault must go some way towards convincing her that he is not the only transgressor.

He takes the top off Butcher's perfume, smells it, grimaces in the mirror and replaces the lid. Then he exits the toilet, holding a bit of toilet paper over his cut.

The Depute Head of Services has her phone to her ear. 'I'm sorry, I'll need to go,' she says. 'Mr Thorn has just come in.'

'I'm sorry that didn't go too well with Mrs Butcher,' he tells her, when she has rung off and put her phone on the table. 'I did think it would be better to speak to her. Maybe it wasn't such a good idea after all.

'What happens now?' he asks. 'I don't suppose I should hang around any longer than necessary. Will I just go home?'

'Yes, I'm sorry, Mr Thorn… Archie. I wasn't expecting Mrs Butcher to react like that. How's your head? Is it okay?'

'Oh, it's okay, I guess,' says Thorn. 'I've got some Steri-Strips at home. I can patch it up. I don't think there will be much of a scar.'

'Are you sure you don't want to see a doctor?'

'No, no,' he says, shaking his head and trying hard to appear reasonable and brave, despite his injury. 'No problem. I'm just glad she didn't get my eye,' he reminds her. 'It could have been a lot worse.'

Realisation that this has dawned on Thorn gives McGoogan obvious concern. She purses her lips, then says, 'Thank goodness it wasn't any worse. You're sure you'll be all right?'

'Yeah, fine. Don't worry. A butterfly stitch, a paracetamol, a sit-down and I'll be fine. No probs. I know what the symptoms of concussion are. I won't be on my own for long.'

'Well, I think you'd best go home. I've just spoken to the Head of Services, to put him in the picture. We'll need to have a chat about the next steps, but I think you should have a few days at home, especially now. We can't have you here in the current circumstances.' She smiles rather artificially.

'No, I think Mrs Butcher's feelings about me are pretty clear.'

The policeman appears at the door. 'Mrs Butcher is in the staff base,' he says gruffly. 'I asked her to stay there. Am I needed here just now?' he asks, with a rather bemused expression on his face.

McGoogan looks at him, then, momentarily, back at Thorn. 'No, I, eh, don't think so, thanks, Inspector Holmes. If you could just wait in the staff base, I think I am just about done with Mr Thorn, thanks.'

The policeman's cap disappears from the door. They hear the clump of his shiny boots as he goes off down the corridor to keep an eye on the head teacher.

'Well then, have you got everything?' asks McGoogan.

'So, am I to understand that you'll be in touch? Or will someone else be in touch?' Thorn asks. 'Should I speak to anyone, I mean, like my union or a lawyer?'

What he sees now is a good deal of apprehension in her face. A blush rises quickly to her cheeks.

'Of course, that's entirely up to you, Mr Thorn. But I'm not sure what you would be talking to them about. I mean, what did you have in mind? I mean, what would you be asking them?' She is increasingly agitated. No wonder.

Thorn is completely aware that what they are talking about now is not that the school has closed on his account – although that is still an important detail. What he and the Depute Head of Services are alluding to now is the violent assault perpetrated by his head teacher upon his person. She must be aware of the potential for scandal. It's bad enough that his earlier overreaction has damaged the school's reputation. It's more than sufficient that his story will be plastered over social media and possibly national newspaper and television reports during the following twenty-four hours. If yet another episode is added to the story – if it emerges that the whole thing has descended into farce, because he has been attacked by the head teacher and pressed charges, then…

'Just for some advice,' Thorn assures her. 'I mean, I usually just come in and get on with my job. I suppose I would be needing some advice about my rights and everything. I can't be out of work, you know. I have a mortgage to pay and kids to support and a pension...'

Here, just now, he is putting it on the line. He wants some reassurance. He is not prepared to leave the building without some gift from the authority. He has to make it clear that he is prepared to go straight to the union or the lawyer or social media – or the press, for that matter. He has been assaulted by his senior leader and, if McGoogan is not prepared to show him some leniency, he must demonstrate to her that he will be calculating and ruthless in his retaliation.

'No one said you would be out of a job, Mr Thorn. I think a few days at home to relax and reflect would do you some good. Then I'll get back to you and we can discuss the way forward. Maybe a change would be good for you. Maybe a position in another school could be available.'

Now she is beginning to make sense. Now the day is starting to look up. She has the awareness to recognise his power to influence outcomes – if he decides to stir the shit. He wants to hold her to her word though. He needs some assurance. He is not prepared to go home and wait. Only if he can exact a guarantee will he leave. He must have a guarantee.

'That would be fantastic!' he says, to sound positive and to put a good spin on things. 'That would likely mean that no one else would need to know about what went on in this office today. I think that would make sense and probably make things much easier – don't you?'

He says this with a pleasant smile, which is completely phoney and is a poor attempt to disguise his coercion.

His smile is met with a tight-faced grimace from McGoogan. She can find no gratification in this type of transaction. But, as well she knows, in her elevated position, she has to be prepared to cut deals and to be pragmatic.

'I am sure we can organise something to suit you, Mr Thorn. I had a quick word with the Head of Services. He said he would delegate the decision-making to me on this occasion, since I am here and he is not.

'And I think, on this occasion, where your actions have been detrimental, but where no one has been harmed...'

'Except me!' Thorn can't help interjecting.

'Yes, apart from you, which you said we were not going to mention again, I am sure we can find somewhere else for you to work very soon.'

'Will you be able to confirm that in writing, please? I would rather know, within a reasonable time frame, so that I can plan. You do understand?'

'I'll email in the next twenty-four hours, Mr Thorn. You have my word on that.'

'You're sure?'

'Mr Thorn, given what I have seen here today, I want to sort things out as quickly as possible. There is no way I want you to feel dissatisfied with the outcome. There have been enough problems in this school already. If I have my way, I will be asking Mrs Butcher to spend a bit of time at home as well. I think the situation has been stressful for her, by the looks of things. What we need to do is get the school back to normal as soon as possible, with the pupils back in class and learning.'

'I wish someone had asked me before,' says Thorn. 'I could have told you what she was like. If she had only been sympathetic with me this morning, when the room was vandalised, things wouldn't have escalated like this. It's so unfortunate.'

'Anyway, Mr Thorn, I think we are agreed,' she says – having cut her dirty deal, she wants to move on. 'We don't need to go into it again just now. You have your things and you said you would be in touch with the principal teacher about your classes. I'll email you tomorrow about the way forward, once I've briefed the Head of Services. I'll go now and have a meeting with Mrs Butcher. I think she's with Inspector Holmes just now. Will you be able to see yourself out?'

Thorn smiles, almost too broadly. 'Sure, I know my way out,' he tells her.

He makes a show of dabbing at his brow with the tissue, to show more evidence of blood, then he puts his jacket on and zips it up.

'I'll hear from you in the next twenty-four hours, then,' he reminds her.

'I assure you, Mr Thorn, I will be in touch.' She is comforted and can be more officious now. She has guaranteed his co-operation. The whole thing has been a headache for her, but he is finally leaving. At the end of such a day, that must come as some relief.

# Wednesday, 1347

As he lifts his bag and walks out of the head teacher's room, for what must surely be the last time, Thorn feels the tension in his shoulders and neck ease. He almost has to stifle a sigh of pleasure. The meeting was certainly quite different from the one he had in the boss's office the previous night. He was almost in control of the whole thing.

Walking down the corridor, past the room in which Mrs Butcher is contained, all he sees is the policeman's fluorescent back standing between her and the door. Great, he thinks, a policeman doing his civic duty and protecting him from further assault.

Deep down, Thorn would love to give her another turn of the screw. A big grin as he passed would have done nicely… a provocative wink…

But the opportunity is gone. No matter, when he passes the door and is making his way towards the front door, he forgets. He forgets because he has other things to look forward to.

Primarily, he is not coming in tomorrow. That, in itself, is reason for considerable delight. But, of course, it's not like every other holiday. He always has a bad taste under his tongue at the start of the holidays, because of the enduring fact that he needs to return to the god-forsaken place.

But not this time. This time, he doesn't need to come back… ever.

Usually, as he walks in these corridors, he feels heavy and trauchled, as if he is carrying extra kilos, bags of dirty grit and ashes, which draw him towards the ground – a dehumanising burden, forcing him down towards his hands and knees.

Now, though, a cleansing breeze of levity passes through him. He is parting from that dire dictator and leaving this place of denigration and belittlement behind.

He has imagined a lottery win. That sort of euphoria must feel something like this, he thinks. He has a temptation to smash a window for the sake of it or to scream his relief in someone's face. On the other hand, he doesn't really need to. With wild and liberating abandon, he has just aimed a blaring fart at the head teacher.

He winks at the photos of the past sixth-year pupils, as he marches purposefully along the hallway. Passing the trifling trophy cabinet and the latest art display of painted paper maché balloons, he breenges through the double doors into the outer foyer...

He will not be back. He will not be in the building, the street or even the town, if he can help it. He has been so benighted with the damned drudgery of this job for so many years, that it is with delight, rather than regret, that he begins a new chapter.

Years ago, Thorn realised that he worked in an environment where no one gave one single fuck about him. Beyond the casual daily pleasantries and the necessary work-related communication, he was a non-entity. He was little more than a number – not much more than a face. He could have been spirited away one day and a sprinkling of pupils might have briefly noticed his absence – even a few teachers – until, without a second thought, they turned back to their lives.

So, not for one moment does he hesitate. He has no qualms, because he knows full well that there is nothing of any lasting value behind him.

*This is it. This is the day. This is the hour*, he thinks, as he fills his lungs one last time with the stagnant air of human disaffection. *This is what it feels like to walk through these doors for the final time.*

*So be it*, he thinks. *Amen. Let it be over*, he reflects, as he finally thrusts into the world.

He does an air spit. Not a big spit, with spittle, just a wee, barely noticeable one, pushing breath through between his lips, with a tiny tap of his tongue. With this, he rejects the bad taste left over from the place.

Last night he felt powerless, trapped, cornered even. He was appalled and overwhelmed. He had his guard down and, when he was vulnerable, he was savaged by his head teacher.

233

She wrecked his evening. She could have wrecked his life. But he struck back today and, touch wood, with impunity.

For so many years, so many, he has been marooned – just a sad, ageing man and a computer – barely managing to keep afloat in the treacherous sludge of hormonal teenage antipathy. It has been such an energy-sapping experience and he is so tired of swimming against that current of adolescent sentiment, when so many are so cussed and unappreciative of any small adult effort.

So, it is with a clear sense of relief that his feet carry him out into the playground.

He does not care that it is overcast and raining. That is of no consequence – considering the enormous weight that rockets from his shoulders into the sky.

For so long, at this time of day, he has wanted to be somewhere else, almost anywhere else. And now, that wish has been made real – not by anyone else's hand but his own.

The contrast with last night is so stark. Exultant might be too strong a word, because his career is not yet stone dead, but elation is not far from the truth.

No matter that he has to go back to Polly and face her concern and affect to be embarrassed and repentant about the social media issue. She will not know the whole truth of the situation and she does not need to know. What she will need to come to terms with is the fact that, in less than twenty-four hours, he has contrived his own escape tunnel and that, this time, his hare-brained scheming appears to have won the day.

He will tell her that he walked into a door. That can be the reason for the blow to his temple. That's what everyone else says about an injury like that. She will likely say that she hopes the bump on the head knocked some sense into him.

*But, oh!* he thinks, as he walks across the playground, *Oh! that fart!* It was a gesture of pure genius. The timing, the execution. That was the mortal blow. It was something that Butcher could never have anticipated. It was an inspirational piece of performance art – a work of distinction, a beautifully formed noise. In its orchestration, it was as if he was touched by virtuosity. But, *Oh!* when it happened, what a masterstroke. *Oh!* what a perfectly pitched ending to a difficult day.

Printed in Great Britain
by Amazon

69183991R00139